Murder *and* Moonshine

Murder *and* Moonshine

CAROL MILLER

MINOTAUR BOOKS

A THOMAS DUNNE BOOK

NEW YORK

A THOMAS DUNNE BOOK FOR MINOTAUR BOOKS.
An imprint of St. Martin's Publishing Group.

MURDER AND MOONSHINE. Copyright © 2013 by Carol Miller. All rights reserved. Printed in the United States of America. For information, address St. Martin's Press, 175 Fifth Avenue, New York, N.Y. 10010.

www.thomasdunnebooks.com
www.minotaurbooks.com

Library of Congress Cataloging-in-Publication Data

Miller, Carol, 1972–
    Murder and moonshine : a mystery / Carol Miller.—First edition.
        p. cm.
    ISBN 978-1-250-01925-7 (hardcover)
    ISBN 978-1-250-01926-4 (e-book)
        1. Waitresses—Fiction.   2. Distilling, Illicit—Virginia—
Fiction.   3. Virginia, Southwest—Fiction.   I. Title.
    PS3613.I53277M87 2013
    813'.6—dc23

                                                    2013025281

Minotaur books may be purchased for educational, business, or promotional use. For information on bulk purchases, please contact Macmillan Corporate and Premium Sales Department at 1-800-221-7945, extension 5442, or write specialmarkets@macmillan.com.

First Edition: December 2013

10   9   8   7   6   5   4   3   2   1

For Manfred,
in loving memory

Murder *and* Moonshine

CHAPTER

1

"You've outdone yourself with this cobbler, Ducky."

"It's the peaches," Daisy explained, pulling out the used filters from a pair of worn coffeemakers. "Georgia Belle. I picked them up at the farmer's market in Lynchburg."

"Lynchburg? When on earth did you have time to go to Lynchburg? You've been working here every shift all week."

"Tuesday." Daisy leaned under the marred diner counter to retrieve a jumbo can of coffee grounds. "Tuesday morning. Don't you remember? I left right after the early boys shoved off, and I came back just as the lunch rush kicked in."

Brenda's chewing slowed, and she gazed thoughtfully at the little bowl of cobbler in her cracked, peeling hands. "I remember you going, Ducky. But I don't remember you saying it was Lynchburg you were going to."

Daisy merely shrugged as she spooned a heap of grounds into two new filters.

"Did you talk to the doctors when you were there?" Brenda asked her.

"I did."

"And?"

The shrug repeated itself.

Brenda took a fresh bite of cobbler before pressing the matter. "What did the doctors say about your momma, Ducky?"

"The same thing they always say. The same thing they've been saying for the last four years. *They don't know. They can only guess.*"

"So far their guesses have been about as good as Hank's chili."

Daisy responded with a rueful smile.

"I heard that!" was the angry roar that followed through the open door leading to the kitchen.

Brenda laughed and Daisy's smile widened as the owner of the roar appeared a moment later, his thick face creased and red from the vigor with which he had been scouring the grill.

"I heard that!" he shouted a second time. "There's nothing wrong with my chili, Brenda. Not a damn thing!"

"There's nothing much good about it either," she replied crisply.

Hank growled as he wiped his grease-covered hands on the white grease-smeared apron wrapped around his almost equally grease-stained jeans. "Everybody loves my chili!"

"They love it so much," Brenda returned, "nobody ever orders it."

"People order it."

"Only strangers passing through. And they never ask for a second helping."

"H & P's Diner has the best chili in the whole Commonwealth of Virginia," Hank insisted stubbornly.

"H & P's got the best chicken stew, the best potato salad and baked beans, and without a doubt"—Brenda nodded approvingly at Daisy—"the very best peach cobbler between Charleston, West Virginia, and Charleston, South Carolina, but I'm afraid its chili is near inedible. Always has been, Hank. Since the day you and Paul first opened this place."

"Paul always liked it."

"Paul never liked it."

Hank turned to Daisy for support. "Your pop liked my chili, didn't he?"

Before Daisy could answer him, Brenda said, "He liked feeding it to the pigs out back maybe."

Daisy sighed to herself as she poured a pot of cold water into the machines and clicked the red start button. It was far too early in the morning for a full-blown battle over the quality of Hank's cooking. He and Brenda sparred frequently—sometimes even violently if flinging hush puppies and pickle spears was included in the discussion—but it was usually much later in the day. Not at six in the morning before the sun was up and the coffee had brewed.

"What's the special today?" Daisy asked Hank, watching a pair of headlights turn from the road into the diner's parking lot.

He and Brenda stopped squabbling long enough to look toward the front bank of windows, curiosity over the identity of the day's first customer winning out over the continued debate regarding the value of H & P's chili.

"Looks like the Balsam boys," Brenda determined, squinting at the shadowy outline of a pickup truck in the gray light of the approaching dawn.

Daisy sighed again, more audibly this time.

Brenda nodded in agreement. "They're always trouble, aren't they, Ducky?"

"Trouble?" Hank looked back and forth between the two. "What do you mean by that? They're just a couple of red-blooded country boys."

"Red-blooded country boys who like to start fires, take target practice at anything that crawls, and cook up heaven-only-knows-what in those beat-up old trailers of theirs back there in the woods," Brenda retorted with derision.

Hank shrugged. "They're just kids being kids."

"They ain't no kids! That older one must be getting on thirty now. Isn't that right, Ducky?"

"I went to school with both of them," Daisy said. "Bobby was my year. So he's twenty-seven like me. Rick is two years older."

"That makes them getting on thirty," Brenda crowed at Hank. "Thirty ain't kids!"

Shrugging once more, Hank started back toward the kitchen. "So long as they pay their bill when they leave and don't drive off other customers, I don't care what they're doing on their own dime or their own property."

"You should care," Brenda snapped. "They always bother poor Ducky."

Hank swiveled on his heel. "Have they been bothering you, Daisy?"

"No more than usual," she answered truthfully.

He frowned.

"And the usual is pretty bad! Every time they're in here that worthless Rick is badgering her to go out with him." Brenda wrinkled her pug nose indignantly. "As if she'd ever stoop that low. It'd be like a beautiful butterfly dating a stinking maggot."

"Doesn't he know you're married?" Hank asked Daisy.

"Of course he knows. At one time he and Matt were

even friends. They played football together in school. But Rick also knows Matt left me and—"

"Matt didn't leave you," Brenda interjected.

"He drove off one morning and never came home again," Daisy returned dryly. "If that's not leaving me, I don't know what is."

Brenda's voice softened. "Oh but, Ducky—"

She was interrupted by the rusty bell strung up above the front door of the diner. It clanked as Richard and Robert Balsam pushed their way inside. They were wearing old faded T-shirts, even older and more faded jeans, along with muddy construction boots. Based on their wild eyes and boisterous demeanor, Daisy promptly concluded that neither one had slept a wink the night before. She wasn't the least bit surprised. All the brothers ever managed to do was drink home brew and plink squirrels. Doing honest work for an honest paycheck and keeping sensible hours were utterly foreign concepts to them.

"G'morning all," Bobby proclaimed brightly as he and Rick plopped themselves down in the nearest emerald-green vinyl booth.

Daisy rolled her eyes to Brenda and Hank, then swung around toward the brothers with the obligatory chirpy waitress smile. "And good morning to you. What'll it be today, boys?"

Rick gave her a quick once-over and grinned appreciatively. "You're looking mighty fine, Daisy McGovern."

"What'll it be?" she repeated, ignoring both the compliment and the accompanying seedy gaze.

"Waffles," Bobby declared.

"With pecans?" Daisy asked.

He nodded. "And sausage."

"Links or patties?"

"Uh, patties."

"Coffee?"

Bobby shook his head. "Chocolate milk. A big glass."

"For you?" Daisy looked at Rick.

"I'll have a heapin' platter of you, darlin'."

She turned away without speaking, having learned long ago that ignoring Rick Balsam's irritating and usually offensive flirtations was invariably the best course of action. Yelling, whining, or slapping his smirking cheek only egged him on, like a hungry pit bull catching a savory whiff of hamburger.

"With plenty of whipped cream and syrup," Rick called after her salaciously.

"The poor girl who marries him one day," Brenda mused, clucking her tongue as Daisy returned to the counter and gave Bobby's order to Hank through the wide rectangular opening above the grill.

"I wouldn't wish it on my worst enemy," Daisy replied, pulling the gallon jug of chocolate milk from the refrigerator.

"At least he tips well."

"I'm not sure that makes it any better. Strippers get good tips too, don't they? And I doubt it helps much with their dignity."

"Ain't that the truth," Brenda said, scooping a generous second serving of peach cobbler from the baking dish into her bowl.

"Dessert's supposed to be for the *paying* customer," Hank chastised her over the sizzle of sausage patties.

Brenda went right on scooping. "If it was pudding or sherbet, I'd agree with you, Hank. But it's not. I'm telling you, this is the best cobbler I've ever tasted in my whole life."

"Well, quit tasting so damn much of it," he growled. "Or there won't be any left for this afternoon when the old dames come in for their tea and cake."

"You can give them doughnuts instead."

Daisy didn't catch Hank's reply as she set a tall glass of chocolate milk in front of Bobby and a mug of steaming coffee in front of his brother.

"Cream as usual?" she asked Rick, depositing a handful of little plastic half-and-half containers on the table before he could answer.

"Thank ya, suga'," he drawled at her.

"You want anything to eat with that?"

She raised a finger of warning at him as she said it. Rick cocked his head to one side and gave a roguish chortle.

"Just toast. Toast with jam. Strawberry if you got it."

Daisy nodded and headed back to the counter once more. As she untied the bag of sandwich bread, the rusty bell strung up above the front door of the diner clanked for a second time that day. Sensing the onslaught of the typical morning whirlwind, she hollered to Hank, "Have you decided on the special yet?"

"Let's make it hash. Corned beef hash with a side of—"

"With a side of what?" Daisy said, not hearing him over the whistle of the waffle maker.

Hank didn't answer.

"What's the side?" she asked again, with a touch of annoyance. Handling the early-morning crowd was tough enough without the so-called chef dragging his feet on the cooking end of the business.

There was still no answer.

"Hank!" Daisy snapped, raising her head from the toaster to give him a sour stare.

But when she saw his face above the grill, she discovered

that it was he who was staring, a spatula frozen in one hand with a sausage patty half-flipped. Brenda was staring too, the spoon from her bowl of cobbler clattering to the floor. They were both staring at the door with an expression of absolute shock, as though a horrifying ghost from their past had suddenly decided to come floating through it. Except a ghost wouldn't have shaken the bell in the process. And a ghost didn't have thudding footsteps like the ones presently trudging toward the counter.

"B . . . Burger . . ." stuttered an unfamiliar voice.

Daisy's mind instinctively clicked into waitress-mode. "With cheese and onions?" she replied, turning toward the new arrival. "Or bacon and egg?"

"Burger . . ."

The usual follow-up question regarding mustard versus mayonnaise vanished from Daisy's lips the instant that she saw the man. He was stumbling across the tile floor toward her, swaying back and forth with his arms stretched out in front of him like a drunken zombie. He had on camel-colored farm coveralls, a black-and-white checkered flannel shirt underneath, and tall rubber farm boots. Based on his sparse white hair and long white beard, it was a safe bet that he was closer to seventy than fifty. Water ran in rivers from his eyes, and his mouth foamed profusely.

"Isn't that old man Dickerson?" Rick said, rising from his booth.

Neither Hank nor Brenda responded. They were still staring and frozen in place like a pair of ice sculptures. Daisy could only shake her head. She hadn't seen old man Dickerson in nearly a decade. But it could be him. The age was right. So was his general shape and size. And he was a farmer. Or at least he had been a farmer before becoming a recluse.

The man tried to wipe the foam from his mouth with his sleeve, but more foam appeared. There was so much of it that his lips were completely covered, and it began oozing over his chin and down his neck almost like runny shaving cream. As he staggered closer to Daisy, she saw that both the foam and the tears streaming from his eyes had a strange yellowish tint to them. She was pretty sure he was ill.

"I think we should call an ambulance," she said.

"You're right," Brenda agreed, waking from her trance and reaching for the phone next to the cash register.

As she dialed, the man tried to speak. His jaw moved rapidly, and a string of incomprehensible syllables followed.

"What's he saying?" Rick asked, coming over and standing next to Daisy.

She shook her head again. "I don't know. I can't understand him." She looked at the man apologetically. "I'm sorry, but we don't understand you."

His watery, befuddled gaze switched from her to Rick, and his expression immediately changed. His face tightened, and his shoulders started to twitch. It was clear that he recognized Rick, but it wasn't at all clear whether that recognition was good or bad. The man was definitely trying to get some point across though. The incomprehensible syllables rolling off his tongue increased both in speed and number. They were joined by two clenched, trembling fists.

"Maybe you should sit down?" Daisy suggested to him.

"That's a good idea." Rick pulled a stool from under the counter.

"Or how about lying down?" She gestured toward the booths. "And a glass of water? That might help."

Before the man could take more than a step toward the proffered stool, his whole body began to shake. His eyes rolled back in their sockets, and the foam gushed from his mouth with an almost startling ferocity.

"Holy hell," Rick muttered.

A moment later the shaking turned into violent convulsions. The man tumbled backward. He hit the floor with a loud, hard thwack. His mouth stopped foaming, and his limbs grew still. A tiny red trickle of blood crept down from his ear onto the tile.

"Is he—" Daisy stammered, horrified. "He's not—"

"I think he might be," Rick said.

Bobby came over and nudged the man's leg with the toe of his boot. There was no response.

"That ain't good," he drawled.

"Should I check for a pulse?" Daisy started to reach down toward the man's neck, but Rick hastily seized her wrist and pulled her back.

"Don't!" he barked.

"Don't tell me what to do!" she snapped in return.

"You don't know what's wrong with him," Rick said. "And you don't know what that stuff is coming out of his mouth and eyes. You shouldn't touch it. Not when he's already down and there's nothing you can do to help."

Twisting her arm free, Daisy turned to Brenda questioningly.

"I think he's right," she replied with a mournful sigh. "Better to wait for the professionals, Ducky. They'll be here in a minute."

The scream of a siren could be heard off in the distance. Closer by, car tires crunched over the gravel in the parking lot.

"One of us should get outside," Brenda went on. "Make sure no one comes in. We don't want anybody to see this, especially not any little kids."

Daisy nodded. "I'll do it. What do you want me to tell them, Hank? Just that we're temporarily closed? The gossips will start their wagging no matter what I say the second that ambulance arrives."

When he didn't answer, she looked over at him and was astounded to find Hank leaning casually against the counter, calmly feeding himself from the baking dish as though nothing remotely out of the ordinary had happened only a minute earlier and there was no man lying motionless on his diner floor. He raised his placid gaze to Brenda, the barest hint of a smile tugging at his lips.

"You know, you're right about this cobbler. Daisy's really outdone herself this time."

CHAPTER
2

Tasty cobbler or not, Daisy didn't exaggerate the speed with which the gossip started. Or spread. It moved with the same swiftness as a swarm of cicadas. And she knew that it would be just as dense, blanketing the neighborhood with no house, cabin, or trailer left untouched. The ambulance hadn't even shut off its blaring siren before she saw the first whisper pass from eager lip to awaiting ear amidst the rapidly growing group of onlookers in the diner's parking lot. It wasn't difficult to guess what they were saying. There had been an incident at H & P's. The Glade Hill Fire & Rescue Squad was on the scene. They weren't letting anyone in. And so far, no one had come out.

No one would be coming out, at least no one requiring medical care. Sue Lowell, the chief paramedic for the squad, determined that quickly enough.

"He's gone," she said, after completing a brief examination of the man who had collapsed on the tile.

Daisy swallowed with an audible gulp. Brenda said a quiet prayer.

"I've got a blanket out in my truck," Rick offered. "Should I bring it in, so we can cover him?"

Sue shook her head. "I don't think that's a good idea."

"Can't you at least close his eyes?" Bobby muttered, growing a bit green about the gills. "Or turn his head? It's like he's staring at us. He looks so . . . so . . ."

"He looks dead because he is dead," Sue said.

Her words may have sounded cold and clinical, but she wasn't a cold person. Sue Lowell was a tall, thick woman with closely-cropped black hair and a penchant for glittery dangling earrings. She had a warm, hearty disposition and possessed an admirable degree of patience. The disposition came naturally, while the patience had been progressively acquired through thirty years of marriage to the Pittsylvania County sheriff.

Sheriff George Lowell appeared just as his wife stood up and began peeling off her protective gloves.

"There's my girl!" he exclaimed.

As if recoiling from a cobra, Rick and Bobby both took two hasty steps backward. Despite the morbid circumstances, Daisy couldn't help chuckling to herself. The Balsam brothers had plenty of experience with the law, particularly the law of Pittsylvania County, and from their perspective, it was never a good experience.

The sheriff, who was even taller and thicker than his wife, gave her an affectionate peck on the forehead, then glanced merrily around at the entire group. "So what's the trouble? Bad case of pancakes? I was getting a clip over at Beulah's, and they heard about it there before I even got a call. Where's the emergency?"

"George—" Sue nudged him with her elbow and pointed toward the diner floor.

"Oh." His laughing face grew somber as he gazed at the recently departed lying before his feet. "Wait a minute. Isn't that—"

"Fred Dickerson," Hank concluded for him.

The sheriff looked over at the counter where Hank was sitting on a stool, leisurely perusing the *Danville Register & Bee* with an occasional bite of peach cobbler thrown in for good measure.

"Howdy, Hank."

"Howdy, George."

The two men exchanged a cordial nod. They had known each other most of their lives, since their much earlier, more carefree days when they used to run around old abandoned tobacco barns together looking for spiders to put in jars and a good afternoon consisted of digging frogs from ponds in the rain.

"Fred Dickerson, eh?" Sheriff Lowell leaned down for a closer inspection of the still face hidden beneath the long white beard. "I think you're right, Hank. It is Fred."

"Surely," was Hank's reply.

"Fred Dickerson," the sheriff mused, rubbing his own freshly trimmed peppered beard. "I can't remember the last time I talked to old Fred. It must be at least two or three years back. Maybe more even. I thought I caught a glimpse of him at the hardware store last fall, but I wasn't sure."

"I used to see him now and then over at the Food Lion in Gretna," Brenda said, "but that was a long time ago."

"He grew corn," the sheriff went on. "Feed corn mostly. Off Highway 40, down by Frying Pan Creek." He inclined his head toward Daisy, who was well familiar with that area. "I don't think he had planted for a couple of seasons though. Last time I drove that way it was all grown over. I never checked on the house, if anybody was still living there. You can't see it from the road. It's back behind—" He broke off midsentence.

"Back behind?" his wife prodded him.

Sheriff Lowell didn't respond. He straightened up slowly, and as he did, his gaze moved from Fred Dickerson to Rick and Bobby Balsam. "Isn't that your land?" he asked, his tone edged with equal portions of distrust and dislike.

Bobby shuffled his feet and took another step backward. His brother wasn't nearly so easily intimidated and held his ground.

"It's mine," Rick confirmed.

Daisy's head snapped toward him. "What do you mean it's yours?"

"I own it."

Her eyes stretched wide. "You own it? The fields north of Frying Pan Creek?"

Rick nodded.

"And the farmhouse too?"

He nodded again.

She stared at him in stunned disbelief. "How can you possibly own it?"

"I bought it," he stated simply.

"You bought it," she echoed. Her hands started to shake, and she pressed them together hard. "When exactly did you buy it?"

"Beginning of the year."

She blinked at him in silence for a moment, then with a clenched jaw she turned to Sheriff Lowell. "You knew about this?"

"Daisy—" Sue Lowell began gently.

Daisy was in no mood to be placated. "You knew about this?" she said again, her voice rising.

The sheriff shrugged somewhat sheepishly. "I just heard about it last week."

"And you didn't think Daisy should be told!" Brenda snapped.

"I thought she already knew," he apologized.

Sue nodded in agreement. "We thought she had to know. We didn't think the property could ever go up for sale without her knowing."

"Well, I didn't know," Daisy informed them crisply, fighting the intense urge to pick up a coffee mug and hurl it across the diner. She spun back toward Rick. "But apparently you knew."

He met her blazing gaze straight on. "I did."

"And you didn't think it might be nice to share the information with me?"

"When have you ever thought I was nice?"

Daisy glared at him, her lips and shoulders quivering with anger. "There was a time when we were friends, Rick," she spat. "And you and Matt—"

He cut her off abruptly. "It's two hundred acres, Daisy. Where the hell would you have gotten the money for two hundred acres?"

It was a slap in the face, sharp and swift. She felt the color rush to her cheeks. The red was half rage, half embarrassment.

"Get out!" Hank snarled, jumping up from his stool. "Get out before I toss you out on your sorry ass!"

Rick didn't respond. His dark eyes were on Daisy, watching her narrowly like a jungle cat. There was no regret in his expression, but no malevolence either.

"Get out!" Hank shouted again, pointing a stiff arm toward the door. "Get the hell out now!"

"We're going. We're going," Bobby said hastily, shrinking from Hank's tattooed biceps and scarred fists.

Just as with the sheriff, his brother wasn't so quickly browbeaten. But Rick had enough good sense and respect for Hank and his flexed muscles to tread lightly.

"I'm not lookin' for trouble." He shrugged.

"You'll get trouble—" Hank warned him.

Rick raised his hands in cool capitulation. "All right. I got the message. But just so we're clear, I'm not trying to hurt anyone's feelings. I'm just stating facts."

Hank grunted, unappeased.

"It had to come out eventually," Rick continued, "so now it's out. I bought the land off Highway 40, along Frying Pan Creek. I own the house, the barns, and the creek too. All of what used to be known as Fox Hollow." He glanced at Daisy for a split second as he said the name, but then pulled his eyes away just as fast.

Hank's eyes also went to Daisy, as did Brenda's and George's and Sue's. It was obvious that they were waiting for her to respond, to give them some sort of an indication how she intended to handle the matter, but Daisy didn't say a word. She couldn't. Her throat was swollen shut, and her stomach twisted painfully.

After a tense minute, the sheriff looked at Rick and raised a questioning eyebrow. "You say you bought the property at the beginning of the year?"

"I did," Rick answered somewhat absently, not looking back at him. He was focused on Fred Dickerson, frowning at the lifeless man with a grave intensity.

"Then what about old Fred?" Sheriff Lowell asked. "I know he used to lease the house and land. What sort of an arrangement did you have with him?"

"I guess you could say he was leasing it from me too, except we didn't have anything in writing. And no money ever changed hands. We never even talked about it."

"You never talked about it? You mean you just let him go on with the old lease?"

"No." Rick continued frowning at the body. "I mean I didn't bother with any lease, old or new."

The sheriff squinted at him dubiously. "You're telling

me you bought two hundred acres—some of the best acres we got in the county—along with a farmhouse and outbuildings and a flowing creek, but you didn't bother with a lease?"

"I didn't bother with a lease," he repeated curtly, finally raising his gaze from the diner floor.

"So then what did Fred think?"

"How the hell should I know what he thought?"

"Well, he must have had some inkling in his head if he was still living there."

Rick's patience was wearing visibly thin. His lips curled back from his teeth like a wolf warning an enemy from its territory.

"Don't test me, boy." Sheriff Lowell puffed out his chest and slapped his hands on his gun belt. "I'm the law around here, and we both know you and your brother ain't done so good with the law over the years."

Bobby gave a meek little whimper. Rick's snarl remained, but he answered the sheriff's question.

"I've no idea what old man Dickerson was thinking. I hadn't talked to him in ages, probably close to a decade. Not since before he moved to Fox Hollow." Rick almost looked at Daisy again but stopped himself this time. "After I bought the place, I figured he'd been living there so long he could just go on living there. It didn't bother me none, and I didn't think it'd bother anybody else."

Daisy sighed. She was furious with Rick for not telling her that the property was for sale. She was even more furious with him for buying it, and buying it in secret. He of all people knew what it was to her, what it meant. She felt terribly blindsided—and more than a little betrayed—but at the same time, she couldn't argue with him regarding Fred Dickerson. It had never bothered her that the old farmer lived in the house or planted the fields or fished in the creek. On the contrary, there had been many moments when it almost comforted her, the thought that someone was taking care of Fox Hollow.

"So you don't know if Fred was sick?" Sheriff Lowell asked Rick.

Rick ground the heel of his boot into the tile with irritation. "Of course not. I just told you I hadn't talked to the man in ten years."

"And you also didn't see him?"

"I couldn't swear in all that time his truck never passed by mine on the road," he replied with a smirk. "Or that we didn't both order ice-cream cones on the same day over at the Dairy Queen."

Sheriff Lowell sucked on his teeth. "You want me to ask you again wearing handcuffs?"

"I. Didn't. See. Fred. Dickerson."

As he said it, Rick cocked his head to one side. No one seemed to notice but Daisy. And she knew what it meant. Rick Balsam only cocked his head to the side when he flirted and when he lied. He had seen Fred Dickerson somewhere, probably pretty recently if she were to hazard a guess, but he had no intention of sharing that information with George Lowell or the rest of the group.

"Are we done? Can I go now?" Rick drawled, partially stifling a yawn. "Or do you want to read my diary first?"

The sheriff grimaced at him. "Go." He waved his hand at Bobby, then at the door. "The two of you just go. Go before I—"

"George—" Sue interrupted him.

He glanced over at her.

"They can't leave," she said.

Both Rick and the sheriff frowned at her.

"They can't leave," she repeated.

"Why not?" Bobby whined. It was the whine of a bored and hungry child, one who had never gotten his waffles with pecans or the accompanying sausage patties and was tired of old man Dickerson staring up at him from the diner floor like a bug-eyed trout.

Ignoring Bobby, Sue spoke to her husband. "I'm going to have to send him to Danville."

Sheriff Lowell's brow furrowed. "Danville? Are you sure?"

She nodded. "I can't do this. I'm not a medical examiner."

"You think—"

"I don't know. That's why I've got to send him to Danville."

"He was old," the sheriff remarked. "And probably sick."

"I don't know," Sue said again. "It might be that. It's possible he had a stroke or his heart just gave out, but . . ." She paused for a moment as she regarded the lifeless body with a scrutinizing eye. "There's that discharge. Especially around his mouth. The color. It's not right."

Her husband shrugged. "Well, you know best. I hate getting them involved, but if you've got to send him to Danville, then send him to Danville."

"So what does that have to do with us?" Rick asked somewhat sharply.

Daisy was wondering the same thing. And to her surprise, instead of answering immediately, Sue toyed with her earrings. It wasn't a good sign.

"If you're thinking about needing a couple of strong backs to load him into the ambulance," Sheriff Lowell said, "I can call the office and get a pair of boys to come over. We don't need them." He stuck his thumb in the direction of the Balsam brothers.

"No." Sue kept on fiddling with her earrings. "That's not what I was thinking. You don't have to call your office." Taking a deep breath, she added, "You have to call the Danville office."

"What! Why the hell should I call them?"

"You have to."

"No, I don't!" the sheriff roared, a tad petulantly. "Not those smug bastards!"

"You don't have a choice," Sue returned with briskness. "We need a forensics team, and they've got one."

George Lowell snorted like an irascible bull.

"It's the closest," she reminded him, "and the only one Pittsylvania County is authorized to use."

He snorted once more.

"A forensics team?" Hank said, folding his arms across his chest and leaning back against the counter. "Does that mean what I think it means?"

"It means she thinks it's suspicious," Brenda said, with a touch of excitement.

"It means I don't want any of us getting in trouble later for not following proper procedure now," Sue argued.

"What it really means is we're going to be stuck here for a damn long time until the fellas from Danville drive up and do what they do." Rick walked over to the emerald-green vinyl booth that he had previously occupied and plopped himself down in it. Lifting his coffee mug, he gave Daisy a hopeful little smile. "Refill?"

CHAPTER
3

"Is that you, Daisy?" Beulah cried at the telltale creaks from the aged front steps.

She was answered by a slamming screen door and a weary moan.

"Oh, I'm glad you're back! We were awfully worried." Beulah came rushing out of the parlor into the entrance hall of the inn. "First the ambulance, then Sheriff Lowell—I was just finishing up his clip when he got the call to go to the diner—and then those police cars from Danville. We were all racing around trying to figure out what had happened, but nobody actually *knew* anything!"

Despite her exhaustion, Daisy grinned. Beulah's untamable mane of flaming red hair was sticking out in every direction, like a cartoon character that had just gotten its finger stuck in an electrical socket. It was pretty funny, especially considering that Beulah owned a hair salon, a really popular hair salon.

"I'm sorry I didn't call." Daisy swapped an air kiss with her friend. "But the whole thing was just crazy. And Sue said it'd be better if we didn't talk to anybody about it until after the police were through."

Beulah and her hair nodded. "But you're okay? You look okay. And Brenda and Hank? They're okay too?"

"They're fine. We're all fine. Everybody except old man Dickerson."

"Old man Dickerson? Is he still living around here?"

"Not anymore," Daisy replied, with a wryness that surprised even her.

"You don't mean?"

"I'm afraid so."

"Oh my God!" Beulah clapped her hands over her mouth in horror.

"I know. I spent half the day staring at his dead body on the diner floor and I still can't believe it."

"I can't believe it either. I thought for sure it had to do with one of the Balsam brothers. They finally got caught doing something even stupider than usual."

Daisy shook her head. "Unfortunately not. But they were both there. And just wait until I tell you what Rick pulled."

Beulah began chewing on a chipped orange fingernail. "He pulled something with old man Dickerson?"

"With Fox Hollow."

The chewing instantly stopped. "Fox Hollow!"

Daisy hastily hushed her. "Not so loud. I don't want my momma to hear."

"She won't. She's out back. With Aunt Emily."

Aunt Emily wasn't actually Beulah's aunt. She wasn't anyone's aunt. Emily Tosh was the last surviving member of the oldest family in Pittsylvania County. It was her kinfolk that had originally settled the area, and there were plenty of roads, cemeteries, and abandoned houses in the neighborhood bearing the name to prove it. The inn had been the grandest of all the houses, a behemoth Victorian with yellow gables and matching wraparound porches. It had been built—and for many decades maintained—by the glorious tobacco plant. But with the inexorable march of time, the once seemingly endless acres of highly profitable tobacco were converted into cheap corn. There was drought, followed by price wars. Land was sold off, and younger generations moved away, enticed by the thrill of the big city. Eventually only Emily and the venerable Tosh house remained, two worn and weathered monuments harkening back to a slightly different era.

Sociable and in need of extra income, Emily turned the family homestead into an inn. But the timing wasn't good. Tourism in southwestern Virginia was on a steady decline. So she began to pick up neighborhood strays instead. Beulah arrived before Daisy. In an attempt to attract a few more visitors—if only just for gossip and a friendly cup of coffee—Emily encouraged Beulah to set up a little salon in an old potting shed on the property. The idea turned out to be remarkably successful for both of them, and soon Beulah traded in her shabby apartment and stale bologna sandwiches for a cheerful room and hot home-cooked dinners at the Tosh Inn.

Not long after, Daisy and her momma moved in. It was a natural enough arrangement. Emily was Daisy's godmother, and Beulah was Daisy's oldest friend. If the circumstances that prompted the move had been a little less unpleasant, everyone would have been quite happy. But as it was, the motley group got along fine, with only a few minor complaints, the most frequent being Aunt Emily's shotgun.

Daisy was just about to slide onto the settee in the parlor and share with Beulah all that Rick Balsam had shared with her that day regarding Fox Hollow when the first thunderous boom emanated from the rear of the inn. It was followed in quick succession by another, which set all the decorative plates lining the walls of the room rattling.

"Aw jeez," she groaned.

Beulah grimaced and nodded. "I told you she was out back."

"But now? Does she have to shoot now?"

"Either she thinks the deer have been munching on her perennials again or she's warning off all those vicious burglars who might be skulking around the neighborhood just waiting for an opportunity to prey on us helpless females."

"But it's the middle of the afternoon," Daisy protested. "The deer aren't out in the middle of the afternoon. Nor are any supposed burglars."

Beulah smirked. "Try explaining that to Aunt Emily."

Daisy rolled her eyes, then settled down on the settee. Beulah curled up in the scuffed leather smoking chair across from her.

"Okay, so what did that weasel Rick do this time?"

"You won't believe it," she began. "I can barely believe it. But Sheriff Lowell says it's true. He saw a copy of the papers and—"

She was interrupted by a second set of thunderous, rattling booms.

"All right. That's it." Daisy popped back up. "My momma's supposed to be resting, not getting her eardrums blasted to kingdom come."

"I tried talking to her about it earlier," Beulah said. "I told Aunt Emily some of my customers have been complaining. The main reason they come to the salon is to relax. They're trying to get away from the fussing men and screaming babies. The last thing they want to do while they're here is be stuck in the middle of an artillery range. But you know

Aunt Emily. She's like a rabid raccoon with that gun. She'll probably insist on being buried with the damn thing."

Daisy headed down the hall toward the kitchen. Beulah followed along. They stepped out onto the back porch just as the rabid raccoon was cracking open the breech of her beloved firearm for reloading.

"Ah, the girls," she cried. "Just in time!"

"Hey there, Aunt Emily. Hey there, Momma." Daisy went over to her mother, who was sitting quietly in a white pine rocking chair, and brushed back a few stray wisps of pale blond hair from her sunken cheek. "How are you today, Momma?"

Lucy Hale looked up at her daughter and smiled. "Hi, honey. I'm okay. I can't complain. I got to come outside."

"It is a pretty day, isn't it?" Daisy frowned at the thick cotton quilt wrapped snugly around her momma's thin legs. "Are you cold? You shouldn't be. It must be at least eighty-five degrees out here."

"With ninety percent humidity," Beulah added sourly, trying without the least amount of success to press down her unruly mop.

"It's those new drugs," Lucy responded, taking her daughter's hand from her cheek and squeezing it affectionately. "They just give me a chill, that's all."

"But are they making a difference?" Daisy asked anxiously. "The doctor said it might take a few weeks to see an improvement. He also said we should watch out for side effects. If you have any shortness of breath or—"

"Oh, let's not talk about that now," Lucy cut her off gently, squeezing her hand once more. "Not on such a beautiful afternoon. The sun shining. The breeze in the magnolias. And look at those zinnias, Daisy. Aren't they the most beautiful scarlet you ever saw?"

Daisy glanced over at the pair of old barrels stationed at the corners of the porch that were overflowing with blooms. "They are lovely," she agreed absently, more concerned with her momma's wan complexion than the crimson flowers.

"The deer haven't gotten them yet," Aunt Emily said, pulling out the spent casings from her Remington.

"And they aren't going to get them," Beulah returned teasingly. "Not unless those deer are geniuses and can learn to climb a whole flight of stairs."

Aunt Emily reached over to her needlepoint bag sitting on one of the empty rockers and began rummaging around inside. "They've taken all the phlox. There's nothing left but a bit of stalk. Every last leaf is gone, not to mention the blossoms."

"I'm sorry about that," Daisy said, trying to be tactful. "But really, Aunt Emily, do you have to start shooting in the middle of the day? It's not as if the deer are eating anything now. And if you keep firing willy-nilly you could actually hit someone."

"So much the better. If they're out there lurking, I hope to hit 'em. Serves 'em right for spying on us."

Daisy and Beulah looked at each other and sighed.

"Nobody's lurking," Daisy argued.

"Nobody's spying," Beulah added.

"They could be," Aunt Emily retorted decisively.

They sighed again. It was a useless debate, one that they would never win. Not with Aunt Emily.

"Found 'em!" She pulled a box of shells from the needlepoint bag. "And you're just in time, girls." She dropped two new shells into the breech and snapped it shut.

"Just in time for what?" Daisy asked hesitantly.

"Just in time to see me frighten the molasses out of whatever's hiding in that holly back there."

"You mean the holly next to the barn?" Beulah squawked.

"Surely."

"But that's got to be at least a hundred yards!"

"I reckon so."

"You're going to nick one of the horses," Daisy said.

"Rubbish." Aunt Emily raised the double-barreled 20-gauge to her shoulder. "I've been shooting since before you girls were even a gleam in your daddy's eye. And shooting good, I might add."

"Well, if we end up having to fetch the vet," Daisy replied tartly, pulling a rocker next to her momma and taking a seat, "don't expect us to make up some ludicrous story like last time. And I'm not fibbing to Sheriff Lowell about it either. He's got enough going on with the diner today."

Aunt Emily swiveled on her heel. "That's right. The diner. I was meaning to ask you about that, Ducky."

"Uh, Aunt Emily—" Beulah stammered, shrinking from the business end of the Remington that was now staring her in the face.

"Oh. Yes." She lowered the gun. "Sorry about that, dear."

Both Daisy and her momma chuckled under their breath. Emily Tosh had a gift for being sharp as a tack one second and scatterbrained as a day-old chick the next.

"So about the diner," Aunt Emily said to Daisy, leaning her precious pet against the porch railing. "What was all the commotion?"

"There was a problem at the diner?" Lucy immediately asked her daughter.

Daisy hesitated, debating what to say. Evidently Beulah and Aunt Emily hadn't told her momma about the ambulance or police cars, and she appreciated it. She didn't want her worried and upset, especially not needlessly. The doctors had made it very clear that extra stress should be avoided at all cost.

Lucy's smile faded to a frown. "You're not having trouble with Hank, are you? Or Brenda?"

"No, of course not. They're great." Daisy shrugged, more to herself than the others. She couldn't think of any reason why the news of old man Dickerson's passing would cause her momma undue stress. "It's Fred Dickerson. He—"

"Fred Dickerson?" she interjected. "Is he still living around here?"

"That's what I said," Beulah remarked, reclining on the porch swing.

"If he is, I'm surprised to hear it," Aunt Emily returned. "I always figured Hank took care of him long ago."

"What do you mean?" Daisy asked.

"What do you think I mean?" she answered with a small smirk. "I'm talking about Hank killing Fred and dumping his body somewhere."

Beulah gasped. Daisy stared.

Aunt Emily clucked her tongue in amusement. "Oh, girls. Don't look at me like that. You're not two toddlers running around with your blankies and pacifiers anymore. This is real life. And real life has consequences."

"Ain't that the truth," Lucy mumbled.

Daisy turned to her momma with a gaping mouth. She knew firsthand that life had consequences, and as far as she was concerned, those consequences were all too frequently unpleasant. But life's consequences or not, she was dumbfounded that Aunt Emily could talk so cavalierly about Hank murdering Fred. And she was even more dumbfounded that her momma didn't appear to be the least bit shaken by it.

"You were saying something about Fred, Ducky?" Aunt Emily reminded her.

"I . . . He . . ." It took Daisy a moment to pick up her jaw off the porch. "Fred Dickerson is dead."

"You're sure?" her momma asked her.

She nodded.

"When did it happen?" Aunt Emily said.

"This morning. At the diner."

Lucy and Emily looked at each other.

"Well, that's another chapter ended." Aunt Emily exhaled, closing the box of shells with firmness and tucking it back into her embroidery bag.

"It's about time too," Lucy agreed.

"Was it poison?" Aunt Emily wondered.

"Poison!" Beulah cried.

"Yes, dear." Aunt Emily shook her well-coiffured head. "How else would Hank do it at the diner? Poison is the most logical choice. He's the chef, after all. A sprinkle of cyanide in Fred's hash browns. A dash of drain cleaner in his tomato soup."

Beulah clutched her stomach with a nauseated expression that clearly stated she wouldn't ever be able to eat another one of Aunt Emily's home-cooked dinners.

"Now if it hadn't been at the diner," she went on, picking up her gun and wiping a smudge of grease from the stock with her thumb, "I would have guessed stabbing. Hank's always been handy with a knife. Tool of the trade, I suppose. But then they'd never have found the body. And you saw the body, didn't you, Ducky?"

Daisy sputtered out a garbled affirmative.

"That's too bad," Aunt Emily said. "It's too bad Hank didn't have time to get rid of it. It's so easy to dispose of a body in these parts. You don't even have to bury it. Just throw it out in the middle of the woods. Ashes to ashes and all that. The only worry you have is a hunter stumbling across it or somebody's dog going digging and dragging. But you can avoid that if you go deep enough on a nice quiet posted property. No hunting allowed and too far off the road for anything to be running around sniffing that's not feral."

Beulah blinked at Daisy. Daisy blinked back at her. It wasn't every day that they got instructions on how best to hide a corpse in the countryside.

Finally Daisy managed to say, "But Hank didn't kill Fred."

Aunt Emily stopped cleaning the Remington. "He didn't?"

"No. Fred came in, had some sort of a stroke or seizure, and then collapsed. He didn't eat anything."

"Huh. That's interesting. So it might not have been poison then."

"They don't know what it was," Daisy told her. "Sue did think it was a little strange, so she had him taken to Danville for an examination—or autopsy—or whatever it is officially. And Sheriff Lowell called in the Danville forensics team."

"Even more interesting." Aunt Emily rubbed her palms together gleefully. "Hank planned better than I gave him credit for."

With a loud snort, Beulah threw up her arms in frustration. "You're talking nonsense, Aunt Emily. Absolute nonsense! Poison? Stabbing? Dumping a body in the middle of the woods? I think you're the one who's eaten some bad hash browns and tomato soup. Because everything you're saying is just nuts."

"And Hank!" Daisy exclaimed, in full accord with

Beulah. "Hank's been cooking at H & P's since I was a baby. He's never made a single person sick. At least not intentionally. Why would he want to hurt Fred Dickerson? It makes no sense. Nobody's seen the man in ages. Everyone's first question today was whether he even still lived around here. So if Fred hasn't had contact with anybody, why would anybody—"

Her words fell away as it suddenly occurred to Daisy that maybe she was wrong. She hadn't seen Fred Dickerson in years. Neither had Brenda or Sheriff Lowell. Rick had initially guessed that the ill man stumbling about the diner might be him, and she had agreed. But it was Hank who had positively identified him. And he did it without any deliberation, even with Fred's long white beard and the foam covering his mouth and the fact that he didn't utter more than a couple of syllables. Which made it seem awfully likely that Hank had seen Fred Dickerson much more recently than the rest of them.

"Ah," Aunt Emily chortled, "the wheels are spinning, aren't they, Ducky? You noticed something today, didn't you? Something odd. Something that makes you think I may not be so out of my gourd after all."

"No," she protested. "I—"

Again she stopped. She remembered Hank's strange lack of reaction. The rest of the group had been horrified at old man Dickerson's collapse. Brenda had called the ambulance. Rick had tried to get a stool for him before he fell. Even the usually oblivious Bobby Balsam had turned queasy after Sue announced that he was dead. But not Hank. Hank had happily eaten peach cobbler and read the newspaper. The corpse lying on his diner floor might just as well have been a muddy sock someone had dropped.

"But—" Daisy frowned. "But why? There's no reason."

"Lucy?" Aunt Emily turned to Daisy's momma.

She voiced no objection.

Aunt Emily looked back at Daisy. There was sympathy in her shrewd blue eyes—and also a hint of excitement—as though she didn't want to hurt Daisy with what she told her but at the same time was eager to finally reveal a long-held secret.

"Frederick Dickerson," she said, "was responsible for the death of your daddy."

CHAPTER
4

"Are you sure you want to be here, Daisy?"

"You've asked me that three times already."

"Yes, but—" Beulah looked at her anxiously.

Daisy lifted her bottle and took a long drink. The beer was cold and bitter. It felt good. Beulah didn't need to be concerned. The crumbling old roadhouse was a good place to be. It was known fondly throughout Pittsylvania County as the General. The true origin of the establishment's name was a long-standing local mystery, but there was plenty of speculation on the subject, the most popular theory being that it was a tribute to Robert E. Lee. There was no question that the building and most of its contents could have easily dated back to the War for Southern Independence. The primitive wooden chairs were short and rickety. The tilting wooden tables were etched with countless signatures and doodles. And everything was water stained. The leaky wooden walls. The cracked wooden floorboards. Even the beamed ceiling. The whole place smelled like damp, musty, smoldering firewood, but in a strangely appealing way.

The General didn't offer much. No exotic drinks in neon colors. No pretty foods with fancy foreign names. There was beer—domestic only, of course. There were hot dogs—spinning ceaselessly under a red heat lamp. And there were three aged pool tables—all with a great deal of scratched felt. No one would have ever claimed that there was anything hip or trendy about the General. But it served the inhabitants of the neighborhood well. There they could sit, drink, and escape the cold, cruel world outside, if only for a little while. And that was exactly what Daisy needed.

Beulah lowered her voice. "After what Aunt Emily said—"

"Sometimes Aunt Emily is a few apples short of a bushel."

"I know. There's no doubt about that. Except—"

"Okay. I'll be honest." Daisy took another swig from her bottle, then she met Beulah's earnest gaze. "What she said did surprise me. Only it's ancient history. Or at least it should be ancient history. That was four years ago. Almost five now. It was a terrible, terrible accident." She swallowed hard, forcing down the thick lump that surfaced whenever she had to utter the horrible words. "My daddy died. Matt's daddy died. But it was an *accident*. I don't know how Fred Dickerson could have possibly been involved. He wasn't at Fox Hollow then. He wasn't anywhere near Fox Hollow when it happened."

Beulah nodded.

"The more I think about it," her brow furrowed, "the more irritated I get. Aunt Emily shouldn't be talking about the accident in front of my momma. She knows better. She knows how hard it's been for her. She shouldn't be dredging up all those nasty memories."

"She shouldn't," Beulah agreed.

"And she shouldn't be talking about Hank that way either," Daisy went on with some vigor. "Hank Fitz was my daddy's best friend. They went through Vietnam together. They started H & P's. Hank did everything he could for us when my daddy died. He gave my momma all the money he had, even though it wasn't a lot. The diner's never brought in much. And he gave me a job when I had to be close by after Matt left and my momma got sick. Hank may be as sulky and tough as a grizzly, but he's been like a guardian angel to us, and I wish Aunt Emily wouldn't say such ridiculous things about him. Poison and murder! It's so disrespectful. Frankly, I'm surprised my momma didn't defend him more."

"She was probably just as stunned as we were," Beulah suggested.

"I guess."

"But in a way—now don't get mad at me for saying this, Daisy—Aunt Emily wasn't really disrespectful. She didn't accuse Hank of being a cold-blooded killer. According to her, if he did anything to Fred Dickerson, it's only because Fred did something to your daddy. She's talking old-school, biblical-style vengeance. Eye for an eye."

Daisy sighed. She wasn't sure how she felt about that. She wasn't entirely sure how she felt about any of it. It had been such a strange, surreal day. Everything seemed topsy-turvy. And she was so painfully tired. Far too tired to think any more about it tonight. Too tired to care much at all. Exhaustion had a remarkable way of deadening even the most poignant emotions.

There was an unexpected hand on her shoulder, and she jumped slightly.

"I'm sorry, Daisy. I didn't mean to startle you."

She turned in her seat and found a heavy-set man with

a thick shock of curly silver hair standing next to her. Daisy suppressed a chuckle. It was Carlton Waters. He was a regular customer at H & P's. Friendly, polite, and a consistently mediocre tipper. Brenda called him the wet poodle. That was how his hair looked. Like a wet poodle had taken up residence on the top of his head.

"I heard about what happened at the diner today," Carlton said in his raspy Appalachian accent. "Is everyone all right?"

Daisy answered with a weary nod.

"I was going to come by for lunch, but you were closed. A pity about Fred Dickerson. Do they have any idea what it was?"

"They're guessing it might have been a stroke," she responded vaguely, careful not to share too much information.

Carlton liked to talk—to everyone, about everyone— and considered it an integral part of his business. In a way, it was. He was the local auctioneer and had disposed of nearly every estate in Pittsylvania County over the last three decades. On occasion there was a home or vehicle involved, but primarily it was household goods. Furniture, knickknacks, dishes, and tools. The old crocks tended to fetch a nice price. So did the guns and knives. The rest generally went for a pittance. But valuable or not, Carlton had a talent for peddling worn wares. His auctions were highly anticipated community events and never failed to be entertaining. The man could sell just about everything, including the leaky kitchen sink.

"We never do know when the good lord will call us back." He ran his fingers through his silver shock of hair. "I wouldn't guess Fred had much property?"

"I don't think so." She restrained another chuckle.

Carlton was already planning what he could auction off. Unfortunately for him, old man Dickerson hadn't been the sort to have any Tiffany lamps or Revolutionary War swords tucked up in the attic. "Maybe some rusty farm equipment."

"Suppose so," Carlton agreed without much enthusiasm. "Well, I'll be off then. I'll probably drop in for dinner on Monday."

When he had departed, Daisy raised her bottle and drained it. Beulah did the same.

"Another one?" she asked.

"Definitely," Daisy replied with a sigh. "Especially if everybody is going to come over and want to talk about Fred."

Beulah signaled Zeke, the all-purpose bartender who both poured the drinks and served them. He shuffled over with a pair of fresh bottles hanging down in between his fingers like a couple of sticks of dynamite.

"Haven't seen ya 'round here fer a long time, Daisy."

"I know." She smiled at him. She was fond of Zeke. "Wish I could get out more often."

He smiled back at her, before coughing. Zeke was an extremely gaunt, middle-aged chap with a permanent hacking cough. Too much coal dust from his last job. "Boss man workin' ya hard?"

"I need the money," Daisy answered simply.

"I hear ya. I know how it is. Ain't easy with all them medical bills." He coughed again. "How's yer poor momma doin' by the by? Haven't seen her fer a long time neither."

"Oh, she's got her good days and plenty of bad ones. But I really appreciate you asking about her, Zeke."

"Well, tell her I say's hey." He exchanged the new bottles for the old. " 'Least ya can save yer pennies with these two. They come from him."

Daisy followed Zeke's boney finger as he pointed toward a table in the far corner of the roadhouse. There she
saw Rick and Bobby Balsam, along with two unidentified
females. Rick inclined his head at her.

"Great," she muttered. "Just what I need."

"I'd watch out fer that one," Zeke advised, squinting
dubiously at Rick. "If ya ask me—which yer not, I know—
but just the same, that boy's gonna get himself mixed up in
a heap of trouble if he ain't careful."

"He's never careful, and he's always in a heap of trouble," Daisy responded dryly.

"But he's foolin' with the wrong folks this time," Zeke
told her. "City folks. Big-city folks."

Both Daisy and Beulah looked at him with interest.
Zeke may not have made it further than the ninth grade in
school, but he knew people and how to read them. Every
night he saw them at their weakest, watched them inter-
act, listened to their stories. If there was anybody new in
Pittsylvania County, if anything whatsoever happened
in Pittsylvania County, if there was an unexpected litter of
pigs or a secret steamy affair in Pittsylvania County, Zeke
was sure to have all the details.

"They were in here last week," he said. "And a couple
of weeks before that too. I didn't like the looks of 'em. Up
to no good. I could tell right off. They were askin' 'bout
people. First time it was ol' Fred."

Daisy blinked in surprise.

Zeke shrugged at her. "I heard 'bout ol' Fred this mornin'.
Hope it wasn't too bad fer y'all."

"Bad enough." She shrugged in return.

He nodded. "Well, I don't have to tell ya none 'bout ol'
Fred. I reckon ya know more than yer share already."

She frowned. She found it rather odd that no one had

mentioned Fred Dickerson in forever and now all of a sudden everyone was talking about him nonstop. But maybe it wasn't so odd after all. Death did have a peculiar way of resuscitating long-forgotten ghosts.

"So these men from the city," Beulah said. "They asked about old Fred. Did they ask about Rick too?"

"They did," Zeke confirmed. "And they met him. 'Least I think they did. They was talkin' 'bout drivin' over that way. To his and his brother's place. Them trailers out there in the woods."

"That's it?" Beulah scrunched up her nose in disappointment. "I thought it was something big. You said Rick was going to be in a heap of trouble."

"He will be," Zeke answered emphatically. "Ya mark my words. Them city boys ain't lookin' to join a nice quiet game of bridge with a couple of sweet ol' country ladies. They come fer business. Big business and big trouble. That's always been my experience. In fifty years of livin', I ain't seen nothin' different."

And from Daisy's experience, Zeke was rarely wrong when it came to judging people's motives and character. She smiled to herself. That was the first bit of good news she'd had all day. If Rick had trouble to deal with—especially a big heap of trouble—then he wouldn't have any energy left over to trouble her.

"Guess I better stop gabbin' like a turkey and get on with the job." Zeke directed a thumb toward the occupants of the neighboring table who had been waving at him for some time. The roadhouse was filling up good, even considering that it was a Friday night. All the tables were now full, and there wasn't an empty stool at the bar.

"I'll tell my momma you asked about her," Daisy said. "I know it'll make her real happy."

"Just holler when ya girls need somethin'," Zeke replied cheerfully. Then he shuffled off, coughing as he went.

As soon as he was out of earshot, Beulah said, "So what do you want to do about the beer? Drink it? Toss it out? Toss it in Rick's face?"

"Tossing it in his face sure would be fun." Daisy chuckled. "I think he'd get plenty of sympathy though," she added, watching the unidentified female who appeared to be Rick's date rub up against him with all the zeal of a donkey in heat.

"Well, we can't send the bottles back. Zeke wouldn't understand, and he'd want to know why."

"And Rick might come over here and start arguing."

"Good point. Speaking of the weasel—" Beulah leaned eagerly toward Daisy. Her hazel eyes were stretched wide with curiosity. "You never told me. What did he try to pull with Fox Hollow?"

"He didn't just try. He succeeded." She shook her head. "Rick bought Fox Hollow."

For a moment Beulah's face was frozen with shock, then it melted in an outpouring of sympathy. "Oh God, Daisy. I don't even know what to say. To have that weasel Rick Balsam own your childhood home. The place where you were born and your daddy died. It's wrong. Just plain wrong. I'm so sorry."

Daisy responded with a desultory shrug.

Beulah sucked on her teeth. "Wait a second. Fox Hollow is a serious piece of land, not to mention the house and creek. Where the hell did Rick get the money from?"

Daisy snorted. "I have no clue. I've been trying to figure that out all day."

"He doesn't work."

"Certainly not."

"He doesn't have family money?"

"Not that I've ever heard of."

"He can't have family money," Beulah said decisively. "Or they wouldn't have been living in those junky trailers all these years."

"That's what I always thought," Daisy agreed.

Beulah sucked on her teeth again. "Is it just Rick? Or him and Bobby?"

"What do you mean?"

"Do they both own Fox Hollow, or only the weasel?"

"I don't know," Daisy answered slowly. "I never thought of that. Rick said— I just sort of assumed—"

"I guess it doesn't really matter either way."

"No, I suppose it doesn't. But . . ." Daisy glanced over at Rick and Bobby playing merrily with their dates like a pair of puppies chewing up some new rawhide, and she dropped her head on the table with a groan. "God help me. That beautiful old farmhouse. Where my momma always cooked Thanksgiving dinner. The barbecues in summer. The sleigh rides in winter. Christmas and New Year's."

Having spent a good portion of her own childhood at Fox Hollow, Beulah replied with a melancholy whimper.

"Now the miserable Balsam brothers are going to turn it into a goddam rodeo and brothel! Can't you just see it?" Daisy seethed, her face pressed hard into the table. "Half-naked girls running around day and night. The boys shooting up the property when they get bored. Burning down half the place when they get too drunk."

"And growing who-the-hell-knows-what in the fields."

"That's probably where they got the money to buy Fox Hollow in the first place."

"You'd have to grow an awful lot of pot for an awful long time to get that kind of money."

"Then maybe they were cooking up meth instead."

"You shouldn't talk about that, Daisy," Rick interjected suddenly. "Especially not here. Meth's a dangerous business. You don't know who'll hear you."

Both Daisy and Beulah started in surprise, not having noticed Rick approach their table. Daisy kept her head down, annoyance winning out over shock, but Beulah attacked him straightaway.

"You've got some nerve!" she cried. "Strutting over here and acting like we're all bosom buddies."

"Nice to see you too, Beulah," Rick returned with a smirk.

She scowled at him. "You're lucky I'm a lady. Otherwise I'd wipe that smugness right off your chin."

"I'd like to see you try, sweetheart."

Out of the corner of her eye, Daisy watched Beulah's fingers twitch and curl into a fist. She wasn't a natural fighter, but she did have a very short redheaded fuse. Daisy figured that she'd better step in before Beulah hurt herself. It was tough to cut hair with a broken hand.

"What do you want, Rick?" she said, sitting up.

"You're not drinking?" he asked, gesturing toward the pair of untouched beers. "Should I take that as a hint?"

Daisy looked at the bottles, then at Rick. His eyes were dark and cloudy. That was always a sign with him to tread gently. She didn't have the strength to battle him. Not tonight at least. And it was just beer. There was no reason to get all huffy over a couple of free beers.

"Thanks for the drinks." She picked one up and took a swallow.

"Well, it's been a hell of a day. Figured you could use a little liquor."

She smiled, reluctantly. He was right. It had been a hell of a day, and she could use a little liquor.

"What you said a minute ago . . ." Rick glanced around,

spotted a vacant chair at a nearby table, pulled it over, and deposited himself on it. "You've got to be more careful, Daisy. People are always listening."

"I know." She did know. Meth equaled money in Appalachia. Serious money. The kind that was jealously, violently guarded. You didn't mess with it unless you wanted to end up either dead or in prison.

"Good," Rick replied sternly. "I wouldn't like to find you in a ditch somewhere just cuz you were yapping crap at the General one night."

Daisy smiled again, more willingly this time. "Gracious. I can't believe my ears. It almost sounds like you're worried about my well-being, Richard Balsam. It must be the alcohol talking, because there's no way you've become such a kind, tenderhearted soul at long last."

He responded with a grunt. Beulah grunted too.

"Don't believe a word that comes out of his weaselly mouth," she told Daisy grimly. "He's just being his usual flirty, devious self. Trying to butter you up, so you forgive him for stealing Fox Hollow."

There was an awkward silence, with everyone staring at the table. Finally Rick shifted in his seat and looked directly at Daisy.

"Let me explain—" he began.

She raised a hand to stop him. "No."

"You gotta know I'd never—"

"No," Daisy said again. Her tone was firm but not angry. Anger required far too much energy. "Please, Rick. Not now. What you said before. It's been too long of a day."

"Okay." He hesitated. "But eventually we're gonna have to talk about it."

"Not now," she repeated. "I can't do it now."

She fully expected him to get up and go back to his

own table, but he remained where he was. Beulah eyed him disdainfully. Daisy took a hearty drink.

"I'm kind of surprised to see you here tonight," Rick remarked after a while.

"Tomorrow is the first Saturday I've had off in . . ." Daisy thought a moment. "Well, let's just say in months, maybe even a year, so I'm trying to enjoy it."

"How's that working out for you?"

She raised an eyebrow at him.

"Why did Hank decide to close?" Beulah asked her, pointedly ignoring Rick. "If it's out of respect for the recently deceased, then you definitely ought to tell that to Aunt Emily. It would throw her murder theory right out the window."

Rick's head snapped first to Beulah, then to Daisy. "Murder theory? Aunt Emily's got a murder theory?"

"Forget it. Aunt Emily's just talking nonsense, as she loves to do, which you well know. And no," Daisy answered Beulah, "Hank didn't decide to close. The Danville forensics team made him do it. They need to run further tests or something."

"Brenda must be happy. She's at the diner almost as much as you are."

"She said she was planning on spending all of tomorrow soaking in her tub." Daisy smiled ruefully. "I shouldn't do it, because it's awfully irreverent, but I think he deserves a toast." She lifted her bottle. "To old man Dickerson. His death wasn't in vain. It gave Brenda and me a vacation day."

Beulah laughed and lifted her bottle too. "I'll drink to that."

"Careful, Daisy," Rick warned, rising from his chair. "If you start talking like that, pretty soon people might think *you* murdered him." And with a parting wink, he walked off.

"He's right," Beulah said, as she watched Rick return to his brother and their dates with a critical gaze. "You better be careful. You better be real careful. Because unless I'm very much mistaken, that weasel wants something from you."

CHAPTER
5

She didn't have to be careful that weekend. Daisy neither saw Rick Balsam nor heard one word about Fred Dickerson. It was the best weekend she'd had in a very long time. On Saturday she and her momma enjoyed a lazy morning on the back porch of the Tosh Inn, followed by a hilarious afternoon at Beulah's salon. And on Sunday the weather was picture-perfect for the annual church picnic, complete with fried chicken, buttermilk biscuits, and plenty of sweet lemonade. Daisy even managed to convince Beulah to sample the fare, after promising her that none of it had been prepared by the poison-talking Aunt Emily.

On Monday she arrived at the diner feeling refreshed and rejuvenated, like she had spent an entire month at some fancy Parisian spa, rather than a few simple days in rural southwestern Virginia. Brenda appeared equally relaxed, and during the lull between breakfast and lunch, the two happily sampled Daisy's newest culinary creation—white-chocolate raspberry scones—until Hank slammed down the phone in a fury.

"Idiots. That's what they are. Goddam idiots!"

Daisy and Brenda swiveled on their stools toward him. Hank was standing next to the cash register, dressed in his usual grease-smeared apron and jeans, glaring at the phone like it was a rat that'd had the audacity to sneak into his storeroom and he was about to take a cleaver to its filthy head.

"Problem?" Brenda said in the untroubled tone of a woman who was eating chocolate and had spent the past three days not serving anything to anybody.

"You bet there's a problem," Hank growled. "They're jackasses."

"Who?" Daisy asked, with only slightly more sympathy than Brenda. She was feeling rather chipper herself. So far her momma's new drugs hadn't shown any ill side effects, and they actually seemed to be helping somewhat. Her energy level had been better than usual that weekend, and she'd even had enough strength on Sunday evening to go for a short stroll through the garden to admire the perennials that the deer hadn't snacked on yet.

"Those fools down in Danville!"

"You mean the forensics team? Did they damage something when they were here?"

As she said it, Daisy glanced around the diner, but she saw nothing out of the ordinary. There was no sign that anything the slightest bit unusual had happened there on the previous Friday. Old man Dickerson's body was long gone, and the spot on the floor where he had fallen was clean. No blood from his head. No foam from his mouth. Not even a lonesome speck of mud from one of his rubber boots remained. It was like Frederick Dickerson had never been there at all, alive or dead.

"They don't know what the hell they're doing." Hank pounded his fist on the counter. "They should mind their own goddam business!"

"Oh, calm down," Brenda drawled. "That's what the police do. They get paid to dig around in other people's business. And you should be grateful for it. Just think of George Lowell. Without him as our sheriff we'd have a whole lot more crime in this county." She offered Hank a scone. "Here. Have one of these."

"Don't tell me to calm down," he snapped. "Or to be grateful neither. And don't stick those blasted cookies in my face—"

"Scones," she corrected him.

"Huh?"

"Scones," Brenda repeated, brushing the crumbs from her fingers. "It's a scone, not a cookie. And you should try it. After one bite your mouth will be too happy for any more grousing." She turned to Daisy. "I've said it before, Ducky, but I'll say it again. You should open up a bakery. You've got a real knack for making pastries. People would drive from all over to buy 'em. And you could sell 'em through the Internet too. Ship 'em out."

She smiled. "Thanks. It's a nice idea. But the only way I'll ever have enough money to open up a bakery is if I win the lottery. And it'd have to be a big lottery, because right now every dollar I get goes to my momma's doctors—"

"If those morons in Danville get their way," Hank interjected with vehemence, "you'll have to win the lottery to pay anybody anything. You won't get another cent from this place."

Daisy instantly fell silent. She and Brenda looked at him.

"That's right." He nodded. "Not one more penny."

"That isn't funny." Brenda's voice was sharp. "You know how hard Ducky works to take care of her momma. If Lucy weren't sick and Daisy didn't have to be with her all the time, she could get a proper job in Lynchburg. Like she used to have before her daddy passed and Matt left. Instead of wasting her days in this old dump serving up pork and beans to lousy folks like those Balsam boys."

"I wasn't saying—" Hank began.

"It's cruel. Just plain cruel," she cut him off, "to even joke that you might fire Ducky. You're lucky to have her! Without her, half the customers wouldn't take a step through that door. They come to see *her* and her fabulous cookies, not *you* and your mediocre hash."

"I wasn't saying," Hank tried again, louder this time, "anything about firing Daisy. Have you lost your mind, Brenda? That's one of the stupidest things I ever heard come out of your mouth." He shook his head at her angrily. "I didn't mean she wasn't going to have a job here because of me." Turning to Daisy, Hank patted her arm with paternal affection. "Of course you've got a job here. You've got a job so long as H & P's is open for business."

"I know." Daisy nodded. "And I appreciate it, Hank. I really do."

He patted her arm again. "But I'm afraid that's where we hit the problem. H & P's isn't going to be open for business much longer."

"What!" Brenda and Daisy cried in unison.

"That's what I've been trying to tell you. Those idiots in Danville want to close the place. They've decided to shut us down."

"They can't do that!" Brenda exclaimed, jumping up from her stool. "They've got no right! They can't go around closing down diners whenever they dang well feel like it." She spun on her heel to Daisy. "They can't, can they?"

"I don't really know, but I don't think so." Daisy looked at Hank. "You're current with all the health inspections, aren't you? I thought they gave you an almost perfect score just a couple of months ago. Wasn't it ninety-eight out of a hundred? And the only thing they found wrong was that bucket you'd been using to dump the old cooking grease. It wasn't even anything food or health related."

"It's health related now," Hank seethed, grinding his teeth.

Brenda marched over to the phone. "I'm going to call Sheriff Lowell. I'll tell him what they're trying to pull. He'll straighten it out. He always does."

"Don't bother," Hank responded. "George is the one who gave me the news. He's the one I was talking to before."

The phone dropped from Brenda's fingers. "But—"

"But you said Danville," Daisy finished for her, equally surprised. "You said it was the folks down in Danville."

"It is the folks down in Danville. The goddam fools! They told George, and George told me."

Daisy's brow furrowed. "And Sheriff Lowell is going along with it? Since when does he agree to anything they do in Danville?"

"He doesn't agree," Hank informed her. "He's mad as hell, same as me. And he's been arguing with them since early this morning. That's when they called the office and ordered him to shut us down."

"Shut us down when?" Brenda asked.

"George wasn't even supposed to let us open today."

"Well, that explains why nobody's here." Daisy glanced at her watch. It was nearly twelve thirty. "I was wondering what happened to the lunch rush. I guess this time the gossip train traveled so fast, it actually beat us. Everyone in the county knew we weren't serving before we did."

"But why?" Brenda shook her head in confusion. "I still don't get why. They're closing us because of an old grease bucket?"

Hank rolled his eyes at her. "No. Don't be a fool too! Of course they're not closing us because of an old grease bucket. They're closing us because of old Fred."

Brenda went right on shaking her head. "Fred? But we were already closed because of Fred. Didn't they finish everything they needed to do on Friday and Saturday?"

"They did finish," Hank explained to her, "but apparently one of the idiots from the Danville forensics team didn't like what he saw. He thought it could be a health hazard, and he reported it to the state disease center."

"Does that mean they're worried Fred died of something contagious?" Daisy said.

"Exactly. So they're locking our doors. A precaution, the morons are calling it."

"For how long?"

"A crew is supposed to come up from the Danville hospital later this week and sterilize the place."

"They're not planning on quarantining us too, are they?"

Brenda gaped at her in horror.

"Bite your tongue, child," Hank reprimanded her gravely. "Nobody's mentioned it, and we don't want to give them any ideas."

There was a heavy silence. Brenda returned to her stool. Hank untied his apron and hurled it into the kitchen. Daisy thought about her momma's new medicine.

"When can the diner reopen?" she asked Hank.

"Hell if I know. They haven't said."

Daisy chewed on her lip. Having one vacation day was great. Having a week, or two, or three was bad. Very bad.

"I know what you're thinking." Hank's thick face was creased with concern. "I've been thinking it too. You need the money."

"My momma's drugs are so expensive," she responded plaintively.

He nodded. "I'd give you an advance, except I don't have it. Frankly, I don't know how I'm going to come up with the money for the cleaning."

"They're making you pay for the cleaning!" Brenda exclaimed indignantly.

Hank answered with a grunt.

"And you're sure Sheriff Lowell can't do anything?" she went on.

"George told me he's going to keep on fighting it, but I don't really think there's much he can do."

"But he's the sheriff!" Brenda protested. "Doesn't the Pittsylvania County sheriff trump some stupid forensics team in Danville?"

"I'm sorry to say it doesn't work that way," Hank replied. "It's not a matter of who has the shiniest badge. Once there's a report to the disease center, a whole huge set of procedures and regulations automatically kicks in. You can't stop the ball when it's already begun rolling. All you can do is try to ride it out."

"And pray you don't get squished in the process," Daisy added without enthusiasm.

Hank grunted once more.

"That doesn't seem right," Brenda insisted stubbornly.

"It ain't right," Hank agreed. "But there ain't nothin' we can do about it neither."

Daisy sighed. It had started out as such a good day, promising even. Fresh scones. New drugs for her momma. Now she couldn't afford the drugs and there wouldn't be any customers for the scones.

The rusty bell above the front door of the diner clanked. In unison, they all snapped their heads toward it. Daisy

expected to see Sheriff Lowell, ready to drive them out of
H & P's like an impudent herd of cattle. She found Sue
Lowell instead.

"Oh my lord!" Brenda gasped. "You were right, Ducky.
They're going to quarantine us too!"

"Nobody's quarantining anyone," Hank declared, cross-
ing his tattooed biceps over his chest in defiance.

Sue looked puzzled, which Daisy took as a good sign. If
the sheriff's wife actually was there to quarantine them,
she wouldn't be confused by the discussion of it.

"Hey there, Sue," she greeted her. "Want a scone?"

"Always, if it's one of yours."

"It is. Baked this morning."

"Ooh, yummy. What kind?"

"White-chocolate raspberry."

"Double yummy." Sue rubbed her hands together greed-
ily. "Make it a big one, please. I skipped breakfast, and it'll
have to be my lunch."

Daisy reached under the counter, pulled out a plate,
and deposited a particularly generous-sized scone onto it.
She genuinely liked Sue, but she also figured that it couldn't
hurt to butter up the sheriff's wife a bit, especially when
that sheriff was in the process of shutting down her only
source of income.

"So if it's not for one of Hank's delectably greasy bacon
cheeseburgers," Daisy drawled, sliding the plate and pastry
in front of the nearest empty stool, "what brings you to the
diner?"

Sue didn't answer immediately. She took a seat and
broke off a bite of scone, but she toyed with it instead of
eating it.

"Just say what you came to say," Hank demanded, not
having the patience to wait her out. "Don't play games.
Give it to us straight."

"All right." With a sigh, she set the scone back down and pushed the plate away. "I'm here to ask for a favor."

"A favor?" Hank's tone was testy. "If your husband closes us up, I won't be able to give favors to you or anybody else."

"I know that, Hank," Sue responded sympathetically. "George is doing his best. He really is. But those boys in Danville—"

Hank snarled. "Jackasses."

She nodded. "Yes, but they've got their rules and orders. We've all got our rules and orders."

"Here comes the bad news," Hank muttered with disgust. "It's just like in the military. The bad news always comes tucked in between talk about rules and orders."

Brenda knotted and unknotted her fingers anxiously. "Are we going to be quarantined or not? Because if we are, somebody's going to have to take care of Blot."

Blot was Brenda's very spoiled, very fat black cat. He was such a monstrous pile of shaggy fur when he sprawled out on her cream-colored carpeting that he looked like a giant ink stain, hence the name.

"Beulah could probably—" Daisy began.

"Quarantined?" Sue interjected, shaking her head. "Nobody wants you quarantined. At least not that I've heard."

Both Brenda and Daisy breathed an audible sigh of relief.

"And I'm pretty sure somebody would have said something to me about it by now," Sue added, "because I was the one who got the closest to Fred when I examined him. Plus it's been four days. Quarantine wouldn't do much good after that long. Consider all the people we've been in contact with since Friday."

"If it's not contagious, then why close the diner?" Daisy asked.

"There's still the possibility of a disease, and the Danville police think the death is suspicious."

"Didn't you think that too?" Brenda said.

"I did," Sue admitted. "I still do."

Daisy's frustration grew. "But how is shutting down the diner going to make any difference with that?"

Sue shrugged. "It wasn't my idea. And for what it's worth, I don't think shutting down the diner is going to do a lick of good. But unfortunately, I don't get a say in the matter. It's completely out of my hands. I'm just a small-town paramedic, and as we all know, they don't listen to anybody small-town. I'm sorry, but we just have to wait for the results from the autopsy. That'll decide everything."

"So even if they do make us close now," Daisy mused hopefully, "if the autopsy comes back saying the death was due to normal, natural causes, then we can open back up?"

"George and I thought that too," Sue agreed.

Daisy looked back and forth between Brenda and Hank. "That's good news at least. I mean, how long can the autopsy take? Like she said, it's been four days already."

Brenda nodded enthusiastically. Hank turned to Sue.

"What's the favor you want from me?"

"Actually"—she brushed the short black hair from her eyes—"it's a favor I want from Daisy."

"Me?" Daisy blinked at her in surprise.

"Let me start by explaining—"

Hank snorted, slumped down on a stool, and grabbed a scone. "Watch out, Daisy. I have the feeling you're about to be asked to donate a pair of kidneys."

Sue tried to laugh, but it was obviously forced.

"I'd be happy to do whatever I can for you," Daisy said. She regretted the offer almost before she'd even finished the sentence. Sue was tugging at her blue crystal earrings with evident unease. It made Daisy nervous.

"The thing is . . ." Sue hesitated.

"Kidneys," Hank mumbled low.

"It's not about my momma, is it?" Daisy became increasingly worried. "Something bad hasn't happened, has it?"

"Oh, Ducky!" Brenda reached out and squeezed her hand in support.

"No, no," Sue replied quickly. "It's nothing like that."

Daisy took a deep, reassured breath. So long as her momma was okay. She still remembered with painful clarity how it had felt when she first received the horrible news about the accident and her daddy.

"The thing is," Sue began once more, "they started an investigation into Fred Dickerson's death."

"Right." Daisy was already aware of that, considering his body was in the process of being autopsied and the Danville forensics team had done a thorough inspection of the diner.

"Which means they need to look at the place where Fred lived. But there's an issue about gaining access to it."

"Gaining access to it?" Daisy frowned. "What's the problem there? Fox Hollow has a driveway. They just follow it until they reach the house."

"Except Fred Dickerson was just a tenant." Sue scrunched up her nose. "A tenant without a legal lease apparently. So they need to get permission from the owner before they go onto the property. And if not actual permission—because the death was suspicious—they at least need to talk to the owner."

Daisy's gaze narrowed as her former angst switched to suspicion. She didn't like the direction that the conversation seemed to be headed.

Sue came directly to the point. "The Danville police don't want to come up again if they don't have to, so they told George he needs to handle it. He's been ordered to talk to the owner of Fox Hollow. That's Rick Balsam."

"What does that have to do with me?" Daisy responded tersely.

"We both know that going to those trailers Rick and Bobby call home out there in the backwoods is never a picnic. You can only guess what you might find or what on earth they'll be doing . . ."

"Probably burning or shooting something," Brenda remarked.

Sue nodded. "They've got all those crazy signs posted. Then there are the dogs. They could be drunk, and I'm afraid they might be just a little too trigger happy when they see the Pittsylvania County sheriff's car pull up in their front yard."

Daisy didn't argue with her. She couldn't. Every word was true. The Balsam brothers did have crazy signs. And dogs. And by law enforcement standards, an uncomfortably large number of firearms, many of which were scoped.

"I suggested to George that I go instead of him," Sue continued, once again tugging at her earrings. "Break the ice, so to speak. Or at least *try* to break the ice. I don't think Rick and Bobby hold any major grudges against me. But George said there's only one person who he's sure Rick won't shoot on sight." She looked at Daisy with some embarrassment and gave her an apologetic shrug.

Hank grumbled a few incomprehensible syllables as he dug into a second scone. Daisy sighed. He was right. Sue was asking for a pair of kidneys. Or a mighty close equivalent.

"So you want me to go to Rick and Bobby's with you?" she said. "That's the favor?"

Sue's face instantly brightened. "That would be great, Daisy. George and I'd both really appreciate it."

Daisy hesitated. There wasn't even a teeny tiny fraction of her that wanted to pay a visit to the Balsam brothers. She saw more than enough of them already. But there was the diner to consider. The sooner the investigation into Fred Dickerson's death ended, the sooner H & P's could re-open.

"Fine," she agreed reluctantly. "I'll go." Daisy raised a shrewd eyebrow. "But the next time there's any trouble here at the diner, I expect the sheriff's office to take care of it lickety-split."

Sue laughed. "Of course."

"And can I also expect someone to stumble across an emergency slush fund to help cover the cost of the supposed sterilization of this place by the Danville hospital?"

"Either that," Sue promised, "or I'll do my durnedest to talk the folks at the hospital out of coming at all."

"Fine," Daisy said again, with a satisfied nod. "I'll go."

Hank grinned and slapped her on the shoulder. "You're a born negotiator, child. Just like your daddy."

She didn't grin back. Her daddy wouldn't have liked her going anywhere near Rick Balsam.

CHAPTER
6

The ambulance bumped over the gravel like a woozy pack mule plodding along an old wagon trail. Back and forth. Up and down. It was enough to make even the most rugged country girl long for a smooth, paved boulevard. But the scenery was lovely. Pine stands as far as the eye could see. Endless rows of majestic, towering trees. It was a dark, almost ominous forest, with only an occasional sunburst breaking through the canopy where a windstorm or lightning strike had created a small natural clearing. Everywhere the ground was covered with a thick carpet of dried, rust-colored needles. And the smell was heavenly. It was fresh and clean, with a hint of sweetness to it, almost like a stick of peppermint candy.

"This is a hundred times better than air-conditioning." Daisy sighed, opening the window and inhaling deeply. "It always amazes me how you can be sweltering to death in ninety-plus degrees standing in the middle of some cornfield, then you take two steps in here and it feels like a completely different season. You can actually breathe again."

"Speaking of breathing," Sue replied, "when we get to the trailers should I prepare myself for being accosted by any animals other than the dogs?"

"I don't think so. Lordy, I hope not, because I only brought goodies for the pups." Daisy patted the bulging bag of ham bones that she had taken from the diner. "When was the last time you were at the trailers, Sue?"

"I was just trying to figure that out myself." She calculated a moment. "It must have been about two years ago. It was that time Rick had to call the rescue squad when Bobby accidentally skewered himself in the knee."

Daisy burst out laughing. "I remember that! He'd watched some old Robin Hood movie and was trying to make his own crossbow."

"A real genius idea that turned out to be."

"I must have teased him about it for a good six months whenever he and Rick came into the diner after that."

"Daisy," Sue said, growing serious, "I want to thank you again for going with me today to talk to them. I was awfully worried about George coming out here all alone. I know it can't be easy for you. I know there's a lot of . . . er . . . history between you and Rick."

Her laughter promptly died, but she was saved from having to answer by the appearance of the Balsam brothers' infamous signs. The first few were nothing out of the ordinary, merely the standard yellow postings ordering no hunting, no fishing, and no hiking. They were followed by a half dozen black-and-orange beware of dog and a similar half dozen black-and-white private property. Then came the serious signs, the ones that made Sue slow the ambulance and shift uncomfortably in her seat. Some were handmade. Others were professionally done. But they were all big and quite clear.

TRESPASSERS WILL BE SHOT ON SIGHT
GOVERNMENT AGENTS WILL BE SHOT ON SIGHT
GOVERNMENT VEHICLES WILL BE SHOT ON SIGHT
SOLICITORS WILL BE SHOT ON SIGHT
STRANGERS WILL BE SHOT ON SIGHT
TURN AROUND NOW OR YOU WILL BE SHOT ON SIGHT

"I think that last one is new," Daisy remarked, half smothering a chortle.

Sue looked at her in surprise. "You think they're funny?"

"No. Of course not. But you said it best when we were at the diner. The signs are crazy. They've always been crazy, and they're always going to be crazy." She shrugged. "So what's the point of getting worked up about them?"

"It's easy for you to be calm. You're not the government agent driving the government vehicle."

"There's probably an unwritten exception for paramedics and ambulances," Daisy joked. "There was when Bobby skewered himself with the crossbow, right?"

A small smile crept over Sue's otherwise tense face.

"Don't worry," Daisy reassured her. "They won't shoot us. So long as we identify ourselves as soon as possible—and the boys aren't too drunk."

"That's not really very comforting."

She shrugged once more. "Honestly, I think there's a higher likelihood of getting mauled by the pups."

"Now I'm even happier George isn't here. He doesn't do so well with dogs, especially not the overly aggressive kind. He gets too many calls about roaming feral packs that shredded the favorite family hen. He has to put a lot of them down."

"The Balsam canines can get pretty aggressive if they feel threatened. Sometimes even Bobby has trouble controlling them. But they always obey Rick."

Sue gulped. "I guess we better hope Rick is home."

"If he's not, the whole trip up here was for nothing. But," Daisy added deprecatingly, glancing at her watch, "it's only midafternoon. The boys are probably still sleeping off whatever depravity they participated in last night."

"How anyone can sleep over that racket is a mystery to me."

From a distance the collective howling, barking, and baying of dogs sounded like the rumble of thunder from an impending storm. As Daisy and Sue drove closer, it rose in pitch and ferocity until it became a din of gale-force intensity, completely deafening every other sound, even that of the ambulance motor.

"Pull all the way into the clearing," Daisy instructed as the gravel road began to widen. "The pups will start jumping at the tires, but don't worry about them. They're way too smart and agile to get trampled. If you stop too soon, it'll be that much harder for us to make it to the trailers."

Sue pursed her lips nervously and nodded. She jumped when the first rottweiler crashed against the door on her side, snarling like it hadn't eaten for a week and was planning on using her as its next meal.

"Just ignore him," Daisy said. "Keep going. Keep going."

Eyeing the snapping beast warily, Sue continued forward. Daisy had no doubt that if Sue had been just a little less worried about the safety of her husband, she would have instantly shifted the ambulance into reverse and squealed backward down the road, getting as far away from Balsam land as possible.

Restraining a smile, Daisy turned to look at the dogs, counting them and seeing which ones she knew. "That's Morgan." She pointed first to the rottweiler clawing at the

door and then to a second rottweiler hot on his sister's
heels. "The other is Captain."

A pack of yowling blueticks bounded over to join the
fun.

"There's Gold—and Green—and Red—and Bl—"

In spite of her anxiety, Sue laughed. "Do Rick and
Bobby name all their dogs after liquor? Cuz if they do, Jack
and Johnnie are going to have to come up with a few more
label colors."

"Not the black and tans. They've got way too many to
name them."

There were at least fifteen—maybe twenty—black-and-
tan coonhounds racing around the ambulance as though
they were trying to tree it. They were all heavy-boned and
muscular, with long ears and heads.

"Good God," Sue muttered. "I knew the Balsam boys
kept a lot of dogs, but I had no idea it was this many."

"Just think about how much kibble they go through in
a week." Daisy frowned at the bag of bones at her feet. "I
hope I brought enough."

"What's the plan? Throw the ham one way and we run
the other?"

She grinned. "Something like that."

"You think it'll work?"

"Sure. Captain and Morgan just need a good pat and
their own set of bones, then they'll be fine. And the hounds
are all big babies. Take a look at those weepy eyes of theirs.
They may sound loud, but it's mostly bark and not much
bite. They're gonna give us a good sniff, then every ounce
of their attention will be focused on the bones."

"I'm glad you're so confident," Sue responded dubiously, as the monstrous pair of rottweilers bared their teeth
at her.

"This is good. Stop here."

They had reached the center of the clearing. It wasn't a pretty clearing with a white picket fence and manicured shrubs. It was a large, oval, man-made break in the forest filled with plenty of stumps and boulders. At some point gravel had been dumped there to make a sort of entrance-way, but it had washed and worn away over the years, and now the ground was mostly red clay mixed with scruffy weeds.

Rick and Bobby's trailers stood side by side at the far end of the clearing. On first approach a stranger could have easily thought they were abandoned. There was no potted plant on the steps, no lawn chair sitting out front, not even a bag of trash waiting to be taken to the dump. Both trailers were ancient and covered in flaking rust. Their formerly white paint had turned dingy gray. The windows were streaked with dirt, and the screens were shredded. It all looked terribly tattered and pathetically forlorn.

"He's got plenty of money to buy Fox Hollow," Daisy mumbled crossly, "but he still won't spend a nickel to fix up this place."

"What was that?" Sue said, parking the ambulance.

"Nothing. Ready?" She took a deep breath. She wasn't any more eager to climb out of the vehicle than Sue, although for an entirely different reason. Sue dreaded the dogs. Daisy dreaded their owners.

"Ready?" Sue echoed apprehensively, gazing at the growling collection of canines awaiting her. "I don't know. You're sure it's all bark and not bite?"

"Positive. Let me go first, and they'll come around to my side. When I've got their attention with the ham, then you can go. They probably won't even notice you once they've started in on the bones."

"Which trailer is Rick's?" Sue asked.

"The one on the right." Daisy furrowed her brow as she looked back and forth between the two dented doors. There was no sign of either Rick or Bobby. "It's strange they haven't come out yet. Their trucks are both here." She gestured at the two pickups parked toward the left in between a fire pit and a scorched charcoal grill.

"Maybe I should keep the engine running," Sue said, "just in case they don't answer and we have to sprint back to the ambulance to avoid getting mangled."

"I think we'll be okay." Daisy suppressed a chuckle. For a robust woman, both in girth and personality, Sue was awfully timid when it came to pooches. Maybe she had gotten a set of razor teeth locked into her thigh once in the past and was now doubly shy. "Well, wish me luck."

Sue watched as Daisy scooped up her bag of bones and opened the door. As predicted, all the dogs immediately galloped around to her side. Before her feet even touched the ground, she was enveloped in a giant woofing, whining, yapping heap of fur and paws. Sue may have cringed in anticipation of the first savage bite, but it didn't come. Tails were wagging. Tongues were drooling. Daisy acknowledged them in their self-determined pecking order. She scratched the thick backs of the rottweilers first, then rubbed the broad heads of the blueticks. The black-and-tan coonhounds came last, pushing their muzzles against her for their share of the affection. Finally she doled out the ham bones, smartly scattering them away from the ambulance and the trailers.

"Okey-dokey," she called to Sue when she had finished. "All clear."

Sue was visibly impressed. "You're like a dog sorcerer."

Daisy laughed and shook her head. "No. It's just basic

doggie hierarchy. I've met Captain and Morgan before, so they know my scent. They're the alphas. If they accept you, all the rest will too. Pack mentality. And a bit of meat bribery never hurts."

While Sue started toward the trailers, Daisy returned to the ambulance and pulled out a second bag.

"More bones?" Sue asked.

"No. This is for the boys. Bribery in the form of baked goods."

It was Sue's turn to laugh. "What's the old saying? The way to a man's heart is through his stomach?"

Daisy grinned. "Hey, you want cooperation. This is the best way I know to get Rick and Bobby to cooperate."

"I'll have to remember that." Sue stopped for a moment and listened. "Gosh, it's awfully nice in here when it's quiet, isn't it?"

In comparison to their former hullabaloo, the dogs were now silent, only breaking into an occasional tussle over an unclaimed bone. A soft Appalachian breeze rustled the crowns of the pines. A woodpecker pounded the bark in search of an insect. On some distant branch a squirrel chattered.

"This is the best part of not having any neighbors," Daisy remarked. "No car doors slamming. No lawn mowers firing up first thing Saturday morning. Not having to hear everybody else's conversation out on the patio."

"There sure is something to be said for isolation," Sue agreed. "But this," she wrinkled her nose at the ramshackle trailers, "is a little too isolated for my taste."

"If they ever try to sell 'em, I know the perfect way to phrase the advertisement. *Peaceful rural retreat. Needs minor work.*"

"That's hilarious!" Sue chortled. "The poor girl who

marries either of them one day. She's going to have her hands full."

"Brenda always says the same thing."

But Daisy knew that it wasn't entirely true anymore, at least not in regard to the elder brother and the family homestead. Now Rick and a future Mrs. Balsam could move to Fox Hollow and ruin the beautiful old farmhouse there, which would be a thousand times worse than ruining a pair of inconsequential trailers here. It was a depressing thought.

Sue climbed the two short steps to Rick's battered door. She squinted at it, then turned to Daisy, who was a couple of paces behind her. "I don't see a bell. Should I just knock?" She leaned her ear close to the peeling paint. "I don't hear anything inside. Maybe he—"

Her jaw froze midsentence. Through the tranquil stillness came the unmistakable sound of a bolt driving a round into the chamber of a rifle.

CHAPTER 7

Like a doe catching the crack of a twig beneath the paw of an approaching mountain lion, Sue's body went rigid. Only her eyes moved. They dashed from Daisy to Rick's door to the scraggy bushes behind the trailer. Daisy studied the bushes too. She saw nothing. No bending branch. No track in the dirt. Not even a fluttering leaf. She knew they had to be there, concealed somewhere in the undergrowth. But she couldn't find them, neither the rifle nor the man who was presumably holding it.

"Daisy—" Sue choked in a barely audible whisper.

Daisy understood her panic. There was a very specific feeling of fright that came with a gun pointed in your direction, visible or not. It was a basic, instinctive desire to survive. And it wasn't lessened in the least by the fact that one half of your brain realized you probably wouldn't actually be shot. The other half of your brain took priority and screamed at you to flee.

"Where . . ." Sue stammered. "I don't—"

With a frown and slight shake of her head, Daisy silenced her. Logic told her that it had to be one or both of the Balsam brothers hidden in the bushes. The most likely scenario was that they had been out in the forest when she and Sue first arrived. They might have heard the ambulance engine and its tires on the gravel. They would have definitely heard the dogs. And they had come home to investigate. They had caught voices and seen people wandering around their trailers, except they didn't catch or see enough to identify them. Which meant that she had better identify herself. And quick. Daisy wasn't sure how Rick and Bobby felt about Sue dropping in unannounced for a visit, but she was pretty confident that they wouldn't knowingly play target practice with her.

"It's me," she cried, raising her hands in half-mocking surrender. "Daisy. Not a stranger, government agent, or unwanted solicitor. Just lil' ol' Daisy McGovern. Your favorite waitress over at H & P's."

Sticks snapped, and a shrub parted. A figure appeared dressed in full camouflage. Hat, shirt, vest, gloves, pants, and boots. Even his face was painted.

"Aw hell, Daisy," he complained. "I almost took your leg clean off."

Daisy heaved a sigh of relief and lowered her arms. It was Bobby, and he sounded sober. That was especially good considering he had a loaded rifle slung over his back. Sue exhaled so hard, she coughed.

Bobby immediately paused. "Who's that with you, Daisy?"

"Sue," she answered hastily. "Sue Lowell. We came in her ambulance."

"Ambulance? I didn't hear no siren. What'd Rick do? Lop off his hand with that new butchering knife?"

Sue grimaced.

"It isn't an emergency," Daisy explained. "And we haven't

seen Rick. He's not with you?" She glanced over at the shrub from which Bobby had emerged to see if his brother had secreted himself there too.

"Naw. I went out alone."

"Well, he's the reason we drove all the way up here, so do you know if he's around somewhere?"

"Ain't you tried the door?" Bobby motioned toward Sue standing in front of Rick's trailer.

"I was just about to knock." Sue raised a timorous fist and rapped the warped aluminum frame gently.

Bobby let out a snort. "How the jiminy is he gonna hear that? I'll get him for ya." He pulled the large-bore rifle from his back and let a shot rip into the woods with a sharp, startling crack.

"Bobby—" Daisy began critically.

"Relax. We got no neighbors. Ain't nobody gonna get nicked."

Sue gazed curiously at the rifle, which matched Bobby's clothing in its perfect camouflage of olive green, gray, and neutral beige undertones. "Did you paint it to look like that?"

"Don't know much about huntin', eh?" he chortled. "You buy 'em this way. They make 'em for all different terrains. Snow, woods, water. This one's supposed to look like real trees. It's for goin' after turkey."

"It's the middle of summer," Daisy said. "Turkey season doesn't open until October."

"I'm just practicin'," Bobby replied with a suspiciously innocent grin.

"With a rifle? Last time I checked, turkey hunting's usually done with a shotgun."

The grin turned sheepish.

Daisy rolled her eyes at him. He was obviously up to

something bad, but in her experience the only one who ever got hurt in all of Bobby's ill-advised and ill-fated schemes was himself, so she let it drop.

"There's noise inside." Sue backed swiftly down the steps and away from the trailer. "I think he heard us."

"Took him long enough," Bobby muttered, massaging the stock of his rifle.

Sue went over and stood next to Daisy. She knew why. It wasn't the gun itself. Sue was used to guns. Her husband was the Pittsylvania County sheriff after all. He carried a pistol most of the time. But George Lowell had been properly trained in the use of firearms, and he was emotionally stable. Whether the same could be said for the Balsam brothers was debatable.

A lock clicked, and the screen door flew open.

"Jesus, Mary, and Joseph! How many times have I told you not to do that, Bobby? You don't shoot at a rustle in the bushes. And if you fire a warning shot, it's always, *always* into the ground. *Never* the trees! You don't know who could be out there. One of those high-powered cartridges you're using can go over a mile."

"I tried to tell him," Daisy said.

Rick gaped at her. She couldn't remember when she had last seen him so stunned. Fred Dickerson's collapse on the floor of the diner had certainly surprised him, but he hadn't looked half as shocked then as he did now. It was like she had metamorphosed into a mermaid right before his eyes and was lying on the clay in her clam shells, flapping her tail.

"What—" he garbled, his jaw sagging so low that it wasn't fully operational. "What are you—"

"What am I doing here?" she finished for him. "I came with Sue. She needs to talk to you."

Turning to her in anticipation, Daisy assumed that Sue would take full advantage of the introduction and jump straight into the meat of the matter. But she was just as speechless as Rick, although rather obviously for a different reason. If Rick hadn't expected to see Daisy standing in front of his trailer, then Sue hadn't expected Rick to come out of that trailer half-naked.

"Gah," was all she managed to say.

It took some effort on Daisy's part not to laugh. Sue was quite evidently admiring a view that her darling portly George didn't provide. It was a good view. That was an unarguable fact. Richard Balsam was tall and tan and lean and muscular. It wasn't anything new to Daisy. She had seen him shirtless before—as he was now—wearing nothing but an old torn pair of athletic shorts. He had a pretty body and a pretty face, and as a result, girls of all ages tended to throw themselves at him. But Daisy was not one of them.

She walked over to Bobby and handed him the bag of sweet treats that she had brought along from the diner. "Wanna cookie?"

Bobby had the same attention span as his hounds. He promptly tossed his rifle to the ground and stuck his head in the bag like it was a feed trough with a fresh load of slop. Daisy was about to tell Rick that he better act fast if he had any interest in obtaining his share of the goodies, but she was interrupted by a breathy giggle.

"Did somebody say cookie?"

Daisy spun back toward the trailer. A woman was standing in the open doorway next to Rick. She was in her early twenties with big hair and big teeth. Her clothing was the opposite size. She wore a cutoff pink tank top and pink polka-dot bikini underwear. The sight of her broke Sue out of her admiring trance.

"Well," she snickered to Daisy, "I guess now we know why he didn't hear the dogs barking."

The breathy giggle repeated itself. "We heard the dogs, didn't we, Rick?" The pink tank top rubbed up close against his side. "But we were right in the middle, weren't we? We didn't want to stop."

"Lovely." Daisy wrinkled her nose in revulsion. "Thank you for sharing that."

"Jealous, darlin'?" Rick drawled. The appearance of his female companion had snapped him out of his stupor too, and he immediately returned to his usual smug self.

"Oh yes," Daisy retorted dryly. "I'm terribly jealous."

"You're welcome in my bed anytime."

"By the looks of it, your bed is already full."

"Just say the word, Daisy. I'd toss all the rest out for you."

"Rick!" the pink tank top protested.

He wrapped his arm around her bare waist. "Go inside and get a drink or something, would ya? I've got to talk business for a minute."

The pink tank top stuck out a pouty lip. "But—"

"Don't fuss." Rick sucked on the lip, then proceeded down her neck. "Be a good girl."

"Okay." She sighed rapturously.

"Go on now." He gave her one last lingering kiss.

"I don't know if I should applaud or vomit," Sue said to Daisy, shaking her head as she watched the pair. "How does he do that? She's like mushy mulch in his hands."

Daisy shrugged, irritated and unimpressed. Although not quite so proficient as Rick, her husband Matt had been a snake charmer too. And look where it had gotten her. She felt sorry for the pink tank top, mostly because she knew what Rick had said before was true. He'd toss the silly girl overboard in a heartbeat, whenever he got sufficiently tired, or bored, or a potentially greener tank top appeared on the horizon.

As she disappeared into the trailer, Rick swatted her backside. The pink tank top responded with a final breathy giggle, then the door slammed shut behind her.

Having evidently heard her remark to Daisy, Rick turned to Sue with a rakish grin. "Never question the magic of the magician."

"Or the stench of the dunghill," Daisy muttered.

He chuckled. "I can always count on you, darlin', to put me in my place."

She answered with a grunt.

"But considering you brought a chaperone," Rick went on, gesturing toward Sue, "I've got to assume you didn't come to play. More's the pity. What time is it anyway?" He looked down at his watch, only to discover that he wasn't wearing one. "Shouldn't you be at the diner serving up slabs of pie right about now?"

"The diner is closed," Daisy informed him.

His grin faded. "Closed? Still?"

"No, closed again. We were open for breakfast this morning, but then the Danville police dropped the boom on us."

"Still investigating old man Dickerson's death, eh?"

Daisy nodded.

"Have they latched on to Aunt Emily's murder theory yet?"

Sue's head whipped toward him. "What!"

Rick looked at Daisy. She raised a cautionary eyebrow at him, and she knew from the way his jaw twitched in response that he understood. Although Rick had many faults, being a fool was not one of them. He had been born much cleverer than his brother. With Bobby every card was already on the table. What you saw was exactly what you got. But with Rick there was invariably the possibility of an ace tucked up his sleeve. It could be in the form of a hidden agenda, a sly secret, or a favor to be cashed in later, and as a result, Daisy could always count on him to know when to talk and when to keep his mouth shut, especially with the Pittsylvania County sheriff's wife.

"What did you say?" Sue demanded.

"Me?" Rick blinked at her like a guileless lamb. "I didn't say anything."

"Yes, you did," she retorted. "About Emily. Emily and a murder theory."

"Oh"—he feigned a laugh—"you misunderstood. I didn't say *murder*. I said *burger*."

"Burger?" Sue repeated skeptically. "What's a burger theory? And why would Emily Tosh have one?"

"Didn't you tell her?" Rick turned his lamb eyes on Daisy. "Doesn't she know?"

Daisy could do no more than frown at him. She was lost.

"I'm sure it's in one of the reports somewhere," he continued to Sue smoothly. "You probably read it—or heard about it—and you just don't remember. The last thing Fred said before he collapsed was *burger*. Daisy mentioned it to Aunt Emily, and she thought he might've had some bad beef. Didn't cook it right. Or it spoiled. That sort of thing. And he was trying to tell us about it when he stumbled into the diner."

"You mean food poisoning?" Sue said.

Daisy choked. It was a marvelous twist of the facts. She couldn't help being impressed by how quickly Rick had turned *murder* into *burger* and then explained his reference to Aunt Emily in such a plausible way. But the funny part—which Rick didn't know of course—was that Aunt Emily had actually talked about poison. It was her original murder theory, except not through spoiled beef.

Sue glanced at her. "Emily thought Fred might've eaten something bad?"

"Yes." And it wasn't a lie. That was indeed Aunt Emily's initial assumption, with a sprinkle of cyanide or a dash of drain cleaner added in.

"Huh." Sue was thoughtful for a moment. "There might be something in that. If not food poisoning, then maybe a food allergy. An extreme one. A hypersensitivity. Honestly, I never really considered either of those as possibilities, but that could explain some of the symptoms he exhibited."

"Well, we'll find out when the autopsy comes back," Daisy chirped, eager to move the conversation as far away from Aunt Emily as possible.

"When is that supposed to be?" Rick asked Sue.

"The physical exam should already be complete. As to the blood toxicology, my best guess is by the end of the week. Next week at the latest. I don't know what all they're testing for, but I doubt it's so extensive that it'll take much longer than that."

"Then H & P's can reopen," Daisy said hopefully.

It was Rick's turn to raise an eyebrow. She didn't like its inference. He clearly wasn't as confident in the results of the autopsy or what effect they would have on the diner.

Leaning against the door of his trailer, he switched topics. "So Daisy said something earlier about you needing to talk to me, Sue?"

"Right." She nodded. "I'm here for George actually."

Rick sucked on his teeth with displeasure.

"I know you two aren't the best of friends, Rick, but

please hear me out. As part of the investigation into Fred's death, they need to look at where he lived. That's obviously Fox Hollow, and since you legally own the place, someone had to talk to you about entering the property."

"You want my permission?" He shrugged. "Okay. Tell your husband to knock himself out. He can go digging around Fox Hollow as much as he likes."

"I'm not sure if it'll be George or someone from Danville."

"Whatever. Doesn't matter either way. The whole damn state police force could—" Rick broke off abruptly and looked at Daisy. "Are you going?"

"Where?"

"To Fox Hollow with the rest of the governmental ya-hoos."

"No. Why would I go?" She added crisply, "It's not my land."

He gave a little grunt, then looked back at Sue. "Go ahead. Tell 'em anytime is fine by me."

Sue squinted at him. Daisy understood why. She was thinking the same thing. It was no secret that Rick hated the law, especially the law of Pittsylvania County. He had several dozen signs posted warning everyone to keep away from his junky old trailers. His brother Bobby was both willing and eager to blow a trespasser's leg clean off. But when it came to Fox Hollow, Rick was perfectly content to let the world wander about whenever and wherever they pleased? He didn't make even the slightest protest? Something wasn't right.

"You're sure?" Sue asked slowly. "You've got no objection at all?"

"Nope."

"And your brother?"

They all turned toward Bobby, who had nearly reached the bottom of Daisy's goodie bag. The camouflage paint on his chin and cheeks was mixed with brownie crumbs and icing. Bobby looked back at them without saying a word, clueless as to the subject of the discussion.

"Don't worry about him," Rick told Sue. "Fox Hollow ain't none of his concern."

"Okay." She seemed almost stunned at how easy her task had been, and she blinked at Daisy questioningly. "So I guess we'll be going?"

"Definitely." Daisy was more than ready to go home. She could only take so much of the Balsam boys at one time. They were like hot sauce. A little went a long way, and a lot burned like hell.

"Rick?" came a plaintive cry from inside the trailer.

Daisy restrained a smile. "Golly, this has been fun. We've got to do it again real soon."

Rick cocked his head at her. "My door is always open for ya, darlin'."

Not bothering to respond, she turned and followed Sue to the ambulance. Rick stopped her.

"Daisy—"

She glanced around. He waited a moment, until Sue had opened the door of the vehicle and was climbing inside, then he spoke in a low tone that only Daisy could hear.

"If the sheriff goes to Fox Hollow, you have to go with him."

"What?" Her brow furrowed. "Why?"

"Because unless you want him to die like old man Dickerson, you gotta make sure he doesn't drink any of Fred's 'shine."

CHAPTER
8

"By the by, Ducky, you never told me how those ham bones worked out last week."

"They worked great." Daisy smiled at the memory. "The pups chewed like maniacs, then they all laid down for a long snooze. And it was a good thing too, because poor Sue was as jittery as a foal wandering too close to a wasp nest. She's not real good with dogs, at least not big ones that bare their teeth and don't curl up in your lap at night like a kitten."

Brenda chortled as she tallied the previous day's receipts on the cash register. "I once saw her run screaming from a snake out in the parking lot. It was just a lil' ol' black rat snake, not a bit scary. But from the way she jumped and tore off, you'd have thought it was one of them poisonous pit vipers that slither down from the mountains now and then. I guess it's a good thing she decided to fix up people for a living instead of critters."

At the mention of poison, Daisy's smile faded. Ever since Rick had whispered the strange warning to her from the steps of his trailer, she had followed the investigation into Fred Dickerson's death as closely as she could. It was partly out of concern for Sheriff Lowell's well-being and partly out of concern for her own. The longer the diner remained shuttered, the longer she remained without income. But then after only three days of closure, the sheriff had announced that H & P's could once more officially open its doors to the coffee-drinking, waffle-eating public of southwestern Virginia.

Although both Daisy and Hank asked for an explanation, neither George nor Sue Lowell was able to give them one. The privileged folks in Danville who presumably had the information were for some reason unwilling to share it with their small-town comrades. There was no report from the autopsy, no further discussion of potential health hazards or sterilizing the diner, no reference whatsoever to a cause of death—natural or not.

After so much initial commotion, all of a sudden the investigation turned oddly still and silent. While that was good news for Daisy financially, it left her other problem uncomfortably unresolved. Sheriff Lowell wasn't headed to Fox Hollow at present. Even though he now had permission from Rick to enter the property, there was no longer any interest in him doing so from Danville. Daisy could only guess how long that would last, and she had to figure out what she should do in the interim.

If only Rick's words had been part of a drunken ramble. Then she could have simply dismissed them. Alas, he had appeared entirely lucid and sober. She debated whether it would be best to just come right out and tell the sheriff. But she really didn't want to stir up a big pot of trouble, and talking to the law of Pittsylvania County about the ominous admonitions from one of the biggest lawbreakers in Pittsylvania County would undoubtedly do that. Plus she had so little information, and it made very little sense. Why would Rick think there was something wrong with Fred Dickerson's home brew? How did he even know that Fred had been making home brew? And why on earth would he imagine that it had the potential to kill either the old man or Sheriff Lowell?

It seemed awfully far-fetched. Granted, home brew was pretty common in that area. Daisy herself had grown up with a variety of locally made wines and brandies, many of which she had sampled with her daddy after Sunday dinner and on holidays long before she was of legal drinking age. Most of the neighborhood had tried their hand at fermentation now and again over the years when some berry bush or fruit tree in their yard produced an unusually abundant harvest. Aunt Emily, for instance, was well known amongst the community cognoscenti for her remarkably tasty gooseberry concoctions. But when Rick said 'shine, Daisy doubted that he was talking about an innocent glass of the sweet and fruity, one which just happened to contain a touch of alcohol. She was quite confident that he was referring to its country cousin with a lot more punch—whiskey.

The name didn't matter. You could call it moonshine, white lightning, mountain dew, red eye, or a hundred different colloquial circumlocutions. The end product was always the same—illegally distilled liquor. That meant unregistered, untaxed whiskey made from corn. Other grains were possible of course, but in Appalachia corn was the unrivalled king. So if Fred Dickerson had indeed been quietly cooking up something at Fox Hollow, it was in all probability corn whiskey.

There were two reasons for distilling your own liquor—home consumption and sale. Sale seemed unlikely with

Fred, considering that he had been a recluse for close to a decade before his death. If no one ever saw him, then there wasn't much chance of them buying his hooch. That left home consumption, which was what puzzled Daisy. If old man Dickerson used to sit alone in his kitchen peacefully minding his own business with an occasional shot of joy juice passing over his lips and between his gums, how had Rick Balsam managed to learn of it, and also that there was somehow a bad batch?

She didn't know anyone who had ever died from moonshine. Sure in theory there was always the possibility of eventual lead poisoning from the solder in an aged still. And there were plenty of stories about crazy toxic additives being thrown in by disreputable distillers, like a splash of lye or chlorine bleach to give their whiskey an extra kick. There were even tales of the occasional pig or possum carcass ending up in the mash, along with buckets of bird droppings and various insects. But that was silliness—or mostly silliness—in modern times with a basic, relatively enlightened understanding of good hygiene and health consequences.

If anything really made moonshine dangerous, it was its potent alcohol content, which more often than not was nearly twice as high as regulated commercial products obtainable from a licensed liquor store. Judicious moderation was the key to proper enjoyment. A sip instead of a swig. A taste rather than a gulp. A tumbler instead of a bottle—or heaven forbid, an entire jug. It was called dynamite and firewater for a reason. Just a drop too much could crack your skull and mule-kick your insides. Daisy had more than one friend who'd spent an aching, nauseated day recovering from an overconsumption of local likker the night before, but none of them had ever stumbled into H & P's with yellow-tinted tears streaming from their eyes or foam oozing out of their mouth.

There was nothing about Fred Dickerson's collapse on the diner floor that made Daisy think of moonshine. Could Rick have noticed something that she didn't? She remembered how he had stared at Fred's body for a long moment right after Sheriff Lowell arrived on the scene. It hadn't been a vague, absent sort of stare where his mind was clearly elsewhere, and it hadn't been a disgusted, shaken sort of stare over the horror of a corpse lying in front of his feet either. It had been a focused, gravely intent stare. The kind that gave Daisy the distinct impression that Rick must have spotted something. Something important. But what? And what connection did it have to the old man's home brew? It had to have been something small and subtle, because none of the rest of the group noticed anything. Fred obviously hadn't been clutching a jar with a skull and crossbones scored into it when he staggered through the door.

Then again, maybe she was wrong. Maybe whatever Rick saw that day didn't have any relation to Fred's 'shine at all. Daisy was pretty sure that Rick's contact with Fred Dickerson had been greater than he let on. She knew that he had lied to Sheriff Lowell when he told him that he hadn't seen the old man before he died. It was from the way Rick had cocked his head as he said it. But she didn't think that he had lied when he told the sheriff that he hadn't talked to the old man in ten years. So Rick had seen Fred, but Rick hadn't talked to Fred?

Daisy was left with a lot of questions. Unfortunately Rick was the only one who appeared to have any answers, and she had absolutely no intention of running after him to get them. Contact with Rick always equaled trouble for

her, as proven once again by the fact that two little sentences from his serpentine mouth had caused her to spend the
entire last week worrying about George Lowell going to
Fox Hollow and accidentally poisoning himself. At least
there was no sign that the sheriff would drive out in the near
future. He disliked having contact with Rick even more
than she did. So unless the folks in Danville forced him to
do it, he'd never voluntarily visit any property owned by a
Balsam brother.

She was so busy pondering the possible links between
Rick, old man Dickerson, and old man Dickerson's likker
that Daisy didn't hear the rusty bell clang as the front door
of the diner opened. But a few moments later when she
glanced up from the yellow mustard bottles that she was in
the process of refilling, she found a man standing just inside the entryway, an enormous foldout map blocking everything between his knees and the wavy tips of his light
brown hair.

"Howdy, stranger," Daisy drawled. "Are you lookin' for
some place in particular, or are you just lookin'?"

The map lowered, and a face emerged. It was a pleasant
face. Clean-shaven, early to midthirties, with a small scar
on the left cheek that had the appearance of being a fond
memory left over from childhood.

The man smiled. "Don't tell me. Let me guess. It was the
map that gave me away?"

"Actually," she answered, "it was your shoes."

"My shoes?" He glanced down at his feet in surprise.

"Don't get me wrong. They're very nice shoes. Probably
quite expensive too, if I were to hazard a wager. But they're
loafers. Spotless—without a single scuff on them—suede
loafers. Not at all useful for herding, digging, sowing, reap-
ing, or constructing anything whatsoever in the rural

hinterlands. So there you have it. It was your purdy shoes that told me you're not from around here."

His smile widened. "I had no idea shoes could be so chatty."

Daisy smiled back. "You can find out an awful lot about a man from his shoes."

"Does that hold true for a woman too?" He looked at her little white cotton sneakers.

She nodded. "Of course."

"And what should I learn from yours?"

"That I spend my days helping handsome strangers in fancy suede loafers get to where they're going."

He raised an entertained eyebrow. "Is that so?"

Daisy blushed as it suddenly occurred to her that she was flirting with a man she didn't even know. She never flirted with men she didn't know. Truth be told, she almost never flirted at all anymore. After Matt, there didn't really seem to be much of a point.

"I'm Ethan." The man crumpled his map together haphazardly and tucked it under one arm. Then he put out his hand. "Ethan Kinney."

"Daisy." She shook the proffered hand and was surprised by its strength. Ethan Kinney's shoes may have been big-city flimsy, but his grip was definitely country-tough.

"Daisy? I like that. What's it short for? Dorothea? Danielle?"

"No. It's not short for anything. My given name is Daisy. Daisy Luck Hale."

"Well, Daisy Hale, I'm sure glad to have met you, because I could use some luck tonight."

There was a sufficient hint of reciprocal flirtation in his tone so she figured she had better set the record straight.

"It's Daisy McGovern now."

Ethan blinked, but just slightly. "Either way, I'm still hoping you've got some luck to share."

"I don't know about that." Daisy sighed wistfully. "But I do have a new pot of coffee if you're interested."

"Sounds like a good way to start." He glanced around the diner. "Where should I sit?"

"Wherever you like. But"—she gestured toward Hank and Carlton Waters—aka the wet poodle—who were engaged in a lively discussion regarding the resale value of used cooking equipment between the grill and the counter—"it'd probably be a lot quieter in a booth than on a stool."

Ethan nodded. "I can see that. And hear it too."

"Pick a table then, and I'll get the coffee. You want a piece of pie to go with it? We have apple-blackberry and chocolate-pecan. They're both fresh."

"Seriously?" This time he blinked twice. "You've got fresh pie? Fresh as in homemade?"

"Technically this place isn't my home, but yes, I did make them."

"Wow." Ethan grinned. "Has an awesome accent *and* makes pies. Your husband must guard you with his life."

The wistful sigh repeated itself as Daisy turned toward the counter. She poured a large cup of coffee, cut a slice of each pie, and topped them off with a generous scoop of vanilla ice cream. Ethan Kinney may have been no more than a stranger passing through on the road to somewhere else, but he had complimented both her name and her accent. That didn't happen to her very often these days, so it deserved two types of pie, with a little something extra on the side.

When she carried her loaded tray to the green vinyl booth that Ethan had selected, Daisy found him leaning studiously over his map. Spread out, it took up nearly the entire table. In his hand was a portable GPS device. Her lips curled in amusement when she saw it.

"I hope you're not looking for anything around here with that," Daisy said, motioning toward the glowing screen with its flashing coordinates and arrows, "because you won't find it."

Ethan looked up at her questioningly.

"It might be wonderful for getting you to the perfect sushi bar in Manhattan, but in this part of the world, it'll just keep taking you in circles. After four hours of driving, you'll finally realize you've passed the exact same haystack, sitting in the exact same field, next to the exact same church eleven times."

"Honestly?"

"Honestly. And I'll give you an honest example. If you type in Tosh, it will come up with a city in southwestern Virginia named Tosh. The only problem is that after you follow the meticulous directions to get there, you'll discover the electronic cartographer's version of Tosh is a collapsed barn across from a bleached-out STOP sign without an intersection to actually stop at."

"Huh." Ethan frowned. "Well, that would explain the trouble I've been having all afternoon."

"And I would guess," Daisy commiserated, setting down the steaming cup of coffee, "you spent about half the time cursing and pulling over to the side of the road because you kept losing the satellite signal in between the mountains?"

He nodded and moaned.

"Don't feel bad. Even the professional delivery guys in this area get confused sometimes. We always have people coming in to ask for directions."

"I can see why," Ethan replied appreciatively as she placed the plates of pie and ice cream before him. "With service like this, I'd bet a lot of guys get lost around here on purpose."

Ordinarily Daisy would have gone back to refilling the mustard bottles, but curiosity kept her at the booth while Ethan sampled her creations. He took a bite of the apple-blackberry first.

"Daisy Luck Hale McGovern," he purred, barely swallowing before digging into the chocolate-pecan, "has anyone ever told you that you make a damn fine pie?"

He was answered with a smile.

"Won't you take a seat?" he asked. "Just for a minute?"

She hesitated. Daisy rarely sat down while she worked, even when she chatted with one of her close friends. But it was quiet that evening. She looked once around. Brenda was engrossed in the previous day's receipts. Hank and Carlton were still engaged in their used cooking equipment discussion. There were no other customers.

"So you never told me," she said, sliding into the seat across from Ethan.

"Told you what?"

"Are you looking for some place in particular, or are you just looking?"

It was Ethan's turn to smile. "Definitely some place in particular. And I'm hoping you can help me find it."

Daisy raised an inquisitive eyebrow.

"I'm looking for Chalk Level."

CHAPTER

9

The hush fell like an anvil. Up until that point neither Brenda nor Hank had paid any attention to the arrival of Ethan Kinney, but that changed the instant the words *Chalk Level* rolled off his tongue. Even though he said it in a normal tone, the name carried such power that a whisper would have had the same effect as a shout. They turned toward the stranger with stunned fascination. Hank's gaze was steely and suspicious. Brenda's mouth hung open like a confused eel. No one uttered a syllable. The only sound in the diner came from Carlton as he chomped on his supper.

"Why?" Daisy asked after a long minute.

Ethan's brow furrowed. "Why what?"

"Why are you looking for Chalk Level?"

His quizzical eyes moved from her to Brenda and then to Hank. The furrows deepened. "I get the feeling I'm missing something here."

Daisy repeated her question with a tinge of sharpness. "Why are you looking for Chalk Level?"

"I assume that means you know the place?"

She didn't answer. She wasn't about to give any further

information until she got some further information. Another long minute passed as the tension in the room grew thick like smoke. Ethan set his fork down quietly on one of the plates and leaned back against the green vinyl of the booth.

"So what happens now?" he said, his gaze changing from quizzical to shrewd.

Daisy sucked on her teeth in annoyance. It was mostly annoyance with herself. She had been friendly to him, talked about his shoes and the neighborhood. She had even flirted with him a bit. But then—after *two* slices of pie *with* ice cream—the truth finally came out. Ethan Kinney was no mere stranger passing through on the road to somewhere else. He was looking for Chalk Level. And from the marked change in his demeanor, it was clear that he knew there was something special about Chalk Level.

"I'll tell you what happens now." Hank's grim face disappeared from the opening above the grill. It reappeared a moment later as he strode out of the kitchen with quick, purposeful steps. He pulled off his grease-smeared apron and flung it next to the mustard bottles.

"Hank—" Brenda began anxiously.

Daisy understood her concern. Hank rarely removed his apron while at the diner, and when he did, it always meant serious business.

He cut her off with a stern glance as he proceeded to the far end of the counter, where Carlton was sitting. "I'm sorry," he said to him, "but we're going to have to finish our conversation some other time."

Carlton raised his head from his plate of chicken livers and onions. "Huh?"

"We're shutting down early tonight," Hank informed him.

"I'm still eating."

"I'm sorry," Hank said again, "but we're closing. Now."

With the expression of a slightly daft sheep, Carlton scratched his silver shock of hair. "Now? It's not even dark out yet."

"Now." As he repeated it, Hank's tone grew hard.

Shrugging, Carlton rose from his stool and reached for his wallet.

"It's on the house today." Hank gestured toward the door.

"Really? Okay. Thanks, Hank." Digging into his pocket, Carlton pulled out two quarters and set them on the counter. "For Daisy."

She gave him an acknowledging nod as he walked past her booth, although she couldn't help thinking to herself that the wet poodle's tips were quickly slipping from mediocre to lousy. Evidently auctioneering hadn't been so lucrative of late.

Hank followed Carlton to the door and clicked the lock behind him. He flipped the red diner sign from open to closed.

"All right," he growled, spinning around. "Now we can talk."

Daisy glanced at Ethan. He didn't say a word during Carlton's departure. He barely moved. He was sitting casually on his side of the booth, with slack shoulders and his hands resting loosely on top of his thighs. Even his jaw looked relaxed. Hank's gristly behavior would have made many men nervous, but if Ethan Kinney was sweating beneath his starched dress shirt, he didn't show it.

"Ducky," Brenda whispered, crooking a finger toward Daisy as a signal for her to come over by the cash register.

"Ducky?" Ethan echoed. His mouth twitched with a hint of a smile. "Where does *Ducky* come from?"

"It's none of your goddam business where it comes from," Hank spat. "It's none of your business what any of us do—or say—or are called."

The hint of a smile switched swiftly to a frown. "I don't think—" he began.

"I don't care one lick what you think." Hank marched to the counter, stopping directly across from Ethan and Daisy's booth.

"I don't think you—" Ethan began again.

"And you sure as hell better not assume what I think!" Hank folded his tattooed biceps over his chest in a formidable manner.

"Ducky," Brenda whispered once more, this time waving her whole hand in an effort to get Daisy away from the booth.

Ethan chuckled. "Apparently I'm of the dangerous variety, Daisy, and you shouldn't be sitting by me."

"Are you of the dangerous variety?" she drawled. "Should I be sitting by you?"

She didn't say it to flirt or to be flip. Daisy was trying to get him to talk. She wanted information from Ethan Kinney, and although she knew that Hank did too, he was going about it all wrong. She could see that as clearly as a black fly floating in a pitcher of lemonade. Hank was trying to bully Ethan, but it wasn't working. From what Daisy could discern, it was never going to work. Ethan's behavior was far too controlled and confident. Even with Hank flexing his muscles and thundering like an angry bear in front of him, he was still lounging calmly in his seat with not the slightest hint of apprehension.

"If you need protection," he answered smoothly, "it's not from me."

"If anybody needs protection around here," Hank snapped, "it's you."

Ethan looked at him. "I hope that's not a threat."

"Call it what you want, but I'm just stating facts. Daisy's got plenty of friends in this place. *You* don't."

"You sure know how to make a guy feel welcome."

"That's because you're not welcome," Hank retorted sharply. "You can get the hell out anytime. H & P's doesn't need your business, and we don't want your business."

Although Ethan had been in the process of packing up his map, he stopped abruptly. "What did you just say?"

"You can get the hell out anytime," Hank repeated with irritation.

"No." He shook his head. "After that. The name. Did you say H & P's?"

Hank scowled. "What if I did?"

Ethan turned to Daisy. "Is this H & P's Diner?"

"It is," she responded, a bit hesitantly. It was the truth. That was the official name of the restaurant, so there was no point in concealing it. But there was something about the way Ethan had reacted to it that put Daisy on guard.

He gazed at her thoughtfully for a moment, then his eyes traveled slowly around the diner. She shifted in her seat, growing increasingly uneasy. First Chalk Level. Now an unexplained interest in H & P's. That couldn't be good.

"You got a problem with the name?" Hank demanded.

"I—"

"Because I'm Hank." He gestured toward Daisy. "And her pop's Paul. So if you've got a problem with the name, then you've got a problem with us."

"I don't have a problem with the name." Ethan shrugged and continued studying the interior of the diner. "But I am surprised. I didn't see a sign when I pulled into the parking lot."

"There isn't one," Daisy explained. "Only the address

above the door. We used to have a big sign out along the road, but it was torn up by a storm earlier this year. And nobody quite got around to—"

"Sign or no sign," Hank broke in, "you heard what I told Carlton. We're closed. That means you need to go."

Ethan didn't pay any attention. He looked at each of them in turn. "So if you're Daisy, and you're Hank, then you must be Brenda?"

Brenda merely grunted in reply.

"You ask a lot of questions for a man who ain't from these parts," Hank snarled.

"And you seem to know an awful lot already too," Daisy added quickly, taking advantage of the opening before Hank went on and slammed it shut again. "So I'm sure you wouldn't mind telling us what brings you to our little neighborhood."

"If you wouldn't mind telling me where Chalk Level is," Ethan returned with equal slickness.

She didn't need to deliberate. It was a deal that Daisy could easily make. There was more than one way to explain Chalk Level, and she would be as helpful to him as he ended up being to her.

"All right," she agreed. "Fair enough."

"Daisy—" Hank warned her gruffly.

She shook her head at him, hoping that he would understand and keep quiet. But he didn't take the hint.

"He's got no right. It ain't none of his concern. You don't have any idea—"

"Hank!" Brenda interrupted him shrilly.

Startled, he turned toward her. Brenda flared her nostrils at him.

"I don't know about that one," she motioned in the direction of Ethan, "and I don't much care. But Ducky's got every right. And there's no doubt about it being her concern. So for once in your life, shut your big fat maw and let her talk."

Hank started to open his mouth in protest but closed it again a second later. With a sullen sniff, he dropped down on the stool behind him. Daisy swallowed a grin. Although it didn't happen very often, it was always entertaining when Brenda got the last word and put Hank in his place. It was like a skunk that got tired of a pushy raccoon constantly shoving his nose where it didn't belong and finally remedying the problem with a pungent spritz.

"Thank you," Brenda said to him. "Now go ahead, Ducky."

Daisy nodded at her in appreciation, then she looked across the booth at Ethan. He raised an anticipatory eyebrow.

"I think we may have gotten off to a bad start," she drawled.

"No," Ethan countered with a smile, "I think we can both agree we got off to a pretty good start."

"That's true." Daisy returned the smile with an extra sweet one of her own. "But along the way we somehow got our signals crossed."

"I wouldn't argue with you there."

"So let's try again." She blinked at him with long lashes. "Let's uncross those signals and see where they take us."

He leaned toward her. "I'm game."

"Why don't we begin," Daisy purred, "with you telling me all about Ethan Kinney. Where does he come from? Why is he here? What does he—"

Ethan tossed his head back and laughed. "Damn, you're good! I've got to give you that. You must have that husband

of yours twisted around those clever little fingers like a du-
tiful worm."

Her smile vanished. It wasn't his smug laugh. It wasn't
even that he saw straight through her syrupy act and called
her on it. It was the way he talked about Matt, and his assumption that he knew all about their marriage. He knew
nothing.

"Fine." Daisy's eyes clouded. "I thought we could handle
this in a polite, civilized Southern fashion, but now I see
we can't."

For the first time since his arrival at the diner, Ethan
seemed slightly shaken, as though he hadn't expected her
to react quite so strongly or shift her attitude toward him
quite so quickly.

"If you don't like my way," she continued crisply, "then
we'll do it yours."

He raised his hands in an apologetic manner. "I think
there's been a bit of a misunderstanding—"

"There's no misunderstanding at all," Daisy cut him
off. "You're looking for Chalk Level, and I want to know
why. So you can either tell me why, or you can get the hell
out of here right now."

"I'm not going anywhere," Ethan lashed back at her.
"And I'll be the one asking the questions, while you'll be
the one giving the answers."

He pulled a thin black leather wallet out of his shirt
pocket and flipped it open. Daisy squinted at the badge inside.

"I should have guessed." She snorted with disgust.

"What is he?" Hank said. "One of those idiots from
Danville? He sure looks fool enough."

"No." Daisy stood up and backed away from the booth
with revulsion, like she had just discovered a very hairy

and ugly tarantula perched on the seat across from her. "He's not from Danville. He's not good enough for Danville."

Hank's eyes clouded over just as hers had a moment earlier. "You don't mean . . . he's not . . ."

"Oh yes." She snorted a second time. "He's exactly that."

There was such undisguised hostility in her voice that Ethan's face paled with astonishment.

Daisy snickered. "What? You thought you'd flash your sparkly badge and we'd all bow down to you in deference? Well, not here. And certainly not with us. We've met your kind before. It's almost five years ago now, but I'll never forget. So you can ask every question you want. You'll never get a single answer from me."

As Ethan met Daisy's and Hank's bitter stares, Brenda reached timidly for the phone next to the cash register.

"Should I call Sheriff Lowell?" she asked.

"Don't bother," Hank replied.

"But he maybe can—"

"He can't. George can't do a damn thing. He's only local. This joker's federal."

"Lord have mercy." Brenda gasped, finally understanding.

Daisy nodded. "A demon in the flesh. He's ATF."

CHAPTER
10

"I'm going home."

Daisy had about as much interest in spending one extra unnecessary second in the same room with Ethan Kinney as she did in licking a lollipop coated with a virulent strain of the plague. He was an agent for the devil. A special agent according to his badge. Her previous experience with another such agent had been closely akin to what she imagined it must be like to suffer in the fiery lake of hell. Years later she was still smarting from the burns, and she had no intention of ever getting close enough to those flames to be scalded again. Once was more than enough. This time the Bureau of Alcohol, Tobacco, Firearms and Explosives would have to find a different victim.

Brenda wasn't always the sharpest knife in the drawer, but on this occasion she managed to comprehend Daisy perfectly.

"That sounds like a mighty fine idea, Ducky. It's been a long enough day, hasn't it? If you wait just half a minute while I go in the back to check on the freezer and grab my handbag, I'll head out with you."

"Okey-dokey." Daisy walked over to the mustard bottles that she had been refilling earlier and screwed on their tops. "I'll finish these in the morning."

"Will you do the ketchup too?" Brenda pushed open the door to the kitchen. "I think some of them might be getting low. Hank, are you planning on shuttin' down the grill tonight? Or do you want me to do it?"

There was a slight pause before he answered, as though he couldn't quite decide whether to play along with Daisy and Brenda or take the exact opposite tack and play rough with Ethan Kinney.

"I'll take care of the grill," he grumbled, his cooler head prevailing for the moment. "I've got to clean out the grease tray anyway."

"I'm looking at the vegetables on the shelf in here," Brenda shouted from the back room. "We better order some more lima beans."

Hank rose from his stool. "Put it on the list."

"Creamed corn too."

"Put it on the list."

Daisy scooped up Hank's apron from next to the mustard bottles and tossed it to him as he headed toward the kitchen. He shook it out with a sharp crack, then wrapped it around his waist.

"And now that I'm really checking," Brenda added, "we're running short on black-eyed peas."

"For God's sake, woman! Put it on the list!"

As Hank disappeared through the open doorway, Daisy glanced at Ethan from out of the corner of her eye. He was looking at her intently, but she didn't look back. Instead she suppressed a grin. It was the perfect method for dealing with a demon. Pretend that he wasn't there. He didn't even exist. That way she didn't have to answer any questions or give any explanations. The longer she ignored him, the better the chance that he would eventually slink back into the filthy hole he had crawled out of.

Ethan cleared his throat. Daisy responded by locking the cash register drawer. He clattered his empty plates and mug together. She clicked off the lights above the counter. He dropped a spoon on the tile with a crash, and she straightened the stack of menus next to the phone. Finally he used a more direct approach.

"Daisy—"

Daisy turned her back on him.

"Seriously?" There was a hint of laughter in Ethan's voice. "Aren't you a little old to be covering your eyes and sticking your fingers in your ears as though I'm not sitting in the booth right behind you?"

She bit down hard on the inside of her cheeks so that she couldn't answer him.

"I thought we had a deal, Daisy."

Trying not to hurl a coffeepot at his head, she took a long, slow breath.

"I thought we had a deal," he said again. "You agreed. And I'd be sorry to see you break your word."

No longer able to stop herself, Daisy whirled around to face him. "Don't you dare! Don't you dare talk to *me* about breaking deals."

Ethan's jaw twitched.

"It's *you* who lies," she seethed. "It's your office that makes promises one minute and smashes them to bits the next. So don't ever, *ever* lecture me about bargains and agreements. Because I've always kept my word. You ATF bastards only know how to lie."

Although his mouth opened, her eyes met his with such vitriol that she could tell it forced down the heated reply that bubbled on the tip of his tongue. They stared at each other hard for a minute, then with a slight sigh, Ethan stood up from his booth. Daisy immediately took a step backward.

"I'm going to guess," he spoke slowly, choosing his sentences carefully, "that another agent from the bureau has been here. I'm also going to guess that it was some time ago and it wasn't a very good visit. I don't know what happened before. I don't know who you met or talked to. But *I* come in peace. I've got no interest in making trouble, either for you or myself. I just want to find what I've got to find, see what I've got to see, and then I'll go away again. Quietly. Without any commotion."

Daisy pursed her lips. She doubted him. She doubted every syllable that slithered out of his deceitful special agent mouth.

"This is just another job for me," Ethan went on. "That's all. I don't want to be here any more than you want me here."

Her icy expression didn't soften, but she didn't spit at him either. He seemed to take that as a positive sign.

"I'm not trying to cause problems," he said. "My assignment is as simple and straightforward as they come."

"What exactly is your assignment?" Daisy asked.

"Apparently you had a man die in here a couple of weeks ago?"

She gave a little grunt of acknowledgment.

"And you know there was some question about the cause of death?"

The grunt repeated itself.

"Well, your Virginia boys sent us a copy of the autopsy report, and I'm here to follow up on it."

Every limb in Daisy's body stiffened. So the investigation into Fred Dickerson's death hadn't actually turned still and silent. It had moved up the food chain instead. From state to federal. From the folks in Danville to the ATF.

"All I need to do is check out this place"—Ethan waved his hand once around—"talk to the people who were present when he died"—he nodded toward her—"and take a look at where he lived."

Daisy heard his words, but her mind was focused elsewhere. ATF. Alcohol, Tobacco, Firearms and Explosives. That's what they handled. Not strokes. Not seizures. Not the ordinary collapse of an aged recluse in Pittsylvania County on the floor of the local diner. So if the bureau was interested in old man Dickerson's death, they had to believe that it had some connection to alcohol, tobacco, firearms, or explosives. Only one of those could reasonably apply to Fred. Alcohol. Or more accurately in his case—moonshine. Fred's 'shine. The same 'shine that Rick Balsam had told her was potentially lethal.

"Which is why I was driving around in circles trying to find Chalk Level," Ethan explained. "And it's also why I needed to find H & P's Diner."

"You found it," Daisy muttered absently.

"I was lucky to stumble in here. There's no doubt about that. I checked one place off my list, *and* I got to meet you."

She didn't respond. She was too busy thinking about Rick. If only she knew everything that he apparently knew. Then she would have had a much better idea of how to handle Ethan Kinney and his assignment.

"I swear to you," Ethan said. "That's it. The diner, the diner's employees, and the deceased's home. My office has no other intention or goal. No hidden agenda. No secret mission."

He sounded honest. He even looked honest. But Daisy wasn't as gullible as she had been five years ago. She didn't trust any agent from the ATF one lick. Except she was gradually beginning to realize that it wasn't really a matter of trust. It was much more a matter of practicality.

"Now that I've answered your question," he prodded her gently, "I hope you'll answer mine?"

Daisy hesitated. Part of her still wanted to hurl a coffeepot at his head, but that was the opposite of practical. She would be acting on pure emotion, and this time she was determined to put emotion on the backseat. She wouldn't let them bamboozle her. This wasn't going to be another opportunity for them to prey on her while she was grieving and in shock. They wouldn't take one more damn thing from her or her family. Bad luck and poor timing may have forced her to be a witness to old man Dickerson's death, but that didn't mean she couldn't have some control over the consequences.

"I can give you directions to Chalk Level."

Although it took her some effort, Daisy spoke calmly, almost casually. Ethan cocked his head at her curiously.

"You can?"

She wasn't sure whether he was surprised by her willingness to assist him or her ability to assist him. It didn't matter to her either way. Ethan Kinney had come, and he obviously wasn't leaving until he got what he needed. The faster she gave it to him, the sooner he would go away and hopefully never return.

"I can show you on your map if you'd like."

"I know it's on here." Ethan sat back down at his booth and smoothed out the crumpled paper. "I saw it before."

"It doesn't appear very often. Not unless it's a Virginia map that's really detailed or really old."

"I dug this one out of the archives at work."

Daisy swallowed hard. She wondered if he'd looked at

any of the files that presumably had been sitting right next to the map. He must not have—or at least not very closely—because otherwise he would have recognized her name when she first introduced herself.

"But the problem," Ethan complained, "is that there's no dot."

"That's always the problem," Daisy told him, as she went over to his table. "They plop the names down in the correct general vicinity, but if there's no dot at an actual intersection or some sort of locatable landmark, the general vicinity in this part of the state equals fifty square miles of winding, unmarked roads that keep crisscrossing without any apparent rhyme, reason, or a useful signpost."

"I learned that the hard way this afternoon."

She leaned over the map and orientated herself. "Okay. This is us."

"Where?"

"Here. This is H & P's."

As Daisy put her finger down to show the location of the diner, Ethan shifted closer to her for a better look. His shoulder brushed her arm, and she felt a strong desire to pick up a fork and jam it into one of his rotten ATF eyeballs. But she restrained herself.

"Now over here is Highway 40," she said. "If you—"

"Have you lost your mind!" Hank bellowed.

Daisy didn't immediately turn around. Hank was obviously livid, and she understood why. He had come back from the kitchen and seen what she was doing. Instead of continuing to ignore their enemy, she now appeared to be cheerfully fraternizing with him.

"Have you forgotten what they did?" Hank snapped his teeth like a frenzied piranha. "What they took?"

Ethan gazed at her inquisitively.

"Of course I haven't forgotten." She spoke in a low tone, trying to find words that would appease Hank while at the same time dampen Ethan's visibly growing curiosity. "I could never forget. I've said that many times before. But this has nothing to do with the past. It's about laying poor Fred Dickerson to rest."

Hank's thick jaw sagged. "Fred?"

"Yes, Fred." Daisy nodded. "That's why Ethan is here. They sent him a copy of the autopsy report, and he's following up on it."

"But George told us there wasn't a report from the autopsy."

She could merely shrug. "You said it yourself, Hank. Sheriff Lowell's only local. The ATF's federal."

"Why would the ATF be interested in . . . in . . ."

He stopped midsentence with a stammer. It startled Daisy. Hank never stammered.

"It's standard procedure." Ethan responded with a shrug of his own.

She didn't believe that for a second. There was nothing standard about sending a special agent to the farthest depths of southwestern Virginia just because there was a question or two about an old man's death.

"As I told Daisy," Ethan went on, "I've got to take a look around here, talk to witnesses like yourself, and see where the deceased lived."

The color drained from Hank's face.

"That's what Daisy was doing when you came in," Ethan said. "She was giving me directions to Chalk Level."

He turned to her for confirmation, but she didn't give it. Daisy was too focused on Hank and his ashen complexion. Hank was always red. It may have been varying shades of crimson or burgundy depending on how hard he scrubbed the grill or how annoyed he got with Brenda, but it was still decidedly red and not white. There was only one time when Daisy could remember him being pale, and that was at her daddy's funeral.

Hank blinked at her for a moment, then with a drawn mouth and pasty cheeks he reached for a newspaper. Instead of asking Ethan any questions or making a single remark about Chalk Level, he leaned against the counter and leisurely perused the Monday edition of the *Danville Register & Bee*, even though the counter lights had already been shut off. It was the strangest behavior Daisy had ever seen from him, until it occurred to her that she had in fact seen it before. The day Fred Dickerson had collapsed, Hank had done the exact same thing. While everybody else had been stunned and horrified, he had merrily flipped through the newspaper and snacked on peach cobbler.

It reminded Daisy of something else strange. Hank had been the first to positively identify Fred, and she had later wondered whether that meant Hank had seen the old man before he died. She had wondered the very same thing about Rick Balsam. And now she suddenly found herself wondering whether Hank—just like Rick—knew a lot more about all of this than he was letting on.

Ethan nudged her with his elbow. "You were showing me Highway 40?"

Daisy looked down at the map, but her mind pictured Aunt Emily instead. She saw her shrewd blue eyes and the unconcealed excitement as she had talked about Hank poisoning Fred. Daisy hadn't believed a word of it then, and she still didn't believe it. But the whole thing was undeniably fishy. Hank's strange behavior. Aunt Emily claiming that old man Dickerson was responsible for the death of her daddy. Rick warning her about bad moonshine. It seemed as though it all had to add up in some peculiar way, except she didn't know how, and she had the distinct feeling that it wasn't good.

Staring at the blurry roads and towns, Daisy came to a decision. If she was going to have any control over the consequences of Fred Dickerson's death, she couldn't toss Ethan out into the night with a set of directions and simply forget it. Not if Hank was somehow involved. And certainly not if Rick was right about Fred's 'shine. If old man Dickerson's home brew really was bad and somehow lethal, and Ethan tasted it, then got sick and possibly even died, not only would it be on her conscience for the rest of her life, but it would surely bring a storm of trouble down on her and everyone she cared for.

She had to be careful. That she understood. She couldn't let the pain of the past cloud her judgment now. Nothing would mend the old injuries. No amount of yelling, or stomping her feet, or even a hefty dose of lovely retribution. Daisy couldn't undo what had happened, and she realized that neither could Ethan. But if she played her cards right and helped him, she might at least be able to obtain a better grasp on the future, if only by finding out what Rick and Hank already seemed to know.

"So are you going to tell me where Chalk Level is or not?" Ethan asked impatiently.

Daisy raised her eyes to him and smiled. "I'll do you one better. I won't just tell you where it is. I'll take you there."

CHAPTER
11

"So you live here? At the inn?" Ethan asked her the next morning as they climbed into his car. "This is your actual address?"

"It is," Daisy answered.

"But you didn't grow up there, right?"

"Why do you say it like that?"

"Well"—he hesitated—"it's kind of an odd place to call home."

"It's a gorgeous old house!" she protested, shifting in her seat to admire it. "With running water, heat and air-conditioning, beautiful antique furnishings, and it's surrounded by a fabulous garden complete with a stable full of horses. How much more do you want? Granted, the floor and stairs do creak and groan a lot, especially in winter. And the wiring isn't the most modern, which we're reminded of every time there's a big storm and we lose the lights. But it's still an awful lot better than some of the places people end up living, like under bridges in cardboard boxes or rat-infested apartments with no windows."

"Of course. I didn't mean it that way. It's a great bed-and-breakfast. But that's just it. It's a bed-and-breakfast. There are people around all the time. Wouldn't you rather be alone with your husband?"

It was Daisy's turn to hesitate. She wasn't sure how much to tell him about Matt. But then she shrugged to herself. What difference did it make really? She might as well just be frank about the state of her marriage.

"Unfortunately my husband doesn't want to be alone with me," she said.

Ethan frowned, not understanding. "So he's gone a lot? Is he a long-haul trucker or something?"

"Or something," Daisy muttered.

"Huh?"

"My husband, Matt, left me. He drove off one morning and never came home again."

Ethan stopped fiddling with his car's GPS and looked at her. "Seriously?"

"Yes, seriously." She shook her head at him with a touch of annoyance. "Why would I joke about that?"

"I don't know. I guess you wouldn't. I just can't imagine someone leaving like that. It's so . . . so . . ."

"So cruel?" Daisy suggested. "So selfish and unkind? So weak and utterly pathetic? Well, you can imagine it now, because that's exactly what Matt did. No hint beforehand. No note or phone call afterward. No explanation. Ever."

"If you don't mind my asking, when was this?"

"About four and a half years ago."

"And you haven't divorced him?" Ethan was incredulous. "Why would you want to stay married to a person who treated you that way?"

She responded with a light laugh. It was a question that

she had asked herself dozens of times, and she had an equal number of constantly varying answers.

"For what it's worth," he said after a moment, when he didn't get more of a reply, "I think you deserve better."

"Thank you. I appreciate the sentiment, but are we going to head out anytime soon? Or should I run back inside and ask Aunt Emily to pack us a lunch and possibly even a supper?"

Ethan returned his attention to the GPS. "I was trying to type in Chalk Level."

"I thought that was why I was here," Daisy remarked dryly.

"It is, but just in case there's a problem."

"Don't you mean, just in case I get you hopelessly lost?"

He grinned. "Electronic navigation is a lot better than following a trail of bread crumbs sprinkled from the car window."

"I wouldn't be so sure about that," she retorted. "Not around here where the satellite gets blocked by every third hill. And anyway, you've got me with you. How could I get you lost without also getting me lost?"

"We could be on a tiny back road in the middle of absolutely nowhere, you could suddenly jump out and dash off to a friend's cabin hidden in the woods, and I'd end up driving around in circles again for another whole day."

"A little paranoid, aren't you?"

Ethan shrugged. "You did make it pretty clear in the diner last night that you hate the ATF."

Daisy restrained a smile. At least he was aware of how she felt.

Having finally finished setting the GPS, Ethan shifted the car into gear and pulled out of the row of parking spaces at the side of the Tosh Inn. They didn't make it more than ten feet down the driveway before he stepped on the brake.

"We'll be okay in a sedan, right? We don't need some heavy-duty truck with four-wheel drive and monster tires?"

Her smile grew so big that she didn't bother trying to conceal it anymore. "Wow, you really are paranoid."

"I saw the condition of some of the smaller roads yesterday," he shot back defensively. "I don't want to get stuck for an entire afternoon in a pile of mud up to my bumper."

"Don't worry," Daisy reassured him. "We'll be fine. Chalk Level may have its quirks, but it's passable by foot and car. An all-terrain vehicle—or tank—isn't required."

With a dubious grunt, Ethan moved his foot to the gas. At the end of the driveway she told him to turn left.

"Are you sure it's left?" he questioned her. "Because the arrow on the map points to the right."

Daisy rolled her eyes. It was going to be a painfully long day if their first half hour together was any indication.

"So right then?" Ethan persisted.

"No, left."

"But it—"

She opened the car door and began to climb out. "Go ahead. Turn right. Don't listen to me, even though I've lived here all my life. Don't rely on my directions, even though I told you I would take you there. Trust the machine and see what convoluted route you wind up following until you suddenly discover you've crossed the border into Tennessee or maybe West Virginia."

"Wait," he said.

Her feet were already on the ground, and she was heading up the driveway toward the inn.

"Daisy, come back!"

She stopped with a growl. She didn't need this crap.

"I'm sorry," Ethan called. "You're right. You know where you're going."

Daisy sucked on her teeth. Hank had given her the day off to deal with Special Agent Kinney, but she was sorely tempted to climb back into bed, sleep through the rest of the morning, and spend a peaceful afternoon on the porch together with a cool beverage instead.

Ethan shifted the car into reverse and pulled up the driveway next to her. He leaned toward the open passenger-side window.

"Do you want me to say it again? I'm sorry. Of course you know the best way to get there."

He sounded genuinely apologetic, but Daisy doubted it. He was probably just being pragmatic. After all, there was no question that she knew a whole lot more about Chalk Level than he did—with or without his GPS—so it was obviously better to have her with him, even if it meant having to defer to her directions.

"Will you get back in?" Ethan stretched out his arm and pulled the latch on the door for her. "Please?"

She wavered but only for a moment. If he could be pragmatic, then Daisy figured that she could too. She reminded herself of the original plan. The faster Ethan got what he came for, the sooner he would leave. Permanently. And she was still hoping to get some information in the process. As she climbed inside the car, Daisy checked her watch. Even with the minor delay, it was early. If she hurried things up a bit, there was a chance that she could get rid of Ethan *and* enjoy a peaceful afternoon on the porch together with a cool beverage.

This time at the end of the driveway he turned left without any prompting or dispute. The next few turns were guided by Daisy's forefinger. Neither of them spoke until they reached the main road.

"Thanks, by the way," Ethan said.

"I told you I'd take you to Chalk Level," she responded curtly, "and I'm taking you to Chalk Level."

"I appreciate that too, but I meant thanks for showing me the inn last night. I'm not sure where I would have stayed otherwise."

"You would have stayed in your car in the diner's parking lot or on the side of the road somewhere. The nearest motel is thirty miles in the opposite direction. It's nearly impossible to find in the dark, and trust me, you don't want to find it. It's crawling with bugs and covered in mold."

He glanced at her sideways. "So you were being nice by recommending the inn? I thought maybe you were trying to keep an eye on me."

"There's that paranoia of yours again."

Daisy said it with a laugh, but she couldn't truthfully deny the accusation. Perhaps a part of her had meant to be kind by providing him with a cool, comfortable bed and a home-cooked breakfast served on a silver tray. If that was the case, it was a very small part. Infinitesimal. The rest of her had done exactly what he supposed—kept a sharp eye on him. If Special Agent Kinney shared the same roof as she, then he couldn't do any snooping or interrogating without her knowing about it.

Her only concern in taking him to the inn had been what her momma and Beulah and Aunt Emily would think—and say—when they learned who Ethan was and why he was in Pittsylvania County. But in that regard Daisy had been lucky. Her momma had been even more tired than usual and gone to bed early. Beulah had been out on a date. Only Aunt Emily had been awake and on the premises.

She had listened to Daisy's hurried, whispered account of the stranger sitting in her parlor, and instead of promptly reaching for her beloved shotgun as Daisy feared she might, Aunt Emily had offered Ethan a room, albeit at an exorbitant rate. Unlike Hank, she hadn't been at all upset that Daisy could stand next to a man from the ATF without trying to gut him like a fish. One look from her shrewd blue eyes and it had been clear to Daisy that Aunt Emily understood her plan. She even complimented her on it.

"It's very clever of you, Ducky," Aunt Emily had said. "That's precisely the way to do it. Watch him, so he can't go rooting around and dig up any turnips we'd rather have buried. It's just like that old saying—keep your friends close and your enemies closer."

Her advice had been simple.

"Get more than you give, Ducky. He'll want to know all about us and the neighborhood. But for every one thing you tell him, make sure he tells you three in return. Then you'll never be the last hog in line at the feed trough or the first at the door of the slaughterhouse."

Pig references aside, Daisy was rather happy to have Aunt Emily's approval. She had begun to feel slightly guilty. Maybe by helping Ethan—even strategically—she was being a traitor to her own family. But Aunt Emily's praise and approbation quieted her conscience. It reaffirmed to Daisy her own conclusion that she wasn't a traitor for taking Ethan to Chalk Level, if by taking him to Chalk Level it kept the ATF from causing her and her friends and relations any more trouble.

"Which way?"

"Hmm?"

"Which way?" Ethan repeated.

Daisy turned to him, almost startled. For a minute she had forgotten where she was and what she was doing.

"Are you okay?" he asked her. "You seem a little—confused."

"I'm fine. I just . . . never mind . . . it doesn't matter. How far have we gotten?"

She looked out toward the road. They were stopped at an intersection. On one side rose the gleaming white spire of the Round Pond Baptist Church. On the other side stood a faded pink double-wide with a dozen matching plastic pink flamingos scattered around the front lawn. It was Highway 40.

"Left," she said.

The car turned left, and as it did so, Daisy took a long, deep breath. She hadn't gone left on Highway 40 in more than four years. It looked the same. The overgrown playing field was still next to the church. Across the way the pastor's house was still painted lemon yellow with a sky-blue door and shutters.

Ethan glanced at her. "Are you sure you're all right?"

Daisy nodded.

"Because you're kind of pale."

"I—" She sighed. "It's been awhile since I've come this way."

He connected the dots as far as he could. "Did you used to live around here with your husband?"

"No."

It wasn't a lie. She had never lived in that area with Matt. But the question came so perilously close to revealing the truth that Daisy realized she had to pull herself together. She couldn't let Ethan know how strong of a connection she had to the place that they were going or how vulnerable it made her.

"So what is it then?" he pursued, his brows knit together.

"What is what?" she returned elusively.

"What's wrong? Something is obviously bothering you. And it started the moment we hit Highway 40."

Ethan was dang perceptive. Too perceptive for Daisy's comfort. So unless she wanted him to uncover all that she preferred to keep hidden, she would have to do a better job of controlling—or at least concealing—her emotions. She took another deep breath to steady her nerves.

"In about a mile we'll go over a creek. Then you should slow down."

As she said it, Daisy silently thanked him for driving so fast. The quicker they got there, the quicker they could leave again.

He nodded, and to her relief didn't press the subject of her agitation any further.

"You can see the bridge up ahead. Just after it on the right is a strip of gravel. You should pull over there."

She looked down as they crossed the creek. The water level was high for the middle of summer. At the center it was knee-deep and flowing briskly.

When they reached the other side, Ethan turned off the road as Daisy had instructed. She climbed out of the car and started up the weedy hill that bordered the gravel. Ethan followed her. With a final few scrambling steps, she made it to the top and stopped.

"Okey-dokey," she said.

Slowly Ethan turned in a circle. "Okey-dokey?" he echoed, perplexed.

"This is it," Daisy told him. "This is what you wanted."

"We're standing in the middle of a cemetery."

"We're standing in the middle of Chalk Level."

CHAPTER
12

"Chalk Level?" Ethan repeated.

"Chalk Level," Daisy confirmed.

His gaze narrowed. "Tell me you're kidding."

"I'm not kidding."

With an unhappy sigh, he folded his arms across his chest. "So I guess I was right to be paranoid."

She frowned.

"Don't play the fool, Daisy. It doesn't suit you."

"I—"

"Are you really going to pretend that you don't understand me?" Ethan cut her off. "That when I said I was looking for Chalk Level, you thought I meant a couple of ancient tombstones scattered on a grassy knoll next to a babbling brook?"

"It's not a brook," she corrected him. "It's a creek."

He shot her a blazing look and started down the weedy slope back toward the road.

"This is Chalk Level," Daisy insisted.

Ethan kept on walking.

"It's Chalk Level," she called after him.

"If you want a ride back to the inn," he said brusquely, "you've got about ten seconds to get into the car."

"But—"

"Get in the goddam car, Daisy!"

Daisy certainly didn't take kindly to being ordered about or shouted at, but it did occur to her quickly enough that aside from her feet, Ethan was her only guaranteed form of transportation. Pride or not, she wasn't eager to possibly spend the next several hours trudging to the inn in the blistering Virginia sun.

"I don't know why you're all in a huff," she grumbled, stumbling down the slope behind him. "I did what you asked."

"I asked you to take me to Chalk Level, not Hillbilly-ville."

That really ruffled Daisy's feathers.

"I took you to Chalk Level," she snapped. "I can't help it if you're too dumb to realize that."

Ethan climbed inside the car and angrily slammed the door. Daisy did the same. He turned to her with clenched teeth.

"You must seriously hate the ATF to go this far," he seethed. "To make up a place out in the middle of nowhere. No wonder you didn't want me using the GPS."

"I didn't make up anything," she shot back. "And when you tried the GPS yesterday, where did it take you? Probably pretty near to here, didn't it?"

His mouth opened, but no words came out.

"That's what I thought," Daisy said smugly.

"I did cross Highway 40," Ethan mused.

"That's because Highway 40 runs straight through Chalk Level."

He squinted at her. "But my file said the deceased lived in Chalk Level."

"Surely."

"Then where's his house? Where did he eat and sleep?

Because I highly doubt he was drinking from the *creek* or making a bed out of the grass and gravestones."

Daisy snorted with derision. "You really are dumb, aren't you? Chalk Level isn't a golf club or subdivision. It's a town."

"Of course I know it's a town!" Ethan threw up his hands in frustration. "But if this is Chalk Level, why don't I see any people or homes or stores or traffic?"

She shook her head at him. "Not all rural towns have a bustling center with a quaint little Main Street running in between the post office and grocery store. Some are just areas and communities. Unincorporated parts of a county. Chalk Level is one of those. And the hill we were standing on a moment ago is smack dab in the heart of it."

For a long minute Ethan just looked at her. Daisy smiled. Sometimes it was awfully fun to be right, especially with big-city know-it-alls.

"Is it nearby?" he asked, almost sheepishly.

"Fred Dickerson's place?"

He nodded.

"On the other side of the creek."

"I don't have an address," Ethan said. "I don't suppose you'd be willing to—"

"I'll show you."

He started the car and pulled back onto the road the way they had come.

"Fox Hollow will be on the left," Daisy told him. "It's the only driveway. You can't miss it."

Ethan frowned. "Fox Hollow?"

Her heart thudded hard in her chest. Now she would have to explain, at least somewhat.

"Is that another town?"

"No." Daisy pushed down the thick knot that welled up

in her throat. "Fox Hollow is the name of a property. It's an old farm with a house and outbuildings. It's part of Chalk Level. Fox Hollow and the cemetery are the two biggest tracts of land in Chalk Level. They make up nearly all of it. There are also about a dozen little parcels scattered around the edges. A few have a trailer or single-wide on them, but most are vacant."

"Oh." Ethan nodded. "I understand now. So that's why all I had for Mr. Dickerson's residence was Chalk Level."

"Fox Hollow does have a street address." She spoke wistfully, remembering how as a little girl she used to love racing her daddy up the dusty drive to the big gray mailbox painted with cardinals and holly berries. "But I don't think Fred used it much."

"He had a post office box instead?"

Daisy shrugged. "I doubt it. I don't know why he would have needed one. He was a recluse for years."

"A recluse?" Ethan glanced at her with keen eyes. "How so? Did he live off the land? Was he often seen digging around Dumpsters?"

She laughed. "You've attended too many seminars on fugitives hiding out in the mountains. Old man Dickerson wasn't running from the law or setting up some wacky compound waiting for the end of the world. He just liked to be alone. That's pretty common around here. I would bet it's pretty common everywhere. So if by living off the land you mean he grew his own lettuce and potatoes, then yes, he lived off the land. But I never heard of poor Fred diving into a Dumpster. Have you seen the Dumpsters in Pittsylvania County? The one we have at the diner is so big, I'm not sure if you jumped into it you could ever get back out again."

"Me personally? You don't think I could get back out again?"

"Not without messing up those purdy shoes of yours."

Ethan snorted in amusement. "But you wouldn't have any trouble? Half my size and you'd climb out no problem?"

"We country girls are scrappy," Daisy answered with a grin.

"And we ATF boys are—"

He stopped, but it was too late. The damage had already been done. Her grin vanished, and Daisy shrunk to the far corner of her seat as though she were trying to put as much distance as possible between herself and a nasty little tick.

There was a weighty pause, then Ethan said, "Won't you just tell me?"

She knotted her hands together in grim silence.

"I don't know what went wrong." His voice was appealingly kind. "I can't even begin to guess."

Daisy watched the blood drain from her knuckles.

"But if you won't explain what happened and why you dislike the bureau so much, then there's no way for me to try to fix it."

There was no fixing it. It was over. It had been over long ago. Time had marched on and wasn't reversible. Daisy knew that even if Ethan didn't. She might have screamed it at him at the top of her lungs, but instead she saw the big gray mailbox painted with cardinals and holly berries.

"You're about to miss it," she said flatly.

He slammed on the brakes and swung into a pebbly driveway. The car stopped.

"Uh—" Ethan eyed a large red metal gate that barred their path. "What about that?"

"I'll get it." Daisy started to climb out.

"Are you sure you can open it?"

She blinked at him. "It's a farm gate, not a high-tech bank safe."

"But are you sure you *should* open it?"

"Worried about being shot for trespassing?"

Not waiting for his answer, Daisy walked to the gate, pulled up the center post, flipped the latch, and pushed back both sides. She waved to him.

"Drive through and I'll close it behind you."

Ethan did as she directed. When she had shut the gate and climbed back inside the car, he turned to her.

"Am I wrong in assuming you've done that before?"

"Nope."

"So you know this place well?"

"Yup."

"How well exactly?"

How well did she know Fox Hollow? Daisy chuckled to herself. It was a silly question. How well did a bat know the cave that it flew out of every night or a sea turtle know the beach that it swam back to summer after summer? She could see the changes. That was what mattered. The driveway was getting low in spots and needed a refill of pebbles. Several of the bluebird houses that were nailed to the fence posts had to be cleaned out and repaired. The boxwoods along the border could have used a good pruning.

She replied lightly, "I know it well enough to tell you the house isn't visible from the road. You have to go over the ridge."

Ethan drove slowly down the long broad drive. Daisy looked at the fields on both sides. Sheriff Lowell was right. They were all grown over. Old man Dickerson hadn't planted there for at least a season or two.

"Speaking of trespassing," Ethan asked her after a while, "you don't actually think there's a chance someone would object to us coming out here without an appointment, do you?"

"I believe it's perfectly safe for you to keep your side-arms holstered," Daisy drawled. Silently she added, "At least until Rick and Bobby decide to leave their beat-up old trailers in the backwoods and move to beautiful Fox Hollow along with all of their crazy signs, dogs, and the entire Balsam arsenal."

"I would have called first," Ethan went on, "but I don't have a number."

"I already told you. Fred was a recluse. He didn't need a phone."

"But wouldn't his family have wanted a way to contact him? Even just in case of an emergency?"

"If he had any family, I never saw them."

"No family?" Ethan raised a curious eyebrow. "No family at all?"

"Of course he had some family at some time," Daisy responded with a tinge of irritation. "He obviously wouldn't have been on this earth without them. But that doesn't mean he remained in touch with them. At his age his parents would have been long gone. And I don't remember ever hearing about a wife or children. I have no clue as to siblings or cousins. You'd know better than I would."

"Why do you think that?"

"You said before you had a file, didn't ya? If it listed where the deceased lived, then didn't it also list the whereabouts of the deceased's kinfolk?"

"Kinfolk!" Ethan chortled. "God, I love the way you talk!"

Her cheeks flamed with a mixture of anger and embarrassment.

"Don't get mad. It's a compliment."

Compliment or not, Special Agent Kinney was lucky they weren't standing near an open well at that moment, because Daisy would have been more than a little tempted to push him into it.

He was wise enough to stifle his laugh, although the remnants of a grin remained. "Well, Mr. Dickerson may have been estranged from his family, but somebody in that family sure must be glad to have been related to him, because they just inherited one heck of a property. Is it as big as it appears?"

"Two hundred acres," she answered quietly. "Two hundred really nice acres."

"They look it. I'm guessing they're pretty valuable as far as rural farmland goes."

"Not to Fred's family."

Ethan glanced at her in surprise. "How come?"

Daisy would have explained that old man Dickerson hadn't ever owned Fox Hollow, that apparently he hadn't even had a legal lease for the last six months at least, but just then they reached the top of the ridge. A purple haze of mountains appeared. Thick stands of pea-green pine. Rolling meadows dotted with cattle. Ponds glinting silver in the sun. It was a magnificent vista. She loved it. But most of all Daisy loved the house.

There wasn't anything the least bit glossy or modern about it. It was a sprawling three-story farmhouse dating to the late 1700s. The paint was bright white with burnt orange trim. The windows on the two lower floors were tall, reaching nearly from the ceiling to the ground. And the entire length of the porch railing was carved with delicate leaves and vines. It sat on the very top of a rise, surrounded by century-old rosebushes and rhododendrons, surveying its grand domain like a king in his gilded castle.

Ethan was impressed. "I'll say one thing for Mr. Dickerson. He knew how to pick a place to live. I'd consider being a recluse too if I could wake up every morning to that view. It's fantastic. They should put it on the cover of a travel magazine. And the house. That old monster must have some great history. Probably for a long time the most important family in the area called this home."

Daisy replied with a melancholy sigh. Fox Hollow was indeed historic. She could have rattled off an entire brochure's worth of notable names and dates from Virginia's past. Except to her the most important family was her own, and it no longer had a home.

The car pulled into the pebbly circle at the front of the house and stopped next to a chipped stone birdbath that had toppled over onto its side. Ethan shut off the engine, stepped out, and admired the view once more.

"I bet this is a good spot for watching sunsets."

"Especially from the swing on the left side porch," Daisy muttered under her breath.

"What was that?"

She didn't repeat it. Instead she said, "What now?"

Turning from the hypnotic purple haze of the mountains, Ethan scanned the rest of the property. "Do you see any corn?"

The question surprised her. "Corn?"

"Maybe around back."

With quick strides he headed toward the rear of the house. Daisy had to hurry to keep up.

"Corn?" she asked him once more.

"They certainly didn't send me all the way out here in search of giant dandelions," Ethan responded dryly as they waded through an unruly patch of weeds.

The wheels in Daisy's brain clicked. Corn. In her dual excitement and sorrow at returning to Fox Hollow after such a long absence, she had almost forgotten who she was there with. Of course Special Agent Kinney from the ATF was looking for corn. It made perfect sense. He had come to investigate Fred's death. A death that was evidently connected to alcohol, which in all likelihood meant moonshine, which no doubt old man Dickerson had cooked up from corn.

"Well, there it is." Ethan halted and pointed.

On the other side of the empty brick patio. Past the former vegetable garden that was now no more than a haphazard assemblage of bowed trellises and warped wire cages without the accompanying snap peas or tomatoes. Beyond the unkempt beds of towering yellow sunflowers and creamy pink daylilies, there stood an unmistakable patch of corn. The plot was sizeable, much larger than one man could ever consume with butter and salt, knife and fork over the span of a year. And it was a healthy well-tended plot. The rows were even and clean. The plants were green, watered, and shoulder-high.

"What's that?" Ethan's focus shifted to a pitch-black and ochre-red building just to the right of the corn.

It was a perfectly square structure made of tar-smeared timber and clay chinking. There were no windows and only a single door. The roof was rusty metal with a narrow stovepipe sticking out of one corner.

"That's a tobacco barn," Daisy said.

Ethan's brow furrowed. "A tobacco barn?"

"Every older farm around here has one. Back when tobacco used to rule the world, that's where they hung the leaves to dry after harvest. You can see them all over the county and half the state. In the middle of pastures. On the sides of highways. Intersections were even made around them. A lot have collapsed by now from too many winters and a general lack of care. But some are still standing and can even be used, like to store hay bales or extra machinery. Wait a minute . . ." Daisy paused and wrinkled her nose. "Why am I telling you this? Shouldn't you already know? I thought you handled tobacco. Isn't it part of your official title?"

"Technically." Ethan shrugged. "We don't do much with it anymore. That's mostly the Tax and Trade Bureau now. They handle all the labeling and permits for both alcohol and tobacco. I'm oversimplifying here, but they're more administrative in the office and we're more enforcement in the field."

"So they come for taxes while you come for corpses?"

Ethan's jaw twitched, but he didn't answer. His attention returned to the old tobacco barn. "That one looks fine. Any idea what it's used for these days?"

"Squirrel nests and enormous cobwebs?"

Daisy said it with hope, not confidence. The last time she had been inside the Fox Hollow tobacco barn was well over five years ago. Then it had been filled with an eclectic collection of tired furniture, empty crates, and broken tools. There was a chance that they were all still there, but by her estimation it wasn't a very good chance. She could tell what Ethan was thinking, and she thought the exact same thing. The corn was planted darn close to the barn. The barn was tucked quietly behind the house. The house wasn't visible from the road. And the road was pretty much in the center of nowhere. That made it a really good place to do something illegal, like distill a big batch of unlicensed likker.

"I guess we better take a look," Ethan said.

As he started toward the barn, he moved his hand toward his lower back. Daisy couldn't see the gun, but she was confident enough that it was there. Ethan was ATF, after all.

He needed to be prepared. Except she couldn't figure out what on earth he was preparing for. There was no one around, probably not for miles. No vehicles. No voices. Only a few noisy goldfinches fighting over sunflower seeds.

When Daisy caught up to him, Ethan nodded at her, but he didn't speak until just before they reached the edge of the corn.

"Daisy?" he asked in a low tone.

"Yes?"

"Is there honestly a difference between a creek and a brook?"

She almost laughed at the inanity of the question. "A brook is smaller than a creek, and a creek is smaller than a river."

"So how do you know that the one over by the cemetery is a creek?"

"From the name. It's called Frying Pan Creek."

"And what about a stream? How does a stream fit in?"

"A stream—"

Daisy broke off, suddenly realizing what Ethan was doing. While she was busy prattling on about various bodies of water and their relative sizes, he was surreptitiously inspecting the tobacco barn. And he was speaking so softly that anyone who might be inside would only catch her voice. They could have heard the car engine, the slamming of the doors, even the rustling footsteps through the vegetation, but they would be expecting her and not him.

"You're a sneaky—"

Ethan tried to silence her with a stiff motion across his throat.

"Cut it out," she snapped. "I'm not playing cloak-and-daggers with you."

"Daisy," he said warningly.

She rolled her eyes at him. "Who exactly do you expect to be in there? A secret gang of bootleggers? We're on an empty farm. How many times do I have to tell you Fred was a recluse? He lived alone. He ate alone. And he drank alone. So if there's anything inside that barn, it's alone."

"Don't!" Ethan exclaimed.

Not listening, Daisy marched to the door, found it wide open, and stepped boldly inside. When her eyes adjusted from the glaring sunshine to the shadowy light, she saw the equipment. A burnished copper pot still. Plastic buckets waiting for mash. Small white oak barrels used in aging. And rows of canning jars lined up clean and neat, like a battalion of soldiers ready to be called into battle. Then she saw Rick Balsam, leaning back in a rickety chair, boots up on a nail keg, jelly jar in hand, smirking at her.

CHAPTER
13

"Hey there, darlin'."

Daisy was too astonished to do more than blink.

"I was wondering when you'd come," Rick went on.

As he spoke, Ethan appeared in the doorway. He moved much more cautiously than Daisy, taking just one small step inside the barn and keeping his right palm steadily positioned at his lower back. If he was at all stunned to see a man lounging in front of him with his boots up on a nail keg and a jelly jar in his hand, he didn't show it.

Rick's smirk changed to a sneer. "I thought you'd probably have Sheriff Lowell with you, Daisy. Clearly I was wrong."

"I . . ." she stammered.

She didn't know what to say. She hadn't expected to find him there. If the gate at the head of the driveway had been open, or Rick's truck had been anywhere in sight, or he had ever even remotely implied that he was going to start spending time at Fox Hollow, she never would have come, especially not with Ethan Kinney.

"I . . ." she tried again. "I'm surprised to see you here."

He gave her an arch look. "I don't know why."

Daisy bit her lip. He was right. She had no real reason to be surprised. Rick was certainly entitled to be there. It was his property. She was the one who didn't belong on the land, not him.

Rick turned his attention to Ethan. "Who's your friend, Daisy?"

She bit down harder. How should she introduce Ethan? Rick was bad enough with the law of Pittsylvania County. How in the world would he handle a federal agent? And in their neck of the woods, Ethan was the worst kind of federal agent.

It took her too long to answer, and Rick's gaze darkened suspiciously.

"You do know the man standing next to you, don't you, Daisy?" he said.

"I was about to ask her the same thing about you," Ethan returned.

The two locked stares like a couple of rank bulls sizing each other up. If they had been at the diner or roadhouse with lots of people in a public setting, Daisy would have simply shrugged her shoulders and let them sort it out for themselves. But the tobacco barn was awfully isolated and she was the only potential keeper of the peace should the situation happen to take an ugly turn, which it often did when one of the Balsam boys was involved.

"Rick, this is Ethan Kinney. Ethan, Rick Balsam."

They acknowledged each other with a slight inclination of the head. The appraising stares continued. Neither spoke.

"Where's your brother?" Daisy asked, searching for a harmless subject that could break the tension.

"Bobby's out trackin' some critter," Rick replied with an exaggerated drawl. "And he's plannin' on shootin' it if he doesn't like what he finds."

It might have meant nothing, but Ethan took it as a rather unsubtle hint. His right arm shifted behind his back. Rick immediately dropped his own arm into an open sack of corn that was leaning against the side of his chair.

"Whoa, whoa, whoa!" Daisy cried. She could guess what Rick had stuffed in his sack just as easily as she could guess what Ethan had tucked behind his back. "Let's all relax. There's no need to get testy."

An uncomfortable silence followed. Without removing his arm from the corn sack, Rick lifted the jelly jar in his other hand to his lips and took a long, slow drink of the amber liquid it contained. When he had drained the last drop, he set the empty jar on the floor and gave a grim smile.

"You're right, Daisy. There's no need to get testy. At least not until you tell me what he's doing here."

"It's none of your business what I'm doing here," Ethan answered for her.

"The hell it ain't!" Rick retorted.

"If you'll just wait and let me explain . . ." Daisy began.

They didn't listen to her.

"I don't like your tone," Ethan said sharply.

Rick snorted. "I don't give a rat's ass what you like."

"I'm only going to ask you this one time. Take your hand out of that bag and—"

"And what? What are you gonna do if I don't?"

In one swift unbroken movement, Ethan pulled a black semiautomatic from the waistband of his slacks, threw back the slide, and pointed the barrel at Rick's chest. If he expected to have the faster draw because of his training with the bureau, then he grossly underestimated the speed and skill of a man from the backwoods who had started handling a pistol the same day that he had learned how to crawl. Before Ethan could even open his mouth to issue the first syllable of an ultimatum, Rick had his arm out of the sack and a revolver with a rosewood grip and cocked hammer directed straight at Ethan's neck.

"Aw jeez," Daisy muttered. This was exactly what she had been hoping to avoid.

Rick chuckled. "He thought he was quicker than me, Daisy."

"Rick—"

He stopped her. "Don't worry. I'm not going to do anything stupid."

"You're already doing something stupid. He's the law."

"The law?" Rick's taut wrist twitched once, but he didn't lower his gun. He examined Ethan closely. "You don't look like one of Sheriff Lowell's incompetent deputies. Maybe a yahoo from Danville? But I didn't think they carried Glocks down there. That's a nine millimeter, isn't it?"

"It is," Ethan confirmed.

"So I suppose that makes you federal," Rick said with unconcealed disdain.

"I am," Ethan confirmed again.

"Hell, Daisy," Rick growled. "What on earth was going through that pretty head of yours? Bringing a federal out here."

"Don't blame me," she scoffed. "I didn't know you'd be around. And it wasn't my idea anyway—"

"It was mine," Ethan interjected coolly. "I asked her to take me to Chalk Level, and she did. Now I'm going to ask you to put down your weapon."

"You first," Rick countered.

"We just covered that I'm the law."

"The law that's trespassing. You got a warrant?"

"I don't need a warrant. You're not Frederick Dickerson."

Rick paused. He looked at Daisy. "Does he understand old man Dickerson's dead?"

She nodded. "That's why he came."

"So how does that change him trespassing?"

"It doesn't," she said. "He didn't read his file. He doesn't know that Fred never owned Fox Hollow and that you do."

Startled, Ethan snapped his head toward her. "This guy owns this place?"

Daisy took a deep breath. "He does."

Ethan frowned. "You could have mentioned that little fact when you introduced us."

She shrugged. "You could have asked too. Or you could have read your file." Secretly she was thrilled that he hadn't read his file—or at least not much of it—because that meant he didn't know anything about her or her family's history with the bureau.

"I did ask," Ethan reminded her crisply. "When we were driving up to the house and talking about how the property was two hundred acres. You never finished explaining why those acres weren't valuable to Mr. Dickerson's family. If you had, I would have known about Mr. Balsam."

His memory was annoyingly good. Daisy frowned back at him. "Maybe I was trying to ease into it. Maybe I was trying to keep you and Mr. Balsam from popping each other full of holes."

He replied with a dubious grunt, then he turned to Rick. "Okay, let me put it this way. Trespassing or not, I've got ten rounds. What do you have in that Ruger forty-four? Five, six, if it's even fully loaded, which I doubt?"

Rick raised an amused eyebrow. "You could have fifty rounds. All I need is one. You wanna bet which one of us goes down first?"

Daisy's purported excuse for not immediately setting forth every detail in regard to the ownership of Fox Hollow may have sounded flimsy to Ethan, but she honestly wasn't interested in witnessing a gunfight between him and Rick. It was common knowledge throughout Pittsylvania County that Rick Balsam had a very itchy trigger finger, particularly when he had been drinking. So unless she wanted to call Sue Lowell and her ace paramedic team over at the Glade Hill Fire & Rescue Squad to come clean up the ensuing mess, Daisy realized that she had better scratch his itch fast.

"I thought you said you weren't going to do anything stupid, Rick."

He directed the amused eyebrow at her. "Are you trying to protect me, darlin'? That's mighty sweet of you."

"Of course I'm not trying to protect you. I'm trying to protect myself. You think I want to spend the rest of the day with the law, answering their hundreds of questions and filling out their endless forms because you couldn't resist arguing about magazines and calibers with a federal agent? Well, I've got news for you, *darlin'*. I have other places I want to be and money I need to earn. So quit being such a dang fool."

She thought the last part would anger Rick and he would do what he usually did when he got mad at her— mumble a choice expletive or two, then storm off and keep his distance for a while. But this time he didn't. On the contrary, he didn't even look irked. His eyebrow went right on being amused.

"If you're not careful, Daisy," he responded with a teasing laugh, "I may just start to believe you like me more than you want me to know."

"Knock it off." Her patience for his arrogant smugness had reached its end. "And for God's sake, put down that gun!

There's been too much death on this land already. Do you really have to add to the body count?"

The eyebrow fell, Rick's face paled as though an arctic wind had whipped across it, and he immediately set the revolver on the ground.

"Thank you." Daisy said it so softly, it was almost a whisper. She had gone further than she intended, but it was the truth nonetheless. She couldn't stomach another killing at Fox Hollow, accidental or intentional.

"I . . . I didn't mean to . . ."

Although Rick didn't finish the sentence, she understood. He may have been a snide, egotistical weasel, but even he had his limits. And her daddy was one of them.

"Ethan?" Daisy turned to him expectantly.

"All right." Slowly and with obvious reluctance, Ethan lowered his weapon. But instead of putting it back in the waistband of his slacks, he kept the gun in his hand at his side. "If he makes one move—"

"He won't," she promised on Rick's behalf.

"I won't," Rick agreed. Dropping his boots from the nail keg to the floor, he scooped up a trio of fresh jelly jars. "And now that we're all friends"—he gave a little cough—"why don't we have a drink?"

"I think you've had enough to drink," Daisy remarked wryly.

"It's never enough when it's this good, darlin'."

He reached toward a row of canning jars that were filled to the brim with amber liquid. After a brief hesitation, Rick selected one, unscrewed the metal lid, and poured a short thumb's worth into each jelly jar. Keeping a jar for himself, he placed the other two on the nail keg for Daisy and Ethan.

"There you go. Don't be shy now."

Predictably, Ethan didn't budge an inch. At first neither did Daisy, but then she changed her mind, walked over, and picked up a jar. She swirled its contents like a fine wine, debating whether or not to take a sip. She didn't drink much 'shine. It was too strong, and she worked far too many hours on far too many days to drink much of anything at all, other than seriously caffeinated coffee. But she wanted to keep Rick calm and content, and she was genuinely curious. She had always known that the Balsam boys dabbled in wet goods, but she had never tasted any of their creations. And she was surprised by how appetizing and artisanal the whole operation appeared. Everything was clean and tidy. There wasn't a cobweb, squirrel's nest, or anything filthy and rotten in sight.

She took a good look. The whiskey was crystal clear, with not a tinge of cloudiness or speck of sediment. Then she took a sniff. There was the expected ethanol punch, followed by a slightly sweet aroma. Daisy couldn't help being impressed. Before he died, Matt's daddy used to play with corn and sugar and malt, but he always ended up with a colorless bubbly swill that smelled like a fetid cross between moldy onions and pig's feet boiled in vinegar. Daisy raised the jar to her lips. No more than a thimbleful touched her tongue. It was warm and spicy, with the barest hint of honey. She swallowed. As the liquid flamed down her throat, an equally intense chill raced up her spine. She suddenly remembered, and her eyes filled with horror.

"Rick?"

"Yes, Daisy?"

"Did you just poison me?"

CHAPTER
14

In an instant Ethan's gun was back up and pointed at Rick's chest. "What did you do?"

Rick ignored him and the Glock. Instead he stared at Daisy.

She put a hand to her throat. It was hot and tight. Her head swam, and her vision blurred. She grabbed the back of an empty chair to steady herself.

Ethan rushed forward. "What did you put in her drink?"

Rick remained silent.

"Tell me, goddamm it!" The barrel of Ethan's gun was no more than a few inches from Rick's heart. "Tell me right now or I'm going to blow a hole the size of a golf ball through your lung!"

Heedless of the threat, Rick rose from his seat.

"Where the hell do you think you're going?" Ethan shouted.

Daisy was going outside. The humid air inside the barn seemed suddenly stifling. She was having trouble catching her breath. She stumbled toward the open doorway.

"Is it the same thing you used to poison Frederick Dickerson?" Ethan bellowed at Rick.

Although Rick's dark eyes had been following Daisy, they shifted abruptly to Ethan. "What the blazes are you talking about? I didn't poison old man Dickerson!"

"Is it arsenic?" Ethan demanded.

Arsenic. Daisy's stomach shook. Arsenic was both an herbicide and pesticide. It was often called the king of poisons, because it was able to kill just about everything, from plants to insects to animals to humans. It could be used on so many types of agriculture. Cotton, rye, barley, millet, rice. And corn. Some people didn't work with it anymore. They considered it too toxic. It contaminated the groundwater and frequently destroyed unintended species. There was no question that arsenic was about as far from environmentally friendly as you could get—not to mention that it was classified as a human carcinogen—but that didn't mean everyone shunned it. On the contrary, members of the old school couldn't seem to get enough of the stuff, even showering it like lethal dewdrops on their lawns.

Fred Dickerson certainly had been old school. It wouldn't have surprised Daisy in the least if he had put arsenic on his corn. There were probably bags of it lying all over Fox Hollow. Then he had used that corn to make his 'shine. He had poisoned himself. And now—with the help of Rick—he had poisoned her too. It was so simple really. Arsenic was readily soluble in water. It was colorless and odorless. Poor Fred wouldn't have even realized what had happened until it was already too late. Afterward the arsenic would be detectable in his hair and nails. Daisy knew that because a few years back there had been concerns about the safety of some wells in the area. Scientists from all over the state had descended on them to do tests. That must have been what old man Dickerson's autopsy showed. That was why Special Agent Kinney was here. He came for corpses, and apparently Fred's corpse contained arsenic and moonshine.

Daisy's wobbly feet stepped onto the grass. The sun hit her cheeks, and she paused.

"If you're waiting for me to turn my back so you can grab your Ruger and run, you can forget it," Ethan spat at Rick. "You're staying with me, and we're going outside. Move!"

Rick complied without dispute. He left the barn first, followed closely by Ethan and the Glock. Daisy's eyes met his. Rick's gaze was utterly blank. There was no mocking laughter, no remorse, not even any sympathy.

"How are you?" Ethan asked Daisy anxiously.

She didn't answer. She kept on looking at Rick. He looked straight back at her.

"We need to get you to a hospital," Ethan said. "Do you know where the nearest emergency room is? One with a trauma unit would be preferable. They're better equipped . . ."

Daisy stopped listening. She wasn't thinking about emergency rooms or trauma units. She was thinking about Rick. His head, to be precise. Rick cocked his head to the side when he flirted and when he lied, always when he believed he had the upper hand. But his head wasn't cocked now, and that was what brought the realization home to her. There were no yellow-tinted tears streaming from her eyes or foam gushing out of her mouth. No paralyzing convulsions forced her to the ground. She hadn't drunk a bad batch of 'shine. Whatever strange symptoms she had felt were a result of the potent alcohol hitting her empty stomach. Rick hadn't tried to poison her after all.

"Why didn't you say something!" Daisy exploded in

anger. "I thought I might be dying. I thought you had poisoned me. And you decided it would be a grand idea to let me go on thinking that?"

Rick frowned at her. "Don't be stupid."

"I guess I am stupid," she hissed. "I'm stupid for believing any word that ever rolls off your lying tongue."

"Are you . . ." Ethan squinted at her in confusion. "I don't . . ."

"I'm fine," Daisy told him. "I'm not sick. I don't need to go to the hospital. But I appreciate your help and concern. Very much." She turned to Rick with a bitter scowl. "I've known Ethan for two days, and he was worried enough to want to take me to the emergency room. I've known you for practically my whole life, and you couldn't be bothered to spit out one simple sentence—*No, I didn't poison you, Daisy.*"

"You're being dramatic," Rick replied coolly.

She glared at him. "And you're being an ass. An even bigger ass than usual, which I seriously didn't think was possible."

He glared at her in return. "You're right about one thing. You've known me for practically your whole life. So you should know I would never poison you. Although I'm beginning to wonder if I've been wrong about that all these years."

Ethan waved his Glock in Rick's direction. "I hope that's not a threat." Then to Daisy he said, "What I want to know is why you thought he had poisoned you."

An hour earlier she would have debated how candid to be with Ethan, but after the appalling scare that Rick had just put her through—not to mention his infuriatingly cavalier attitude about it—she felt not the tiniest bit of loyalty toward him.

"I thought he had poisoned me," she answered frankly,

"because last week when I told him that George Lowell—
the Pittsylvania County sheriff—might drive out to Fox
Hollow sometime in the near future, Rick informed me
that I needed to go with him. When I asked why, he responded that unless I wanted the sheriff to die like old man
Dickerson, I had to make sure he didn't drink any of Fred's
'shine. I remembered what Rick had said just as I drank the
'shine, and I naturally assumed that now I was going to die
like Fred."

"Traitor," Rick muttered.

Daisy raised a resentful eyebrow at him. "I'm the traitor? I don't think so. Whose name is on the deed to this
place? It certainly ain't mine."

"I tried to explain that to you—"

Ethan interrupted him brusquely. "How did you know
there was a problem with Mr. Dickerson's product?"

"How did you know?" Rick retorted.

"They sent us a copy of the autopsy report. The arsenic
in the man was off the charts. When combined with the
alcohol in his system, it wasn't too difficult to figure out
what had happened. We've seen it before."

Rick grunted.

"So I'm going to ask you again." Ethan's voice was sharp
and commanding. "How did you know there was a problem with Mr. Dickerson's product?"

He didn't immediately reply. Instead Rick clenched and
unclenched his fists. Daisy understood why. He didn't want
to talk to Ethan. Ethan wasn't just the law. He was federal.
To Rick that was like mixing typhoid and cholera. You
didn't voluntarily help typhoid and cholera.

"Just tell him," she said.

"Maybe I've got nothing to tell," Rick returned.

Daisy wrinkled her nose. "Yes, you do. I saw it."

"What did you see?"

"I saw you stare at him. Right after Sheriff Lowell arrived. You were staring at Fred's body. I know you noticed something. And I'm willing to bet it's the reason you thought he drank some bad 'shine."

Rick grunted again.

"Just tell him," she repeated. "He's going to figure it out eventually anyway. It's better if he hears the truth from you now. Then they can't invent some ludicrous story later on. And we both know how the ATF loves to do that."

"ATF!" Rick gaped at her. "He's ATF?"

Her face reddened.

"You really are a traitor," Rick snarled.

"Don't you dare judge me!" Daisy snarled back at him. "I lost everything because of them. You lost nothing."

"Does your momma know what you're doing? How about Aunt Emily? Or Hank! You can't honestly expect me to believe they're all hunky-dory with you standing merrily next to him and acting like—" Rick halted midsentence as he glanced toward Ethan and saw his perplexed expression. He turned back to Daisy. "He doesn't know, does he?"

She sighed. "I told you already. He didn't read his file."

"Huh." Rick rubbed the stubble on his chin thoughtfully. "What game are you playing, darlin'?"

"I'm not playing any game," she responded, more fatigued than offended. "I'm trying to get Ethan the information he needs so he can finish up his investigation into poor Fred's death and go home."

"And I'm grateful for it," Ethan said.

Rick went on rubbing his chin.

Daisy shrugged. "Tell him. Don't tell him. Do whatever you want, Rick. Just make up your mind—and be quick about it too—because it's hotter than Hades standing out here in the sun."

"I thought I was the only one melting," Ethan agreed. He turned to Rick. "Since we'd all rather be somewhere with air-conditioning, let's just cut to the chase. If you make it easier for me, I'll make it easier for you. Don't forget, I'm ATF and you've got a barn full of what I'm assuming is unregistered, untaxed, illegally distilled corn whiskey behind you. I'm sure you don't need me to do the math for you."

With a shrug of his own, Rick said, "He had the lid to a canning jar."

"Who did?" Ethan asked. "Mr. Dickerson?"

He nodded.

"When was this?"

"When he collapsed at the diner."

"You were at H & P's when Mr. Dickerson died?"

"I was. Right next to sweet li'l Daisy."

Ethan looked at her. "You didn't mention that."

"You didn't ask," she replied.

"You seem to use that answer a lot." He frowned.

"Maybe so, but it's true."

Although the frown continued, Ethan directed his attention back to Rick. "So when Mr. Dickerson died at the diner, he had the lid to a canning jar?"

Rick nodded a second time.

Daisy shook her head at him. "Fred wasn't holding anything. I'm positive of that. I looked at his hands."

"It wasn't in his hands. It was in the pocket of his coveralls. I didn't see it until he fell on the tile. Then it slipped partway out. That's what I was staring at."

"The lid to a canning jar doesn't explain how you knew there was a problem with Mr. Dickerson's product," Ethan said.

"It was pink."

"Pink?" Daisy and Ethan echoed in unison.

"I get that she wouldn't know"—Rick gestured toward Daisy—"because the only wildcat she usually drinks is a polite glass of Emily Tosh's gooseberry brandy after Sunday dinner. But you"—he curled his lips at Ethan with contempt—"are from the almighty, all-powerful, all-knowing ATF. You should understand what pink means."

"Well, I don't," Ethan informed him sourly.

Rick's contemptuous smile grew.

"So are you going to enlighten us?" Daisy asked, more for the sake of her own curiosity than to temper the rising hostility between the two men.

"I'll show you," Rick said. "It's better that way."

He started walking toward the house. Daisy promptly followed him. Ethan joined her but stayed carefully behind their leader, maintaining a clear shot in case Rick tried to pull something tricky. When Daisy realized that he was taking them around the far side of the house, she slowed to a shuffle.

Ethan glanced at her questioningly. "Is something wrong?"

"No."

It was a lie, but Daisy didn't care. She was too concerned with keeping her head down and her eyes glued to her feet.

"Are you sure?" he pressed her. "Because you look like you just saw a ghost."

That was precisely why she had her eyes glued to her feet. She didn't want to see a ghost. And they were getting close to one. Too close. They had already passed the far corner of the empty brick patio. It was just beyond that.

Suddenly Ethan stopped. "What the heck happened there?"

Daisy didn't have to raise her gaze. She knew what he was referring to just the same as her own name. Like a brand, the image was seared permanently into her brain. It was a large circular burnt patch. Soulless black at the center, growing gradually lighter gray until it was almost violet at the edges. The earth was so deeply and violently scorched in that spot, no green would grow there for many years.

"That must have been a bad fire," Ethan remarked.

"It was," Rick responded solemnly. "It's where Daisy's daddy died."

CHAPTER
15

"I'm sorry."

"You should be."

Ethan glowered at Rick. "I wasn't speaking to you."

"That's good, because there's no way in hell I'd ever forgive you."

"Forgive me!" Ethan snorted. "Forgive me for what? I haven't done a damn thing to you. Not yet anyway."

"Maybe." Rick shrugged. "Or maybe not. But there's no arguing you've done plenty to Daisy and her family."

"What are you talking about? I don't even know her family."

"You would—or at least you'd have a clue—if you had read that file of yours."

"Enough with the blasted file already," Ethan snapped. "Okay, I admit it. I didn't do my homework like I should have. My boss handed me the case. It looked like a simple, straightforward, accidental hooch and arsenic combo. And I came here to do the obligatory follow-up before closing the file. It was supposed to be quick and easy. No background or research necessary. I see now I was wrong about that. So if you've got something to say to me, just say it. Don't keep talking around it like I'm supposed to decode an ancient riddle, because I can't."

"Well?" Rick looked at Daisy. "It's your call."

She didn't look back at him. Her gaze was locked on a desolate clump of white clover that was struggling to survive just beyond the violet edge of the charred circle. It seemed to her like a little flag of surrender. Only she wasn't sure if it was the blackened earth that was capitulating or her.

"I don't know what Daisy's told you," Rick said to Ethan. "It can't be much if you didn't know about her daddy."

"He . . ." Ethan paused and glanced at her, but she didn't look back at him either. "He died here? In a fire?"

Rick nodded.

"Was anybody else hurt?" He glanced at Daisy again.

"If you're checking for burn marks," Rick responded with crispness, "you won't find them. She wasn't here when it happened. But there was another person killed. Her daddy-in-law."

"When was this?"

"About five years ago."

"Five years ago? Isn't that around the same time her husband left? Was Matt involved?"

Rick's body stiffened. "How do you know about Matt?"

"Daisy told me." Ethan smiled at him with condescension. "I have spent the last two days with her. She has shared a few things."

"She might seem friendly to you now, but make no mistake about it, Daisy ain't your friend."

The smile grew. "Does she blame you?"

"What in God's name would she blame me for?" Rick retorted.

"Isn't it obvious? It's your property. Her father and

father-in-law died here. It sounds to me like you'd be the perfect person to blame."

"That just shows how little you understand. It wasn't my property then. It belonged to Daisy's family."

"If that's true," Ethan said, frowning, "why did they decide to sell it? Too many bad memories?"

"Sell it?" Rick laughed. His tone was harsh and cynical. "To get away from bad memories? That's a good joke."

Ethan's face hardened. "Do I really have to remind you about the gallons of unlawful liquor you're producing on this land?"

The laughter promptly died.

"Because the potential consequences—"

"You don't need to threaten me." Rick cut him off sullenly. "I know all about your consequences. Everyone around here does. We understand what happens when you boys at the ATF get mad or feel like teaching somebody a lesson. We've seen it before. Daisy and her momma have felt your wrath."

There was a slight pause, then Ethan replied with frosty composure. "I'm not threatening you, and I don't teach people lessons. I meant what I said earlier. If you make it easier for me, I'll make it easier for you."

"And how exactly do I make it easier for you?"

"You can start by explaining to me what happened the last time someone was here from my office."

"Okay. But don't blame me afterward. *You'll* have to deal with these consequences, not me." Rick gestured toward the burnt patch in front of them. "The last time someone was here from your office, they had been sent to investigate that."

"The fire?" Ethan showed mild astonishment. "The fire that killed Daisy's father and father-in-law?"

"Yes," Daisy said. "The fire that killed my daddy and Matt's daddy."

As she spoke, both men turned to her. Her eyes met Rick's first. If he expected tears, there were none.

"Daisy . . ." he began.

She shook her head at him, and her gaze moved to Ethan. Her face bore no anger or grief. Her expression was entirely void of feeling.

"It was an accident," she told him. "A terrible accident with a large propane tank. But for some inexplicable reason—known only to the ATF and the Almighty above—you decided differently. You called it a felony. A whole long list of felonies actually. Everything you could possibly imagine involving the manufacture, use, and storage of explosives. All illegal, of course. And as a penalty for that supposed illegal manufacture, use, and storage of explosives, you chose forfeiture. The house. The land. The crops. You took them. You took everything. It was all forfeit. The bank holding the mortgages eventually worked out some sort of a deal with you. Old man Dickerson in turn leased it from them. And then earlier this year, Rick bought the property free and clear. So that's what happened the last time someone was here from your office. My momma and I buried my daddy—who you branded as a criminal—and we lost Fox Hollow."

Ethan gurgled. He was clearly too staggered for any other response. Daisy found herself almost smiling because of it. He had probably seen a lot during his time with the bureau. Ethan probably already knew from past experience that still waters could sometimes run remarkably deep. But he obviously hadn't imagined anything like this. That sleepy, bucolic Fox Hollow was quietly a nest of arsenic, moonshine, explosives, and deadly fires.

To her own surprise, Daisy felt a very welcome sense of

relief. Now that she had told him, she could stop dreading having to tell him. She turned to Rick.

"Could we go back to you explaining the pink canning jar lid in Fred's coveralls?"

He blinked at her for a long moment. Then he drawled, "I think we can do that, darlin'."

"Good. And please tell me that wherever you're taking us, it's in the shade. Because it's positively roasting out here today. With this humidity I would swear a storm must be coming, except there's not a cloud in the sky. It's as blue as blue gets."

"Do you remember what we used to do on days like this?"

"We used to go swimming in the creek."

"Skinny-dipping in the creek," Rick corrected her.

"That happened once." Daisy rolled her eyes at him. "When I was seven and you dared me to do it. I've been telling you ever since not to expect a repeat performance."

"I can keep hoping."

"And I can hope for an army of penguins to waddle up from Patagonia with buckets of ice in their wee flippers. But hoping ain't gonna make it happen."

Rick chuckled and once again started walking toward the farmhouse. Daisy accompanied him. Ethan followed a short distance behind. He was silent and appeared to be in deep contemplation.

Gesturing toward him, Rick said quietly to Daisy, "So how cozy have you gotten with our federal friend?"

"Not as cozy as you've gotten with that charming woman Sue I saw at your trailer last week."

He grinned. "She is charming. Only not as charming as you."

"I bet," Daisy remarked dryly.

"But seriously"—Rick lowered his voice even further—"is he our friend? I have to know."

"If you're worried about how much trouble that pot still and those brimming barrels in the barn are going to cause you, you probably don't need to be too concerned. I think if Ethan was really interested in you and what you were doing in there, he would have locked you up by now. Or shot you."

"You could have warned me," Rick replied gruffly.

"That we were coming out to Fox Hollow? How was I supposed to know you'd started cooking up 'shine here? And Sue told you the sheriff might drop by. He's the law too, even if he's not federal. You can't count on him turning his head all the time just because it's less work and he wants to keep the peace."

Rick grunted.

"Daisy—" Ethan said suddenly.

She glanced at him.

"Did you fight it?" he asked her. "I mean, did you fight us?"

"That bastard has got some nerve," Rick growled.

Daisy sighed. "I did."

"And?" Ethan prodded.

Rick's fingers curled into fists. She put her hand on his arm to calm him.

"And have you ever tried to fight you?" She didn't wait for his response. "Now imagine doing it when you're twenty-two—without any money or political connections—while you're struggling to put yourself through college, take care of your momma in the hospital, and find a decent place to sleep at night after your husband decides to go gallivanting off."

"Oh," Ethan mumbled.

Removing her hand from his arm, Daisy raised a weary

eyebrow at Rick. "I could really use a jelly jar of yours right now."

"Tonight," he promised. "You and me, two jelly jars and our feet in Frying Pan Creek. Just like the old days."

She sighed again. They had reached the house, and Rick motioned toward the blissfully shady side porch. Trudging up the steps, she collapsed into one of the primeval wrought-iron chairs.

"Mind your elbow," Rick cautioned her.

Daisy looked at the matching wrought-iron table next to her seat, and to her surprise, she found a pair of canning jars standing on it. The first jar was completely full and shut tight. The other was about a quarter empty and missing its lid. Unlike the canning jars inside the barn, the liquid in the jars on the table wasn't amber. It was colorless and as perfectly clear as the sky.

With a little jerk, she shrunk away from the table and the jars. "Are those . . . Is that Fred's . . ."

Rick nodded. "I wouldn't recommend sampling it."

"And the pink thing?" Ethan came up for a closer inspection. "The reason you knew there was a problem with it?"

"Watch and you'll see," Rick said.

He picked up the open jar, moved it carefully away from them, and poured a small stream of liquid onto the table. Both Daisy and Ethan leaned forward, waiting for something to happen. But it didn't. The liquid trickled across the black iron just like normal water. There was no discernible difference.

"I don't . . ." Ethan began.

"Watch and you'll see," Rick repeated tersely.

The liquid dribbled over the edge of the table onto the porch floor. The boards had been painted white, and the first few drops that hit them looked the same as spring rain. Then suddenly Daisy saw the change. It wasn't a bright burst of color, but the formerly hueless liquid had an unmistakable tinge of pink.

She raised her furrowed brow to Rick. "I've never seen pink whiskey. It is corn whiskey, isn't it?"

"It is," he confirmed.

Rick reached over and unscrewed the lid of the full canning jar. He held it up for them to see. Instead of creamy white or ivory as the inside of the lid should have been, it had a distinct pink tint.

"And the pink means there's arsenic in there?" Ethan's brow was even more furrowed than Daisy's.

"Not necessarily arsenic," Rick replied. "But it means there's something wrong with it. Something's *really* wrong with it. Any man who knows his wet goods and sees it change color like that when it hits wood or rubber, knows not to touch a sip of the stuff."

"So you noticed the lid in Fred's coveralls after he collapsed at the diner," Daisy said, "and because it was pink you realized he had drunk some bad 'shine?"

"At the time I didn't know it was arsenic that had got him." Rick sealed up the full jar again. "But I figured whatever it was, it had to be awful bad, considering how sick the old man got and he died from it."

"Poor Fred," Daisy muttered.

"I can understand," Ethan said, "how you saw the lid in his pocket. I can also understand how because the lid was pink you knew there was a problem with his product. What I can't understand is how you connected that pink lid to this canning jar." He gestured toward the partially empty open jar.

Rick's lips curled into a smile. "I wouldn't say I recognized the lid. A lot of folks use the same jars, after all. But since I'm the one who made the 'shine—and I gave it to Fred by personally putting it on this table—I was pretty sure the lid in his coveralls matched my jars."

CHAPTER
16

Ethan took a step backward and firmed his grip on the gun that he continued to hold at his side. "You do realize you just admitted to poisoning a man, don't you?"

"I told you before," Rick drawled indignantly. "I didn't poison old man Dickerson."

"You can say it a dozen more times. I don't care if you hum it, whistle it, or sing it at night like a lullaby. It doesn't change the facts. You distilled the whiskey. You delivered the whiskey. And the whiskey killed him. That's poisoning a man by any definition."

"So that's why he recognized you," Daisy interjected.

Rick turned to her.

"I knew Fred recognized you," she said. "When he first stumbled into the diner, before he had the seizure and fell. Fred looked at you and seemed to want to say something to you, except he couldn't because he was already so sick. I wondered about it, but I couldn't figure out why he'd recognize you. Now it's obvious. You gave him the 'shine, and he was trying to tell you it was bad."

"I do think he was trying to warn me," Rick agreed.

"Or accuse you," Ethan countered.

Daisy disregarded the latter remark. "You gave Fred lots of 'shine, didn't you?"

Rick answered with a grin.

"Why did you lie about it?"

"What do you mean?" he asked her, feigning innocence.

"If you gave Fred lots of 'shine, then I can't believe you didn't see him, at least once in a while. You had to come here pretty often to cook up all that likker you've got sitting in the barn. So even if you didn't ring the bell and swap stories with him every time, you still must have caught a glimpse of Fred on occasion. And you told Sheriff Lowell you hadn't seen him in ten years. I thought you were lying when you said that."

His grin grew. "How did you know?"

Settling back into her chair, Daisy folded her arms across her chest. "I've known you long enough, Richard Balsam. I can always tell when you're lying."

"As I recall," he said, cocking his head at her, "there was a time when we knew each other quite well."

She laughed because by cocking his head, Rick had proven her point. "You also told Sheriff Lowell you hadn't talked to Fred in a decade. Did you lie about that too?"

"No," he said firmly.

"Then why," Daisy said, returning to her original question, "did you lie about seeing him?"

"Aw hell, I didn't lie. I just didn't tell the whole truth." Rick leaned against the porch railing. "I honestly didn't talk to Fred. But I did see him now and again. I'd wave. He'd wave. That was the end of it. I didn't tell the sheriff because I didn't think it mattered. And it wasn't any of his goddam business either."

"If you didn't speak to Mr. Dickerson," Ethan asked, "how did you know to leave the jars for him?"

He shrugged. "After I finished my first batch, I set a jar up on the porch as a courtesy of sorts. I had seen the old man drink out here before, so I thought he might like a taste of mine. When I returned a week later, the jar was empty. I took that as a sign he enjoyed it, and I left a couple of new jars for him whenever I came back."

Ethan frowned. "But isn't what you've got in the barn aged? With the barrels and the amber color?" He gestured toward the jars of hueless liquid on the wrought-iron table. "This isn't aged."

"I do usually age what I make for me and my"—Rick chortled—"fancier friends. But did you ever meet Fred Dickerson?" He didn't wait for Ethan's reply. "The old man lived life plain and simple. He didn't want subtle hints of flavor or bouquet. He wanted the lick of fire. So I gave him the lick of fire."

"All right." Ethan's frown continued. "You gave Mr. Dickerson some of your unaged whiskey. Later—from the events at the diner—you discovered the whiskey was tainted, deadly even. Why didn't you throw it away? Why did you let it sit out here for everybody to drink? You knew how dangerous it was."

Rick responded with another chortle. "Look around you. Do you see anyone? Who would possibly drink it? A horsefly might decide to buzz over and take a sip, but I'd be glad if it died. One less bloodsucker flying around the county. When I heard there was a chance the sheriff could drop by, I told Daisy straightaway to watch out for him and make sure he doesn't pour himself a glass."

Ethan merely grunted.

"Believe it or not," Rick went on, "I feel lousy about

what happened. I didn't poison him, but it was still my 'shine—and old man Dickerson drank it—and it killed him."

"It's not your fault Fred was using arsenic on the corn," Daisy said.

He looked at her. "Fred was using arsenic on the corn?"

"Of course. How else would it have gotten there? He probably thought it was working wonderfully. The corn by the barn sure looks good. Except poor Fred didn't realize that by putting arsenic on the corn, he was also putting it in the 'shine. He poisoned himself."

Rick and Ethan glanced at each other.

"Daisy," Rick responded slowly, "Fred didn't use arsenic on the corn by the barn."

"He didn't?"

"No. I planted that corn. And I tended that corn. He had nothing to do with it."

"But"—she blinked at him in confusion—"if he had nothing to do with it, then how . . . how did . . ."

"I don't know," Rick answered. "That's the problem. I don't know how the arsenic got there. I do know, however, Fred wasn't responsible. There's no arsenic on the corn, next to the corn, or anywhere near the corn. I'm sure of that because the rest of the batch is clean. I appreciate you saying it wasn't my fault, but it wasn't the corn's fault either."

"The arsenic didn't just magically appear in the jars," Ethan remarked dryly.

"That's the main reason I didn't throw them out," Rick told him. "I was hoping if I kept everything the way it was, maybe there would be a clue somewhere. I figured when the sheriff came, he might be able to find it."

"You're positive . . ." Daisy blinked at him once more. "You're positive there's no arsenic in the rest of the batch?"

Rick smiled slightly. "Yes, I'm positive. I'm still standing—and Bobby's still standing—and you're still standing."

"Do you think Mr. Dickerson was the target?" Ethan asked him.

"I think he had to be. Anybody who was paying any attention would have known I was putting the two jars up here on the porch for him, while I was drinking from the jars in the barn. And the jars in the barn are all fine and untouched. I've checked. Trust me, I've double- and triple-checked. But that brings me back to what I said before. Look around you. Do you see anyone? Who would possibly be paying any attention? I can't for the life of me imagine. Except somebody must have been."

"Somebody must have been," Ethan concurred. "The real question is—why? Why would they put arsenic in these two jars and only these two jars?"

"Are you saying it was intentional?" Daisy stared at him. "Someone intentionally put arsenic in Fred's 'shine?"

Ethan gave a little snort. "You're just catching on to that now? Of course I believe it was intentional."

Her stare widened. "That can't be right. Nobody would poison old man Dickerson. Not deliberately."

"Apparently they would," Ethan retorted, "because they did."

Daisy looked at Rick. He nodded.

"But it's not logical." She stood up. "Poor Fred was a recluse. He was old and never bothered a soul. Why would you poison a person like that? There's no reason for it."

"Well, there had to be some reason for it." Ethan turned to Rick. "And since he lived on your property—and you're the only one we know for certain ever saw him—you probably have the best chance of figuring out what that reason was. Or at least pointing me in the proper direction."

"Hell if I know." Rick shrugged. "I've thought about it. I've thought about it a lot actually. But Daisy's right. The man was old and never bothered a soul. Whenever I was here, Fred was always alone. He didn't have any visitors."

"Never?" Ethan said. "Not once?"

Rick rubbed the stubble on his chin. "I can't remember a time—"

Daisy walked slowly down the length of the porch. Fred Dickerson had been poisoned. Intentionally. She was having a hard time believing it, but it had to be true. Logical or not, there was no other explanation left for his death. Rick and Ethan were obviously convinced. Aunt Emily too. Granted, she had envisioned a sprinkle of cyanide in Fred's hash browns or a dash of drain cleaner in his tomato soup, but arsenic in his moonshine had worked just as well, evidently.

It was no longer a ridiculous murder theory. It was actual murder. Except the reason for it still baffled Daisy. There was no cause to hurt old man Dickerson. He hadn't been in contact with anyone for ages. He hadn't seen anyone either. Only Rick. And Hank. Hank might have seen Fred too. He was the first to positively identify him at the diner. Then there was his strange behavior, twice. Hank had to know more than he was letting on.

She caught a snippet of Rick and Ethan's conversation.

"Anyone could have come onto the property," Rick said. "The gate at the road isn't locked. And I'm not here every day. I wasn't here at all the week Fred died."

"So whoever put the arsenic in the jars didn't have to worry about you catching them, only Mr. Dickerson."

"They didn't have to worry about Fred either," Rick replied. "Not in his feeble condition. He couldn't fight a flea. If they wanted to kill him—"

"Which we have to assume they did," Ethan interjected.

"Then why use arsenic? You've got to get it, mix it in
the 'shine, wait for the old man to swallow a glass and finally die. Why not shoot him—or stab him—or strangle
him instead? They're all much simpler and quicker. And
they guarantee the who and when."

"Unless you need it to *look* like an accident."

"That's what I was thinking," Rick agreed. "Because if
you just wanted Fred dead, you could have hit him in the
head with an axe and buried him somewhere in the fields.
Or better yet, dumped him in the middle of the woods.
There are two hundred acres of land out here, most of
which aren't being touched. I wouldn't have found his
body. No one would have probably ever found his body."

With a sigh, Daisy rested her head against the corner of
the house. Dump him in the middle of the woods. Rick
sounded just like Aunt Emily. Only he didn't have a sus-
pect in mind, or at least he didn't name one. Aunt Emily
had promptly pointed her finger at Hank, because Fred was
supposedly responsible for the death of her daddy. But even
if that were true—which it couldn't possibly be—why would
Hank wait nearly five long years to seek his revenge? Why
would he use arsenic in moonshine? And why on earth
would Fred then go to H & P's of all places as he was dying?
It made no sense.

The wood was rough on her cheek from the paint splin-
tering off the boards. The house was in desperate need of
love and attention. Surveying the condition of the porch
in the corner where she was standing, Daisy clucked her
tongue in irritation. Rick might not want to repair the property, but he could at least keep it from becoming a trash
heap. She bent down toward a dirty rag with the intention

of depositing it in the nearest garbage can. As she scooped it up, it reminded her of something. The smell and stains. She squinted at it, puzzled. Then the realization suddenly hit her, and her eyes flared open.

"Daisy?"

She crumpled the cloth into as small of a ball as she could.

"What is that?" Rick asked her.

"Hmm?" she answered vaguely.

His footsteps started toward her. "What do you have there?"

Turning around to face him, Daisy held the ball behind her. "This? Nothing. Just some junk I found. I was about to throw it out."

"What kind of junk?"

"I don't know. Junk."

"Daisy . . ."

Reluctantly she raised her eyes to meet his. Daisy knew that Rick would see right through her. She was an abysmal liar. He took hold of her wrist to get a better look at the supposed junk in her hand, but he didn't recognize it.

"Where did you find that?"

"Over there."

Daisy pointed toward the spot. A quartet of bowed rusty nails stuck out from one of the boards like a group of tipsy sailors. A tiny torn piece of matching cloth remained attached to them.

"The nails must have snagged it," Rick said. "What is it?"

She didn't respond. He tried to take it from her, and she resisted.

"Leave it," Daisy whispered sternly.

Rick frowned but let go of her wrist. She immediately tucked the ball behind her back once more. She wished that she had a better way of getting rid of it. Except it was too big for a pocket. And there was no trash bag on the porch that she could pretend to dump it in now and collect it again later in private.

Astute enough to realize that something was amiss, Ethan walked over to them. He held out his palm.

"May I see it?" he said.

Although Daisy tried to think up an excuse, there was none. How could she justify not handing over a purported piece of junk to a special agent from the ATF—and his Glock—standing a half foot in front of her? Her only hope was that he wouldn't recognize it any more than Rick had.

With the speed of a geriatric snail, Daisy lifted the ball of cloth and set it in Ethan's waiting hand. He gazed at it for a long moment, then raised a questioning eyebrow at her. She gulped. He unfurled the ball with a quick snap. The cloth hung from his fingers like a limp flag, soiled and wrinkled. Ethan gazed at it for another long moment, and the questioning eyebrow turned toward Daisy again. This time it was joined by an unhappy—and painfully perceptive— twitch of the jaw.

"You were planning on hiding this?" he demanded.

She instinctively retreated a step.

"I assume by your efforts to conceal it you know what it is," Ethan continued gruffly, "and what it means."

"It doesn't mean anything," Daisy replied.

"It sure as hell means something."

"But it doesn't prove—"

"Yes, it does. It proves he was here."

Rick looked back and forth between the two. "Will somebody tell me what the blazes is going on?"

Ethan swung the cloth in Rick's direction. "Look familiar?"

He studied it for a few seconds, then shook his head. "No."

"Look again. I didn't recognize it at first either. But it's such a dirty white. With those stains. And there's the shape. The shape was what gave it away for me. Was it the shape for you too, Daisy?"

She pressed her lips together hard.

"Then there's the fact it reeks like hamburgers," Ethan went on.

Rick squinted at the cloth. "Is that—" The squint turned to Daisy. "That's not—"

"It is." She sighed.

"Holy hell," he muttered. "Hank's apron."

CHAPTER
17

It was Hank's apron. There was no question about that. Daisy knew it from the grease. It smelled just like him and the diner. The inimitable scent of frying oil. And it had all those creases from the day before when he pulled it off and flung it next to the mustard bottles. She had picked it up and tossed it back to him, and he had wrapped it around his waist before heading into the kitchen. Hank had been wearing the apron yesterday at H & P's, but somehow it had ended up on the porch of Fox Hollow today.

"How in the world did it get here?" Rick said.

"I think the better question," Ethan replied, "is when did it get here?"

Daisy constructed a timeline in her head. She had last been together with Hank the prior evening at the diner. He'd had the apron on while closing down the place for the night. This morning she didn't go to work. She went straight from the inn to Chalk Level with Ethan. They didn't drive by H & P's on the way.

"I haven't seen Hank since the day Fred died," Rick mused.

"I saw him yesterday," Ethan said, "in this very apron."

"How can you be sure?" Daisy retorted. "It could belong to anyone."

"Covered with that much grill grease? I doubt it." Ethan draped the apron over the porch railing. "And it's still wrinkled from when he got mad at me for asking about Chalk Level and hurled it at the counter."

Rick half-grinned. "The man's got a temper, doesn't he?"

Daisy glared at him.

He shrugged. "There's no need to get mad about it, darlin'. It's the truth."

"Truth or not," she snapped, "it doesn't prove anything—"

"You can argue all you want about his temper," Ethan interjected, "not his apron. I said it already, but I guess it bears repeating. The apron proves Hank was here."

"Not necessarily." Daisy straightened her back. "Somebody else could have left it on the porch."

Ethan smirked. "We both know that's a load of crap."

"It is not! It's entirely possible someone took Hank's apron from the diner last night and brought it here."

"Someone such as space aliens?"

Rick burst out laughing.

Daisy's face went crimson with fury. "What are you hooting about? Hank could beat you—and your brother—to a pile of mulch with one fist tied behind his back!"

The laughter continued. "I'd love to see him try."

"I'd love to see it too, because in less than a minute you'd be flat on your belly, wiping the blood from your chin and begging for mercy."

Ethan jumped in before Rick could respond. "You sure are loyal to Hank, Daisy."

She didn't deny it or apologize for it. She was loyal to Hank. Unwaveringly loyal. Hank had been there for her and her momma at the lowest point of their lives, and he had done it without expecting anything in return. If that didn't engender loyalty, she couldn't begin to imagine what did.

"You probably have no idea what it means to be really loyal," Daisy growled at Ethan. She shot Rick a bitter look. "I know you don't."

Rick's laughter died, and his eyes grew cloudy. Daisy turned away from both men with a scowl.

In an apparent attempt to appease her, Ethan said mildly, "Okay. Let's assume for a moment you're right. Hank wasn't here. Somebody else left his apron on the porch. Why would they do that? Were they trying to send him a message, or were they hoping to make it look like he was here?"

Daisy's brow furrowed. That was a good question. Why would someone bring Hank's apron to Fox Hollow? It did seem a rather strange and pointless thing to do.

"I think we can safely rule out it being a message," Ethan went on, "because how would Hank even know his apron had been put on the porch? He doesn't usually come here, does he?"

Both Daisy and Rick shook their heads.

"So then there's the possibility somebody is hoping to make it look like he was here. But I agree with what Rick said before." Ethan pointed toward the quartet of bowed rusty nails and the tiny torn piece of cloth that remained attached to them. "The nails snagged the apron and probably ripped it off, considering how close it was to them when Daisy picked it up. That means it wasn't left behind on purpose."

He was going full circle. Daisy could see that. Ethan was methodically ruling out any reasonable chance that someone else had brought the apron to the porch.

"Fine," she drawled with annoyance. "You want to believe Hank was here? It's his apron, and it got caught on the nails and pulled off? So what? That only means he was on the porch at some point between the time he shut up the diner last night and we arrived at Fox Hollow this morning. Maybe he was here looking for Rick. Maybe he was looking for me or you. You heard me tell him where we were going today. Maybe he was even looking for Sheriff Lowell, who he knew was eventually planning on coming out here too."

Rick cleared his throat. "Hank could have been looking for me."

Daisy suppressed a smile. Rick was just as well aware as she was that Hank would never go looking for him, especially after learning that he was the new owner of the property. But Special Agent Kinney didn't need that piece of information.

"Whoever—or whatever—he was looking for," Ethan remarked equably, "I'd be interested in knowing whether he found it."

His coolness made Daisy nervous. She chewed on the inside of one cheek as she watched Ethan study the apron, then the quartet of nails sticking out from the board, and finally the length of the porch leading back to the wrought-iron table and two jars of arsenic-laden moonshine. She wondered what he was thinking, but he gave no clue. She glanced at Rick. He was leaning against the railing, both eyes closed.

"How well did Hank know Mr. Dickerson?" Ethan asked.

Daisy stiffened. He had already connected Hank with the porch. Was he now trying to connect him with Fred's death?

"How well?" he repeated.

She glanced at Rick again. His eyes remained closed, but his mouth was drawn tight. He was obviously ignoring the question, forcing her to answer it.

Ethan folded his arms across his chest in anticipation.

"I can't really tell you." Daisy feigned a shrug. "Hank never talked about Fred. Not when I was around. And aside from the day he died, Fred didn't come to the diner. At least I never saw him there. I don't think Hank visited him here either. I don't know when he would have had the time. He spends nearly every waking hour at H & P's."

Turning from her, Ethan studied the apron, nails, and jars on the table once more. After a long minute he said, "And we think the reason Mr. Dickerson came to the diner the day he died was to tell somebody about the tainted whiskey?"

"That's my best guess," Rick replied, not opening his eyes.

"But why the diner?" Ethan pursued. "It's a long way from here to there, especially for a man who had just been poisoned. Why not go somewhere else instead?"

"There is nowhere else." This time Daisy didn't have to feign the shrug. "Not between Fox Hollow and H & P's at that hour of the day. It was so early in the morning when Fred stumbled in, I doubt he would have found anyone anywhere else."

Ethan gave a slight nod. "Did he speak?"

"Who? Fred?"

"Yes. Did he say anything when he stumbled into the diner?"

"Sort of." Daisy frowned. It wasn't a very pleasant memory. "He wanted a burger."

"A burger! You mean a hamburger?"

It was her turn to nod.

"A hamburger?" Ethan repeated skeptically. "For breakfast?"

"It's not uncommon," she told him. "We've got a crew of roofers in the area who pass through twice a week, and they always order burgers for breakfast. Most of them like theirs under a couple of fried eggs with a double serving of bacon."

"And did you give Mr. Dickerson a burger?"

"No. I started to ask him what he wanted on it, like I do with everybody who comes in, but his mouth foamed . . . and his body began to shake . . . and he fell down—" Daisy stopped.

Puzzled, Ethan scratched his neck. "That seems odd."

"I just explained—"

"Not the burger," he said. "The fact that Mr. Dickerson wanted to eat. He must have known he'd been poisoned. Or at the very least that he was seriously ill. I'm certainly not an expert on the subject, but I'd wager most people don't think about food when they're in the process of dying."

Daisy found herself agreeing with Ethan. Although she had never considered it before, it was indeed a puzzling last request.

"I can't tell you why he wanted it." She shook her head. "But I couldn't have misheard him because he said it twice."

"Fred asked for a burger," Rick confirmed, finally opening his eyes. "I heard it also. Hank and Brenda must have too."

"What was Hank doing then?" Ethan asked.

"Cooking," Daisy replied swiftly.

"Just cooking?"

"Hank's the cook. He was at the grill when Fred came in."

"What did he do after Mr. Dickerson came in?"

"He was just as shocked as the rest of us."

"But what did he *do*?" Ethan pressed her.

Daisy hesitated. She couldn't outright lie, because her lie would probably be different from Hank and Brenda's lie if Ethan posed the same question to them. She also couldn't tell the truth. How could she possibly say that while everyone else had been in a panic calling the ambulance and worrying about the blood seeping from old man Dickerson's head, Hank had been sitting peacefully on a stool at the counter skimming the *Danville Register & Bee* and shoveling peach cobbler into his mouth? It didn't sound good.

Ethan blinked at her expectantly.

"I don't know!" She threw up her hands in frustration. "I was paying attention to Fred, not Hank. I don't know the exact second when he put down his spatula—or shut off the grill—or ran out from the kitchen."

"That's understandable," Ethan responded with sympathy.

As he turned to the apron draped over the porch railing, Daisy breathed a sigh of relief. She saw Rick's lips curl into a barely perceptible smile. He had been at H & P's too. He knew precisely how Hank had behaved. But he didn't say a word.

"Well," Ethan said, picking up the apron, "I think I've accomplished all that I can here. Now I need to go talk to Hank."

More than ready to leave, Daisy headed toward the porch steps. She was tired of the heat. She was tired of Rick. She was tired of having to craft answers to Ethan's delving questions. She was even tired of Fox Hollow.

"Do you want to go to the diner with me, Daisy?" Ethan asked, following her. "Or should I drop you off at the inn?"

"The inn would be great."

The inn was cool. The inn had iced beverages. The inn had a comfortable settee to flop down on and moan.

"What about you?" Ethan glanced at Rick. "Do you need a ride somewhere? I didn't see a car when we pulled up."

"My truck is parked behind the barn."

Rick accompanied them across the mixture of grass and weeds at the front of the house. No one spoke until they reached Ethan's car.

"I assume I'll be able to contact you if needed," Ethan said to Rick.

He snickered. "I won't go into hiding if that's what you're worried about."

Ethan climbed inside the car. Daisy was already seated, but she kept her door open, waiting for him to start the air-conditioning. Rick leaned down toward her.

"Are we still on for tonight?"

She frowned at him.

"You and me, two jelly jars, and our feet in Frying Pan Creek," he reminded her.

"Oh, I don't think that's a very good idea, Rick."

"Why not?"

"Why not!" Ethan snorted. "Maybe because the woman has higher hopes for her evening than spending it together with a gallon of mosquito spray and a barrel of homemade whiskey."

The darkness that eclipsed Rick's eyes was so fierce, Daisy instantly decided that it would be wiser—and far safer—not to discuss the matter further. She reached over to close the car door, but Rick slammed it shut before striding off in the direction of the old tobacco barn. He didn't look back.

Ethan pulled the car around the pebbly circle and onto the driveway. Daisy watched the house shrink in the side mirror as they headed toward the ridge and the road beyond. It seemed almost like a helium balloon that someone had released and was now floating up into the ether, growing gradually smaller until only a speck of porch and white paint remained. It was a sad, trifling speck.

"Thank you."

"Huh?" She wasn't listening. Daisy was too busy wondering if she would ever see the house again. She doubted it, and in a way she hoped that she wouldn't. Nothing good could come of it.

"Thank you," Ethan repeated, "for showing me Fox Hollow."

Daisy didn't respond.

"Is there any way," he went on after a brief pause, "I could talk you into coming with me to the diner? I know you said you'd rather have me drop you off at the inn, but I have a feeling it'd go a lot more smoothly with Hank—and Brenda—if you were there with us. I would really be grateful."

His gratitude was of little interest to her. Neither was she inclined to help make anything go more smoothly for Ethan in regard to interrogating her friends. But when Daisy reflected further, she realized that it might be better for Hank and Brenda if she was at H & P's. Then maybe she could steer the questions—or answers—to benefit them, particularly in relation to Hank—who clearly knew something about something—and his apron.

"I guess I could go to the diner if you think it might do some good." She tried to make it sound like she was acting for Ethan's benefit. "I'm hungry anyway."

"Great—" Without warning Ethan stepped hard on the brakes. "Sorry. I thought I saw—"

He leaned toward her side of the car and peered out the window. Daisy's eyes traveled with his. They had reached the top of the ridge and were just starting down the other side toward the road. There was a narrow field to the right of the driveway, followed by a line of dogwoods, then a brush border leading to the creek, which curved in at that part of the property.

"You saw something?" Daisy asked. She didn't see anything except untilled ground and a thicket of forsythias mixed with hollies.

Ethan put the car into reverse and crept backward until he suddenly slammed on the brakes again. "There it is! I knew I saw it."

"What?" She followed his outstretched finger. "What am I supposed to be looking at?"

"There. In between those two bushes."

"You're going to have to be a bit more specific. It's a whole row of bushes."

"You see that big boulder?"

Daisy nodded.

"About four feet to the left. There's a pair of bushes with red berries."

"You mean the hollies?"

"Hollies?" Ethan shrugged. "Is that what those are? Well, smack in the middle of them."

She was about to answer that his vision must be playing tricks on him, because there was only clay and clover in the middle of the hollies, but then she saw it too. The glint of sun on metal.

"It's too big for trash," he said. "Don't you think? A bunch of beer cans wouldn't reflect the light like that. And they'd be flat on the ground. It's too high."

"I guess." Daisy had never once in her life pondered how beer cans reflected the light. Nor did she really care.

"We should take a closer look," Ethan decided.

He shifted the car into park and turned off the engine. Climbing out, he glanced at her. "Aren't you coming?"

"I guess," she replied, with even less enthusiasm than she had a moment earlier. The car was just beginning to cool off nicely. Now it was going to get hot and sticky again, and so was she.

Ethan waded through the field toward the line of dogwoods.

"Watch out for ticks," Daisy muttered, marching after him.

"Watch out for what?"

"Never mind. I—" She squinted at the hollies. "Are those berries, or is that a red light in there?"

Quickening his speed, Ethan reached the brush border a dozen paces ahead of her.

"It's a light," he called. "And it's blinking."

"Blinking?" she echoed, perplexed. "How could it be blinking? How could it even be a light?"

"I think . . . Damn!"

"What? What is it?"

Daisy jogged over to him and saw the answer for herself. Up close the metal was blindingly bright in the sun. A red signal light flashed ceaselessly on and off. It belonged to a motorcycle. A black-and-chrome Harley-Davidson. A seriously smashed-up black-and-chrome Harley-Davidson.

"It must have hit that tree." Ethan motioned toward a nearby dogwood with its trunk freshly cracked almost in half. "Then it slid into these bushes."

"But how—"

"And there's the path it took from the driveway." He pointed behind them into the field. "You see where the grass is shorn down? He must have been really out of control. Look at how it zigzags."

"But how—" Daisy began again, only this time she cut herself off when the full meaning of his words hit her. "He was out of control? Oh my God, where's the driver?"

Ethan's eyes widened, and he looked around hurriedly. "I don't see . . . Do you?"

She looked around too. "I don't either. Could they have walked away?"

"It's possible I suppose." He sounded doubtful. "Anything is always possible. Except that bike is pretty much destroyed. The front end's totally mangled, and the handlebars might as well be a pretzel."

"If they didn't walk away, then shouldn't they be around here somewhere?"

Ethan started pushing his way into the thicket. "The driver was probably thrown off."

"So maybe they're okay. Maybe they flew away safely."

"It's not the flying that's the problem," he responded. "It's the landing."

Together they searched through the forsythias and hollies, but there was no sign of anyone—injured or not.

"It must have happened relatively recently," Ethan said, heading further into the brush. "The lights are still on, so the bike's battery isn't dead yet."

"We should have heard the collision," Daisy told him. "Everything echoes around Fox Hollow, including the sound of a motor when someone comes down the driveway."

"Then it had to have been before we arrived."

"And we missed it the first time we passed by?"

"We almost missed it this time too. The sun hit that chrome at just the right moment for me to catch it. Daisy—"

She stopped picking her way through the shrubs and looked over at him.

"I hate to ask you this"—Ethan cringed slightly—"but do you recognize the motorcycle?"

"No. I don't think so." There was something vaguely familiar about it, but nothing definitive that she could place. "It's a beat-up old Harley. There are a lot of beat-up old Harleys in this area, and to me they all kind of seem the same."

"Okay. That's good. Given the circumstances."

"We're almost at the end of the border," Daisy said. "Could the driver really have gone this far?"

"It's not actually that far," he corrected her. "With enough speed . . . Wait!"

Ethan dashed toward the creek. She quickly lost sight of him but soon heard the sound of shoes splashing in water. Daisy rushed to catch up. When she reached the curving bank, Ethan shouted at her to stay back.

"Don't! Don't come any closer!"

She didn't need to come any closer. Daisy could see it all before her with gut-wrenching clarity. The water looked just the same as it had that morning when they drove over the bridge. It was high for the middle of summer, knee-deep at the center and flowing briskly. And there he was in the heart of it, sprawled facedown with his limbs stretched out like a scarecrow. Hank was lying motionless in Frying Pan Creek.

CHAPTER

18

The funeral was quiet. A dreary, drizzly day would have been appropriate, but it was sunny and scorching instead. There had been no rain in Pittsylvania County for nearly a month, and everything was slowly becoming withered, dusty, and browned. The sick irony of it was that in another week or two Frying Pan Creek would most likely be dried to a muddy trickle. Then Hank Fitz wouldn't have been able to drown in it.

His only blood relations were very distant and lived on the opposite side of the country. Brenda and Daisy were Hank's family in Virginia, so it fell to them to handle the arrangements. They did it without fuss or excessive ceremony. Brenda had already buried a husband, and Daisy had buried a parent. They knew how to lay to rest a person they had loved. Afterward, they invited the small group of mourners back to the diner for one final meal.

"It was only last Monday." Brenda sniffled, peeling off the cover to a large bowl of potato salad. "Was it Monday? Or was it Tuesday?" She didn't wait for an answer. "We were talking about reordering peas and beans. And now he's gone. Can you believe it, Ducky? Hank's gone!"

Daisy replied with a sigh. She was the one who had put the wreath on his grave. She was the one who had informed Brenda and her momma and so many others of the dreadful news. She was the one who had helped drag his wet, limp body from the water. And she was the one who had been on her knees next to Ethan when he had checked for signs of life and found none. Daisy had done all those things, but somehow she still couldn't quite believe that she would never again see Hank pop his thick, red, creased face through the opening above the grill. Never again would she have to badger him to decide on the breakfast special. Never again would she be able to plead with him for more stories about his outrageous adventures with her daddy long ago when they were young.

"We were squabbling," Brenda went on. "Squabbling just like a couple of spoiled children about how many cans of this to get and how many cans of that." She turned to Daisy and sniffled once more. "Now we won't place another order. Never!"

"Oh, sweetie." Daisy set down the aluminum tray filled with Brunswick stew that she had just pulled from the oven and wrapped a consoling arm around Brenda's shoulders.

"It's why there's that old saying," Aunt Emily interjected. "God laughs at those who make plans."

With a soggy handkerchief, Brenda dabbed at a tear creeping out from the corner of one eye. "God laughs? Surely God wouldn't laugh at a good, generous man like Hank Fitz."

Daisy frowned at Aunt Emily, who was standing in the open doorway leading to the kitchen. Sometimes she could be a little too blunt and satirical.

Quick to catch the hint, Aunt Emily said, "Hank was a

good man, wasn't he? I'll always think of him fondly for how he helped out our darling Ducky—and her momma too—in their time of need. Speaking of which, what's going to happen to the diner? Have you heard anything?"

Brenda shook her head. "We're gonna have to shut it."

"You are? Why?"

"Hank was the cook."

"Couldn't you do the cooking?" Aunt Emily replied. "You and Ducky together. One or the other of you already prepares most of the breads and sides, don't you? I know Ducky does all the delicious desserts. Couldn't you just hire somebody to handle the grill?"

"Hire somebody to replace Hank?" Brenda stared at her in dismay.

"It's not as easy as it sounds," Daisy told her. "Aside from not having a stitch of cash to hire anyone for even an hour—let alone full-time—all the necessary state licenses and health department certificates are in Hank's name. Plus every piece of equipment belongs to H & P's, and we have no idea who now owns H & P's. Technically I think we're trespassing just by being here today."

"Trespassing? Rubbish!" Aunt Emily waved her hand like she was swatting away a bothersome gnat. "How could you possibly be trespassing in a place your daddy helped build and who's one-half of the name? As to the equipment, we could get Carlton to rig an auction for you. Buy it all cheap! He's sitting out there now, if you want me to go arrange it with him."

"Thank you, but I don't think we're quite at that stage yet." Daisy smiled. "And I'm not worried about trespassing, not when the sheriff and his wife are also sitting out there, sipping tea and trespassing right along with us. I wasn't talking about today. I meant tomorrow. Tomorrow H & P's will be closed, and it's going to have to remain closed until somebody tells us who inherited it and what that person wants to do with it."

"I suppose you're right." Aunt Emily's brow furrowed as she walked toward the long table on which they were organizing the food. "Except what are you going to do in the meantime?"

Daisy and Brenda looked at each other. It was a question that they had already begun to discuss. They had a few ideas percolating, but today was about Hank.

"Well, I'm sure you'll figure out something grand," Aunt Emily declared with her usual chirpy assurance. "At least you don't have to worry about going hungry in the interim. My dining room is always open for you. And your momma will be thrilled to see more of you, Ducky. You've been working so hard lately, you're hardly ever at the inn. And while we're on the subject of the inn, do you know how long Special Agent Kinney is planning on staying with us?"

"I'd like to know that too," Beulah chimed in, taking Aunt Emily's place in the open doorway. "Because if he's going to hang around for a while . . ." She let the sentence trail away with a grin.

"Seriously?" Daisy pursed her lips. "You want to start flirting with Ethan?"

"Why not? If you're okay driving everywhere in Chalk Level with him, there can't be anything wrong with me inviting him to have a couple of drinks." Her grin grew. "He is pretty easy on the eyes. Don't tell me you haven't noticed, Daisy."

"Just make sure those drinks are all legal," she retorted dryly. "Lest you forget, he's ATF."

"It's a good thing then I'm not Rick Balsam and I don't

have a giant secret stash of 'shine." Beulah shook her head with a mixture of amusement and disdain. "I still can't believe he's been using the old tobacco barn at Fox Hollow to cook up white lightning."

"I can," Aunt Emily retorted. "Pittsylvania County is the moonshine capital of America, after all."

"I thought that was Carroll County," Brenda said.

"Carroll. Franklin. Pittsylvania." Aunt Emily shrugged. "Might as well be the same thing. It's not like those boys with their stills out there in the backwoods know where the county lines are anyway."

"Ain't that the truth," Brenda agreed.

"I think Rick knows exactly where the county lines are. And all the other lines too." There was a marked sharpness to Beulah's tone. "He's a clever weasel, and he's always playing a weaselly game. One that's full of trouble. I've said it before, but I'd bet every last drop of shampoo in my salon that the weasel's looking for something from Daisy."

Daisy snorted. "He can keep right on looking. I've got nothing to give him."

Beulah smirked at her. "You've got plenty."

The snort repeated itself. "Rick certainly doesn't need *that* from me. He's got a whole heap of girls constantly throwing themselves at him. You saw the one he was with at the General. Did she look to you like the type who'd be holding anything back for holy matrimony?"

"Now, Ducky," Aunt Emily drawled, "don't be so green. Just because a man can pluck every one of the chickens pecking at his ankles in the coop, doesn't mean he wouldn't prefer the cute little hen sitting aloof in the corner."

"Oh, Aunt Emily." Daisy and Brenda groaned in unison.

Aunt Emily chortled.

"I'm not surprised you'd take the weasel's side." Beulah

chortled back at her. "You two Pittsylvania moonshiners have to stick together. He's got his whiskey and you've got your gooseberry brandy."

"What I make isn't moonshine," Aunt Emily corrected her. "It's medicine, dear."

Even Brenda had to laugh at that, although it didn't last long. In a moment she was pressing the handkerchief to her wet cheeks.

"I wish it were medicine," she choked. "Then it could have helped Hank."

"Nothing could have helped Hank. He hit a tree with his bike and landed in the creek," Daisy reminded her gently. "He didn't drink bad likker like Fred."

Aunt Emily clucked her tongue. "It's cursed."

They all looked at her.

"It's cursed," she said again. "Fox Hollow is cursed. Four dead on the land, and who knows how many more there'll be. You and your momma were lucky to get away when you did, Ducky."

Daisy's mouth sagged open.

"You're being silly, Aunt Emily," Beulah snapped, "and very inconsiderate to bring it up at a time like this. What happened with Daisy's daddy and Matt's daddy was an accident. Plus old man Dickerson didn't die at Fox Hollow. It was here at the diner, which you know full well. And with Hank . . . well, that was an accident too."

"Accident or murder," Aunt Emily insisted, "four dead is still four dead. And Fred was poisoned at Fox Hollow. Isn't that right, Ducky? Isn't that what you and Mr. Kinney found at the house?"

Beulah angrily tucked an unruly red curl behind her ear. "Is it really necessary to talk about this now! Can't we enjoy a peaceful meal together with friends—"

"How do you know Hank's crash was an accident?" Aunt Emily cut her off impatiently. "Has anyone determined that officially? Doesn't it seem a bit suspicious to you? Since when does Hank drive out to Fox Hollow? He probably didn't go there more than once in the past five years. And why was he in such a rush? He was driving awfully fast when it happened, wasn't he, Ducky? Didn't Mr. Kinney say that last night? I know *he* thinks it's suspicious. That's why he's still here. He thinks it's all connected somehow."

Brenda let out a startled gasp. "He thinks . . . he thinks Hank is connected with . . . it wasn't an accident . . . someone intentionally—"

"Precisely," Aunt Emily declared. "If it wasn't an accident, someone intentionally—"

Daisy shot her a stern, silencing glance and hurriedly put her arm around Brenda's shoulders. "Of course it was an accident. Nobody would hurt Hank. Why would anybody want to hurt him? Everyone loved Hank. We're not going to discuss it any further. Aunt Emily is just talking nonsense."

Aunt Emily squeaked in protest, but Daisy shot her a second glance, this time making it doubly stern.

"Now I think"—she gave Brenda's shoulders a comforting squeeze, then gestured toward the aluminum tray filled with Brunswick stew that was sitting on the table before them—"it'd be a good idea if you took this into the other room before it got cold. We both know how much Sheriff Lowell likes his stew."

Brenda didn't look very comforted. Her face and neck were florid, and her mouth was drawn tight. But she acquiesced to Daisy's suggestion. Her hands shook as she picked up the tray.

"I . . . I'll come back for the potato salad."

"There's no need. I'll bring it out in a minute," Beulah told her.

"Okay." With wobbling arms and legs, Brenda walked slowly toward the doorway. When she reached it, she looked back with some uncertainty.

"I'll bring it out," Beulah repeated, nodding.

Brenda nodded in return and wobbled off with the stew. As soon as she had disappeared around the edge of the front counter, Daisy spun toward Aunt Emily.

"Why did you do that?"

Aunt Emily blinked at her. "Do what, Ducky?"

That only increased Daisy's irritation. "You know perfectly well what!"

"I was simply pointing out the facts of the matter."

"You didn't have to point them out to her right now."

"Brenda's a tough old biddy like me," Aunt Emily responded with a touch of haughtiness. "She can handle the truth just fine."

"Normally, yes. But not today. Not five minutes after Hank's funeral!" Daisy exclaimed. "He was her closest friend in the world. They spent practically every waking minute for the last decade together in this diner. Brenda's grieving, and she doesn't need to hear your murder theories while trying to host a memorial luncheon."

"Would you rather she continued to waddle around like an ignorant hippo and ended up having the next *accident*?"

"What a ridiculous thing to say!" Beulah chastised her.

Aunt Emily turned to her. "Now don't you start sticking your head in the sand too. It's bad enough Ducky takes me for an aged fool and doesn't listen to a single word from my wrinkly lips."

Daisy stuck her hands on her hips. "I do not take you for a fool, Aunt Emily. And I listen to every word from your lips."

As she said it, she remembered how Aunt Emily had been the first person to realize that Fred Dickerson had been deliberately poisoned, so perhaps it wouldn't be such a bad idea to listen a little more closely to those aged and wrinkly lips.

"What I mean is"—Daisy took a deep breath—"we all value your thoughts and opinions very much. Except maybe today you can share them only with us and not Brenda." She lowered her voice. "Or the rest of the group out there. I'm not so sure how the sheriff would react if you told him you believe the death of his oldest childhood pal may not have been an accident."

Aunt Emily patted Daisy's head affectionately. "There you go. Finally thinking smart like your momma."

She squinted at her. "My momma thinks Hank's death wasn't an accident?"

"I don't know about that. But I do know she doesn't automatically assume something's an accident just because someone happens to calls it an accident. Your momma makes up her own mind. She asks questions and looks at facts. Which is why early this morning—when everybody else was racing around getting ready for the service—Lucy was picking Special Agent Kinney's brain."

"What!"

"Now don't get all panicky." Aunt Emily patted Daisy's head again. "It didn't hurt her none. Quite the opposite. She seemed almost energized afterward. A little like her former spunky self. She and Mr. Kinney must have had a good conversation."

"Well." Daisy hesitated, wondering if that was supposed to reassure her or cause her even more concern. "I guess what matters is she was feeling better."

Beulah concurred with a grunt. But it was a dubious grunt. And Daisy knew why. There was an unmistakable hint of excitement in Aunt Emily's shrewd blue eyes, and that always made it difficult to discern whether she was being brilliant or bobbing up a few apples short of a bushel.

"I reckon you girls will sort it out soon enough," Aunt Emily said.

It was Beulah's turn to squint at her. "Sort what out?"

"Everything, of course. All of it." This time she patted her own head, smoothing down a few stray wisps. "And I have no doubt Mr. Kinney will be of great help. Or at least some help."

Both Daisy and Beulah were too busy squinting to respond.

"Just remember what I told you once before already, Ducky. Get more than you give. He's going to want answers, and so will you. Keep him close. Don't let him go wandering about unsupervised."

"But he's got every right to wander about unsupervised," Daisy replied. "He's ATF. And as you may recall from my family's past dealings with the ATF, their agents do what they want, when they want. We don't get a say in it."

Aunt Emily's nose twitched. "Then you better get a say in it."

"And how exactly do you suggest I do that?"

She smiled. It wasn't a broad, supercilious smile. It was a soft, sage smile. Picking up the bowl of potato salad, Aunt Emily headed toward the open doorway. Her clicking heels paused for an instant as she glanced behind her.

"Either sleep with the man, Ducky, or get some of the answers before he gets 'em."

CHAPTER
19

Ethan looked up from the scuffed leather smoking chair when Daisy entered the parlor. "How was it?" he asked.

"It was a funeral." She sunk down on the settee across from him. "In my experience all funerals are pretty much the same. Same pretty speeches. Same pretty flowers. Same grim company."

"I can't argue with you there."

She heaved a troubled sigh. It had been a difficult day. And Aunt Emily had made it even more difficult by insisting on discussing curses and accidents that might not really have been accidents.

"Want to talk about it?" Ethan offered politely.

Daisy shook her head. What she wanted was a drink. Several drinks preferably. Too bad she couldn't get one of Rick's jelly jars without also getting Rick in the process.

"Where's everybody else? Didn't they come back with you?"

"Beulah's checking on something in her salon. Aunt Emily's upstairs enjoying her nightly soak in the tub. And my—" She stopped. "I heard you and my momma had a lengthy conversation this morning."

"We did," Ethan confirmed.

Although Daisy waited for him to elaborate, he didn't.

"What did you talk about?" she pursued after a minute.

He smiled slightly. "Didn't your mom tell you?"

Her gaze narrowed. She didn't like his evasiveness.

"We talked about Fox Hollow," he said.

That made Daisy's gaze narrow even further. "My momma's not in good health. Surely you're aware of that. The last few years have been extremely hard on her, and I would greatly appreciate it if you didn't add to her stress by bringing up the past. Especially after what just happened to Hank. It's too much for her to handle."

"I didn't bring up the past," Ethan informed her. "She did."

"I doubt that."

"You can doubt it all you want, but it's the truth. Your mom wanted to know about the changes at Fox Hollow. She said she hasn't been there in a long time. She was interested in learning how it looks now. And for the record," he added, "I think your mom can handle a lot more than you think she can."

"Are you a doctor?" Daisy snapped. "Because the doctors keep telling me any extra stress should be avoided at all cost. The very expensive doctors," she muttered glumly under her breath.

Ethan shrugged. "I'm not a doctor, and I don't pretend to know what exactly causes your mom extra stress. But it doesn't seem to be Fox Hollow."

She remained skeptical.

He shrugged again. "That's just my opinion from how she was this morning. She didn't appear the least bit upset when I told her about the condition of the place."

"The condition of the place?"

"The house and gardens and such. What obviously needed work. What might have been different from the last time she saw it. Your mom asked if Mr. Dickerson had been maintaining the property. She also asked about Rick Balsam."

Daisy sat upright. "What about Rick Balsam?"

"Apparently she heard from someone that he was there the same day we were, and she was curious to know why. I don't think your mom realizes he owns Fox Hollow."

"You didn't tell her, did you!"

"No, I—"

"Good," she cut him off. "Don't."

Ethan raised an eyebrow at her.

"Don't tell her!" Daisy repeated with emphasis.

"She's going to find out eventually. Especially if everybody else knows."

"Everybody else doesn't know. According to Rick, he bought the place at the beginning of the year. But he kept it quiet. So quiet we weren't even aware the property was up for sale. It didn't come out until Fred died, and then it was only because Sheriff Lowell happened to see a copy of the papers and asked Rick about it. As far as I'm aware, there are still just a few of us who know. And we aren't going to share the news with my momma."

"Why not?"

Daisy grimaced. "Do you want to be the one to tell a sick, penniless widow the new owner of her former pride and joy is a seedy, womanizing bootlegger?"

"Not particularly. Not when you put it that way."

"There's no other way to put it."

"I still think your mom's going to find out eventually," Ethan said. "But if we ever have another chat like we did this morning, you don't have to worry about the news coming from me."

"Thank you." She paused for a moment, then asked, "Did you talk about Hank too?"

"You mean with your mom?"

Daisy nodded.

"He didn't come up. Why?"

She answered with a frown. Aunt Emily was wrong. Ethan and her momma hadn't discussed Hank's death—accident or not. Their conversation had been all about Fox Hollow. That was strange. Or was it? Daisy wasn't sure. Her momma rarely mentioned the property. On the day Fred died she hadn't even known whether he was still living there. Why would she suddenly talk about it with Special Agent Kinney from the hated ATF and not her own daughter? Was the timing mere coincidence, or could there be more to it?

A lengthy silence followed. Daisy tugged absently at a snag in the fabric on the settee. Ethan returned to the files he had been reading when she first entered the parlor. A whole big box of files had arrived for him yesterday at the inn. Daisy didn't ask about them, and he didn't volunteer any information. She wondered if there was some mention of her family in the copious pages. She supposed there had to be. Her eyes went to the marble mantel. Old photographs in tarnished silver frames stood in a crooked row like a long line of seashells washed up onto the beach after a storm. Battered and faded, they were eagerly collected but quickly forgotten.

Ethan glanced over at her. "Any relatives up there?"

"Oh, no. I don't have kin still alive in these parts. Other than my momma, they're all gone. But I'm unusual that way." Daisy smiled. "Around here you've got to be careful.

There aren't any so-called seven degrees of separation. It's closer to three. So you better find out who everyone's relations are real fast, or you could pretty easily end up marrying your second cousin without even knowing it."

He laughed. "I'm glad to hear that didn't happen to you."

She laughed with him. "It's bad enough Matt and I went to the same grade school. I don't recommend picking a spouse who remembers what you looked like in plaid rompers and pigtails. All the mystery is gone."

"I bet you were awfully cute in plaid rompers and pigtails."

"Evidently my husband didn't think so."

"Your husband is an idiot."

Daisy could only shrug. "I won't dispute that."

Closing the file in his lap, Ethan tossed it to the floor with a thud. "I can't read another word tonight. You want to do something?"

"Such as?"

"Such as go out and get a beer somewhere. There are actual bars and restaurants in this area, aren't there? You don't have to go down to the creek with a jug of home brew tucked under your arm like your buddy Rick suggested the other day, do you?"

"Of course not. Of course there are bars and restaurants. And Rick isn't my buddy—"

The unexpected wail of the telephone in the entrance hall interrupted her. Beulah came racing up the front steps of the inn and slammed open the screen door.

"I'll get it!" she cried.

The ringing promptly ceased. There was a bit of mumbling.

"Daisy?" Beulah called.

"In here."

She popped her red head into the parlor. "It's for you."

"For me? Who is it?"

"Zeke."

"Huh?"

"Zeke," she repeated. "From the General."

Daisy was so surprised, her lips parted but not a syllable came out.

"Weird, isn't it?" Beulah agreed. "I had a lot of trouble understanding him. I don't think I've ever talked to Zeke on the phone before."

"I know I haven't." She rose from the settee. "He probably wants to give his condolences."

"You're right." The red mop nodded. "I bet that's it."

As Daisy headed into the hall, Beulah turned toward the occupant of the scuffed leather smoking chair.

"Hey there, Ethan," she cooed.

Daisy smiled. No doubt Beulah would be happy to show Special Agent Kinney where he could get a beer. She picked up the phone from the inlaid table.

"Hello?"

Zeke came straight to the point. "Daisy? Daisy, I gotta talk to ya."

"You need to speak up, Zeke. I can barely hear you."

"I can't. They might be listenin'."

"What?" There was too much background noise, and his voice was garbled. "Somebody's listening?"

"I'm workin', and they're here."

"Who's there?"

"City folks." Zeke coughed. "Big-city folks."

"Okay." Daisy didn't know what else to say.

"They were askin' 'bout—"

"I can't understand you, Zeke."

He coughed again. "Ya gotta come here, Daisy."

"To the General?"

"Uh-huh. Will ya come tonight?"

"Oh no, not tonight." The only place she planned on going that evening was up the stairs and into bed.

"But it's gotta be tonight!" he exclaimed.

"Zeke—"

"I gotta talk to ya, Daisy!"

She was really unenthusiastic about going to the road-house, but there was such an odd urgency in his tone that it forced her to reconsider. Plus Zeke never called. Something was definitely going on, and she decided that she had better find out what it was.

"Do you want me to come now?" Daisy asked with a sigh.

"In an hour." He sounded relieved. "After we close."

"All right. I'll see you in about an hour, Zeke."

The line crackled and went dead. As she set down the phone, Daisy checked her watch. It was late. She should have been sleeping. At least she didn't have to wake up early to make fresh coffee at H & P's.

Grumbling to herself, Daisy trudged to her room. She needed to change her sandals and get her purse. She had to drive. When she came downstairs again a few minutes later and passed by the parlor, she saw Beulah curled up on one arm of the smoking chair like a cuddly little kitten. Ethan looked over at Daisy standing in the hall. His eyes went to the keys in her hand, and his jaw twitched.

"Going out?" he said.

"Going out," she replied.

His jaw twitched once more. "Don't tell me you've chosen the creek and jug of home brew?"

"The creek and jug of home brew?" Beulah echoed, perplexed.

"No." Daisy shook her head, but she wasn't inclined to explain the reference to Rick and his 'shine. "I've got an errand to run."

"Now?" Ethan asked incredulously.

"Yup."

Beulah frowned at her. "What kind of an errand? You're not going to the General, are you?"

"I am."

The frown intensified. "By yourself at this time of night! Why?"

Daisy hesitated. Should she tell Beulah what Zeke had said? Should she ask her to come with?

As though he could read her mind, Ethan said, "Want some company?"

Considering how odd and agitated Zeke had sounded on the phone, Daisy couldn't help thinking that having Ethan along might be good. But then she remembered what Aunt Emily had told her at the diner. Get some of the answers before he does. Well, maybe Zeke could give her those answers.

When she didn't respond, Beulah's curiosity grew. "What on earth did Zeke say to you, Daisy?"

Ethan turned to Beulah. "Who's Zeke?"

"He's the bartender at this roadhouse everybody goes to. It's called the General. We were there a couple of weeks ago and—"

Not waiting for her to finish, Daisy mumbled, "See you later."

Both Ethan and Beulah shouted after her as she pushed open the screen door and jogged down the front steps, but Daisy didn't stop. She headed straight for her car. She figured it was better that way. Beulah could flirt with Ethan as much as she wanted. Ethan could flirt back or read his files. And she would go talk to Zeke alone.

It was a clear night. The moon was nearly full, and the stars were large and bright. Daisy was grateful for it. Driving through rural southwestern Virginia wasn't so easy after the sun went down. The roads were nearly all unlit, and the intermittent reflectors pasted on posts and mailboxes weren't much help in navigating the snaking curves. It was dark out. Really dark. The kind of dark that made you stretch your eyes as wide as they would go like some nocturnal creature peering out from the inky depths of a cavern.

Daisy didn't take much notice of the occasional vehicle that zoomed by her. No doubt they were all heading home, which was precisely what she would have preferred to have been doing. She was tired from the events of the long day and much more interested in a soft pillow than a crumbling roadhouse. There were still a few cars and trucks at the General when she arrived—spread out in the corners of the unpaved parking lot—but that didn't surprise her. Somebody always left the place with somebody else. Either they wanted to share that soft pillow or one of them could no longer stand, let alone safely operate any machinery more complex than a toaster.

The bar was closed for the evening. Daisy was sure of that. The neon advertising signs were shut off, and the front door was locked with a thick metal bar across its middle. That meant she had to go around to the back of the building, which didn't thrill her. There was only one orange security light on the premises, and it was at the opposite end of the parking lot, the farthest point from where she needed to go.

The instant Daisy stepped out of her car, she felt a warning prickle on the nape of her neck. Someone was there. Someone was watching her. She glanced around hastily but saw nothing. No person. No movement. Not even the shadow of a cat's tail slinking behind the Dumpster. She took a deep breath as she walked across the gravel. It was probably just a patron trying to sleep off the evening's enjoyments in the bed of his truck. A harmless drunk. No cause for concern.

Daisy had almost succeeded in stifling her anxiety when she caught the sound of a footstep. She froze and looked around once more. Still nothing. Not even a slight breeze. She tried to laugh at herself. Aunt Emily had made her paranoid. That was the problem. She was always prattling on about people lurking and spying and skulking around the neighborhood just waiting for an opportunity to prey on helpless females. It was silly. There wasn't anyone lurking or spying or skulking around the General. And Daisy certainly wasn't helpless.

All the same, she quickened her pace. She also found herself wishing that she were in possession of Aunt Emily's shotgun. Nobody preyed on a female holding a double-barreled 20-gauge. There was another footstep. This time Daisy was positive. But she couldn't tell what direction it came from. For a second she debated spinning around and sprinting back to her car. Then she shook her head. What good would it do? The owner of the footsteps might be expecting her to do exactly that. It made more sense to keep going. She was almost there. Zeke was inside waiting for her. They would talk, and she would go back to the inn. That would be the end of it.

She turned the corner of the building. It was black behind the roadhouse. Solid black. Daisy couldn't even make out the outline of the back door. But she knew that it was there somewhere. Over the years she had used it on more than one occasion, always to pick up Matt when he and

Rick had been too intoxicated to crawl out the front. The footsteps were close now. They crunched over the gravel like plodding doom. With a fearful lump in her throat and her heart hammering at triple speed, Daisy ran her fingers along the pitted wall. The knob. The knob. Somewhere there had to be the knob for the door.

Suddenly the footsteps stopped. The last crunch was directly in front of her. At the same moment Daisy's palm touched the knob. She turned it, and the door opened a few inches before a hand grabbed her arm. She responded by throwing her shoulder against the wall of the building, squashing the unwanted hand in the process. There was a rewarding yelp of pain.

"Damn it, Daisy! What the hell did you do that for?"

It was Ethan. Ethan's voice and his face in the crack of light streaking out from the gap in the door.

"What the hell are you doing here?" Daisy hollered right back at him.

He shrugged. "I wanted a beer."

CHAPTER
20

She stared at him, furious and relieved at the same time.

Ethan rubbed his aching hand. "You sure do pack a wallop for a little thing."

It wasn't enough of a compliment for Daisy to forget her fear from a minute earlier. "What are you doing here?" she demanded.

"I told you already. I told you before at the inn. I wanted a beer."

"And you thought the best way of getting one was by stalking me through the countryside in the middle of the night and scaring the pants off me?"

He looked down at her legs and grinned. "Daisy, you're wearing a skirt."

If his hand had still been on her arm, she would have squashed it against the wall a second time.

The grin was replaced by a shrug. "You said you were going to the General. Beulah said the General was a bar. I thought I could tag along and get my beer."

Daisy glanced around. "Did Beulah come with you?"

"Do you really think that would have been a good idea?"

She wasn't sure what he meant by that remark, but she didn't have the opportunity to ask him. Just then Zeke's thin head appeared in the gap of the door.

"Hey, Daisy. I thought I heard ya out here." His even thinner neck stretched out like an ostrich. "Who's that ya talkin' to?"

"I'm Special Age—"

"This is Ethan," she cut him off briskly.

"Ethan?" Zeke echoed. "I never met no Ethan before. He a friend, Daisy?"

Was Ethan a friend? She didn't quite know. He acted like a friend. Sort of. Sometimes. But could any agent from the ATF ever truly be a friend?

"Yes, I'm a friend," Ethan answered when she didn't.

"Hmm." Zeke peered at him in the darkness.

"I came with Daisy."

"Hmm."

"I'm staying at the Tosh Inn."

Zeke turned to Daisy. His voice was thick with suspicion. "What's he want?"

She was wondering the same thing. What did Ethan want? But there was no point in debating it at this time of night standing in the shadows behind the General. They might as well go in and sit down. Ethan included.

"Don't worry about him, Zeke," Daisy said. "You needed to talk to me?"

"Not out here." His eyes darted about nervously, and he waved for her to enter.

It wasn't that much brighter inside the roadhouse than it was outside. The lights were all turned down. Without them, Daisy couldn't see the water stains on the walls or ceiling. She could still smell the dampness though. It was like stepping through the door of a musty log cabin after a heavy rain. A couple of brass oil lamps were burning on the bar, and there was also one at a small tilting table. Zeke pointed to it.

"I lit that fer ya. Ya need anythin' to wet yer whistle?"

"Not me. Thanks." She added with a smirk, "But Ethan's been looking for a beer all evening."

Grunting in response, Zeke shuffled off toward the bar. Daisy sat down at the designated table with the dim lamp. Ethan followed her. His rickety wooden chair creaked precariously beneath him.

"This place is pretty old, huh?" he said.

Daisy chuckled. "What was your first clue? The moldering interior or the moldering exterior?"

"So why does everyone come here? Beulah told me it's darn popular."

"She's right. It is popular. I think its age and sad state are exactly why people like it. They can wear what they want. They can talk how they want. They can be any way they want to be. There's no pretense or ceremony. You come for a drink. Maybe a little company. Life is complicated enough. The General is real simple."

Zeke returned with a beer bottle dangling from one hand and a glass filled with a generous three fingers' worth of some mahogany liquid clutched in the other hand. He used his foot to pull out the chair across from Daisy and plopped himself down on it with a guttural groan.

"You okay?" she asked.

He answered with a halfhearted nod. "I ain't young no more. That's the problem. Parts hurt. Lots of 'em. My knees 'specially. Hips and elbows too. All the ol' bones. People keep tellin' me I gotta go see a quack. But what's a quack gonna do fer me? Tell me I'm gonna die one day? I know it already. I see everybody else dyin'. We all gonna pass eventually. Some sooner, some later. I don't need to pay good money to hear 'bout that."

Daisy nodded back at him.

"Well, I surely don't have to tell ya none 'bout quacks and them medical bills. Ya know fer yerself. Ya got yer poor momma." Zeke set the beer on the table and slid it over in front of Ethan.

"Thank you," he said courteously, picking up the bottle.

To Daisy's amusement, before taking a drink Ethan examined the label from out of the corner of his eye to see what exactly Zeke had given him. But he was smart enough not to comment on it.

"So why did you want me to come here tonight, Zeke?" she prodded, figuring that if she didn't get to the crux of the matter soon, she'd still be longing for her bed and soft pillow at dawn.

"I told ya on the phone—"

Breaking off, he swiveled in his seat to check that both the front and back doors of the roadhouse were shut tight. It gave Daisy a twinge of apprehension. Zeke was edgy, and he was never edgy. Normally he was about as calm and sluggish as a drowsy tortoise. But on this evening he acted much more like a jumpy hare, one who apparently thought he'd caught the whiff of a coyote prowling through the neighborhood.

"I told ya on the phone," Zeke began again. "They were here."

"City folks?" she said.

"Big-city folks."

Ethan looked from Zeke to Daisy, then back again. "Big-city folks?"

He did an admirable job of not laughing, but she could see the hint of a smile tugging at his lips.

."Big-city folks," Zeke confirmed in earnest, evidently ignoring the fact that Ethan was also a big-city folk.

"But you get people from the city in here all the time," Daisy replied. "Big cities, little cities, and everything in between. Whoever happens to be driving by and decides to stop. What made these people different?"

"They were askin' 'bout things."

She gave a soft sigh. He had sounded so urgent when he called, like it was an emergency of some sort. Not that anybody had severed a limb or couldn't rescue their baby from a burning building, but a Pittsylvania County crisis nonetheless. Clearly she had misunderstood.

"How did you know they were from the big city?" Ethan asked Zeke.

"By them shoes they was wearin'."

This time Ethan didn't restrain the smile. "Shoes?" He turned toward Daisy. "I seem to recall the two of us having a similar discussion once before."

Her smile matched his. "I explained it to you at the diner. You can find out an awful lot about a man from his shoes."

"I'm starting to learn that."

"They were askin' 'bout ol' Fred," Zeke said.

"Old Fred? Wait a minute—" Daisy's smile faded. "Didn't you tell me this already? When Beulah and I were in here a couple of weeks ago? You were talking about some folks from the big city who'd come through a couple of weeks before that. They were asking about people, including Fred Dickerson."

"That's right." Zeke took a swig of the mahogany liquid in his glass.

"And Rick Balsam," she went on. "They asked about him too, didn't they? Didn't you say something about them driving out to Rick and Bobby's trailers in the backwoods?"

"I ain't certain if they went. But they was talkin' 'bout headin' over that way."

Daisy frowned at him in annoyance. "Zeke, why did I have to come here tonight when I already knew all of this?"

"Cuz they were askin' 'bout Fox Hollow."

"You didn't mention the Fox Hollow part before."

"They didn't ask 'bout it before."

She looked at him. In the short chair and poor lighting, Zeke appeared even more gaunt than usual. He gazed back at her with weary, sunken eyes. But Daisy knew that behind those eyes there sat an excellent judge of character and motives.

"You think something was wrong with them asking about Fox Hollow?" she said.

He sniffled. "Up to no good I tell ya."

"What exactly did they want to know about the property?" Ethan inquired.

The weary, sunken eyes turned to him. "And what business exactly is it o' yers?"

Ethan pulled out the black leather wallet from his shirt pocket and flipped it open to reveal his badge. "It's my business since I'm investigating two deaths in relation to Fox Hollow. That makes it a matter of *official* business."

Zeke barely blinked in response. Instead he took another swig of mahogany liquid.

"Ethan was sent here after they did an autopsy on Fred," Daisy explained apologetically. "He followed me to the General tonight—"

"Ya don't got to be sorry, Daisy. It ain't yer fault he's a durned revenooer."

"I'm not a revenuer," Ethan snapped. "I didn't come to tax or confiscate anything. And I haven't smashed a still or dumped a single pint of whiskey into the creek. So you can knock off the hillbilly attitude and quit pretending you hate the big bad government. We both know it's a load of bullshit. You're perfectly willing to take all kinds of money and benefits from the government when it suits you, let the government build your roads and hospitals and airports, and cry for government assistance the instant there's some homegrown problem or natural disaster that affects you."

Daisy bit the inside of her cheeks, enormously grateful at that moment that Zeke had a strict policy of not allowing any firearms in the roadhouse. Regardless of what the law might permit, he was adamant that guns and alcohol were like chlorine and ammonia and should never be mixed.

There was a lengthy silence. Zeke coughed, sucked down the final few drops in his glass, then coughed once more. Ethan watched him warily.

"The way I see it," Zeke remarked at last, "every man's entitled to his own mind and opinions. That's what makes this land great. Just remember, Mister Government Agent, yer in the heart of that land right now. This"—he rapped his boney knuckles on the edge of the table—"is the blood and muscle of the country. Our boys be the ones losin' arms and legs and lives fightin' wars halfway 'round the world. And our boys be the ones diggin' up the coal and growin' the food them big-city folks take fer granted when they flip on them lights and eat in them la-di-dah restaurants. I just wish somebody'd show a little appreciation once in a while. But that ain't how it works. In all them years I've been livin' and workin' in these parts, nobody's said one blasted word of thanks fer nothin'. And they never will neither. In my experience the only people comin' down to southwestern Virginny are those plannin' on stirrin' up trouble and botherin' good solid folks like Daisy and Hank and their kin."

Ethan nodded in acknowledgment. "I promise you, sir, I didn't come down here to stir up trouble or bother any good folks. But somebody has. There doesn't seem to me to be much doubt about that, considering what happened to Mr. Dickerson and Mr. Fitz."

Zeke nodded back at him. "And there's gonna be more trouble too. A heap of it I reckon. It's why I called Daisy. She knows Fox Hollow better than all of 'em."

That startled her. "You think the trouble has to do with Fox Hollow?"

"I do. And I'll tell ya why. They was talkin' 'bout who owns the place. At first they thought it was ol' Fred, but then they realized it wasn't ol' Fred. He was just stayin' there. After that they thought it might be Rick, but then they was at Fox Hollow—"

"They were actually at Fox Hollow?" Ethan interjected.

"They was *at* Fox Hollow," Zeke repeated with emphasis, "and somethin' wasn't right. Somethin' there gave 'em trouble."

"Was it something or someone?"

Daisy's mind went immediately to Hank. For the life of her she couldn't figure out why he had gone to Fox Hollow on that fateful day. But she could very easily envision him causing the big-city folks trouble while he was there. Hank had been just the sort of tough, grizzly person to give strangers grief if he found them nosing about the place uninvited. She wondered if Ethan was thinking along a similar vein.

"When you say *someone*—" she began.

"I mean Hank," Ethan told her. "I can't be certain he was the trouble of course, but if he had information about these people and a confrontation with them, it would explain a lot—why he was there, why his apron was ripped off on the porch, why he was going so fast on the way out and crashed his bike."

She was in full agreement. Daisy was convinced that Hank had known much more than he ever let on, not just about Fred but also Fred's connection to Fox Hollow. Aunt Emily had even alluded to that. Maybe it went further. Maybe Hank had known something about Fox Hollow itself. That made sense, especially if Zeke was right and the big-city folks were asking about Fred and Rick and who owned the property.

"Zeke," Daisy said, "how sure are you those big-city folks were talking about who owns Fox Hollow?"

"As positive as I am them Hokies are gonna win the championship this year!"

That was as confident as Zeke got. He loved Virginia Tech football. It ranked just under God, the United States of America, and the General.

"And how sure are you someone or something gave those big-city folks trouble at Fox Hollow?"

"I ain't sure what it was, but I'm durned sure it gave 'em trouble. They was complainin' they had to leave right quick. Too quick. They didn't get 'nough time to finish what they was doin'."

What were they doing? They might have been looking for Rick. That seemed to Daisy the most logical possibility. They had previously talked about driving out to Rick's trailer, so instead they could have gone to Fox Hollow to confirm whether he was the owner of the place. Except why would they care who owned it? Perhaps they were interested in buying the property. When she had lived there, her parents had occasionally received offers for the timber, but they never sold it. They never sold even a fragment of Fox Hollow. Her daddy had been particularly proud of that fact. He always detested the idea of carving up the land like it was a Thanksgiving turkey.

Rick, on the other hand, might be fully amenable to slicing and dicing. Daisy didn't know. She could only guess. She had no doubt, however, that if Hank had discovered Rick peddling parts and parcels of Fox Hollow, he would have done everything in his power to stop such a sale, especially if it involved big-city folks. But that was where the logical possibilities came to an abrupt end. Timber, or hunting rights, or even a few acres chopped out of one corner of the property to create a pretty little farmette weren't in any way important enough to result in Hank's supposed accident or Fred's poisoning. There had to be more to it. A good deal more. And there was one person who most likely had the answer.

"Rick," she muttered.

"I told ya before," Zeke reminded her. "That boy's foolin' with the wrong folks this time. They come fer business. Big business. And he better watch out. Ya better watch out too, Daisy. If they're lookin' at Fox Hollow now, then eventually they're gonna come lookin' at ya. Ya and yer momma."

He made it sound so ominous, she gulped.

"I think you and I need to have a chat with Rick," Ethan said to her.

Daisy nodded. When it came to Rick, she appreciated the assistance.

"We'll go first thing. The sooner, the better."

She nodded again.

Finishing his beer, Ethan rose from his chair and stretched. "Time to leave."

It wasn't clear whether he was referring to only himself or her as well, but Daisy didn't care. She had not an ounce of energy left for further reflection or conversation.

Mind-numbing exhaustion pounded down on her like a crushing wave of boulders. With a prodigious yawn, she pushed herself up from the tilting table and took a couple of lurching steps in no specific direction.

"Whoa there." Ethan put a hand on her shoulder to stop and steady her. "You better let me drive you."

"Why? I haven't had a sip to drink."

"No, but you're as bad as drunk. Ten seconds on that dark road and you'll be snoring like a duck with your head flopped down on the wheel. I'd prefer not to have to inform your friends and family that you careened off into a ditch."

"Like a duck . . . what?" Another giant yawn cut short her protestations.

"We'll come back for her car tomorrow," Ethan told Zeke as he steered Daisy toward the exit.

"Don't much matter when, just that she be gettin' home safe."

"She will."

Zeke followed them with his keys to lock up afterward.

Just as he was about to guide Daisy through the door, Ethan paused and looked over at Zeke. "You don't happen to have any idea where those big-city folks were headed after they left here?"

"Well," he rubbed one sunken eye, "I didn't catch no name, but I did hear 'em say somethin' 'bout wantin' a burger."

"A burger?" Ethan squinted at him. "Like a hamburger?"

"I reckon so." Zeke shrugged. "Ain't no other kinds of burgers unless ya talkin' cheese."

The squint turned to Daisy. "Didn't you tell me Mr. Dickerson wanted a hamburger when he stumbled into H & P's on the morning he died?"

She was listening, but her brain was only half-processing. "Huh?"

Ethan simplified the question. "Did Fred ask for a burger at the diner?"

"He did."

"So Mr. Dickerson wanted a burger and these big-city folks wanted a burger. Don't you find that to be a somewhat strange coincidence?"

This time Daisy squinted back at him. "Not unless the big-city folks were poisoned too."

CHAPTER
21

Daisy didn't think at all about burgers, poison, or any other potentially strange coincidences on the drive back to the inn. She slept. Before Ethan had even pulled his car out of the General's parking lot, her head was already slumped against the seat like a pooped puppy that couldn't possibly manage one more step and simply flopped down where it stood. She was so far gone, he could have deposited her on the side of the road fifty miles south across the border in North Carolina without her taking the slightest notice of it.

She regained consciousness briefly when they arrived at the behemoth Victorian. It was enough for her to register in a dazed sort of way that Ethan was carrying her across the aged porch, up the flight of stairs, and into her room. Daisy felt his thumb rub against her cheek as he laid her down on the bed. And then there were his lips.

The kiss entered her dreams. It was deep and strong and seemed to last for a very long time. She liked it. It felt good, so good she didn't want it to stop. That she was sure of. She tried to pull him closer, except she wasn't sure who was leaning over her. At first he had Ethan's wavy brown hair and the small scar on the left side of his face, but then the hair became shorter and blond like Matt's, and when Daisy opened her eyes to look at him, she found Rick's dark, penetrating gaze staring back at her.

The instant she blinked, it was gone. They were all gone. Ethan, Matt, Rick, and the warm lips. Daisy was alone in her bed and room at the Tosh Inn. It was still dark out, but she could tell that dawn was approaching. A mourning dove cooed plaintively in the redbud outside her window. Drowsy and befuddled, she blinked some more, not entirely certain what had been real. She wondered whether the dream would return if she fell back asleep, and she was just on the verge of dozing off when there was suddenly a muffled bang. A second bang came in swift succession.

Firecrackers? That's what it sounded like. But it was too early for firecrackers. Maybe she had dreamt it. Footsteps thudded clumsily down the stairs. A door on the lower level of the inn slammed. More footsteps down the stairs, fleeter ones this time. The door slammed again. Then there was a boom. It was a thunderous boom that made the whole house shake. Daisy's eyes popped open. She wasn't dreaming, and it definitely wasn't firecrackers. She could identify that noise without any question. It was Aunt Emily's Remington.

Another boom followed, and the house shook even harder. There was yelling. Aunt Emily's yelling. Daisy burrowed her head under the pillow. Stupid deer. Stupid perennials. Stupid shotgun.

A door opened. It was a door upstairs, down the hall. There were no audible footsteps, but the floorboards creaked. Somebody was up. They were probably going to check on Aunt Emily. Daisy closed her eyes. Maybe it wasn't too late for an extra little snooze. Maybe those warm lips would still make a repeat performance. It didn't really matter who they belonged to. It was only a dream. An awfully nice dream even if it had ended with Rick Balsam. That part she could just ignore.

The floorboards continued creaking. Then came the click. The patent metallic click of a slide being drawn back on a semiautomatic. Daisy sprang out of bed as fast as if she had found a cottonmouth coiled up in the sheets next to her. It was Ethan's semiautomatic, and Ethan wasn't fully familiar with Aunt Emily's hatred toward the nibblers of her pretty phlox. Hearing her shots, he would naturally assume that something much more serious was going on. Daisy had to get to him before he spooked her, because Aunt Emily had the tendency to blast away even more willy-nilly than usual when she got spooked.

Grabbing her robe from the hook by the armoire and wrapping it hastily around herself, Daisy flung open her door and scurried into the hall. As expected, she found Ethan standing there. He was pressed close to one wall, both hands in front of him gripping his black Glock. He was wearing jeans but no shirt. Daisy had never seen Ethan in a pair of jeans or without a shirt on, and she made a mental note that the new view wasn't at all bad. Although his chest may have looked inviting, his face was grave and concerned, so she got straight to the point.

"It's nothing to worry about," she told him. "It's only Aunt Emily. She and the local deer are in a permanent state of war in regard to her garden. Sometimes she can get a bit overwrought and too enthusiastic with her Remington."

Ethan shook his head. "I don't think—"

He was interrupted by more shouts from Aunt Emily.

Daisy couldn't make out her words, but they were loud and angry. The shouts were closely succeeded by another pair of thunderous, rattling booms. Daisy growled with irritation. At the rate she was going, Aunt Emily would wake half the county before the sun rose.

"I'll go talk to her." Grumbling, she headed toward the stairs.

"Wait!" Ethan called after her.

Daisy glanced back.

"I don't think it's deer," he said.

"It could be rabbits too, I reckon." She started down the hall again.

"Daisy, stop!"

She stopped in front of her momma's door, but it wasn't because Ethan told her to. It was because the door was ajar. Daisy frowned at it. Her momma didn't normally get up so early.

"Momma?" She tapped on the door.

There was no answer.

"Momma?"

Still no answer. Daisy pushed open the door and looked into the room. The bed was empty and rumpled. The top two drawers from the dresser had been pulled completely out and were turned upside down with their contents strewn around. The chubby lamp from the nightstand lay on the floor. So did her momma.

The walls spun, the furniture went blurry, and Daisy's knees lost all strength. She swayed like a birch in a tornado. Ethan caught her just as she toppled over sideways. He lowered her gently to the ground.

"Daisy? Daisy, are you okay?"

He didn't have to ask her twice. She snapped out of her haze in an instant and darted across the throw rug to her momma, who was flat on her stomach in an apricot-colored lace nightgown.

"Momma!"

Lucy Hale didn't respond. Nor did she move when her daughter grabbed her arm. But Daisy let out an immeasurable sigh of relief a moment later when she saw a little puff of air blow some wisps of hair away from her momma's pale cheek. The puff repeated itself. She was breathing.

"Will you help me get her up, Ethan?"

Not waiting for his assistance, Daisy rolled her momma onto her side. She gasped when she saw her face. A welt the size of a golf ball protruded from her left temple. It was turning an ugly shade of puce.

"She must have hit her head on the bedpost," Ethan said.

Daisy nodded in agreement. "The rug probably slipped out from under her, and she fell. But why are those drawers—"

Just then Beulah appeared in the doorway, yawning raucously. "I'm telling you, Daisy, we've got to take that damn gun away from Aunt Emily before—" Her sentence ended abruptly as she saw Daisy's momma lying on the floor. "Oh my God!"

Stirring slightly, Lucy murmured a few incomprehensible syllables.

"Momma?" Daisy cried. "It's me, Momma! I'm here!"

"Is she all right?" Pushing past Ethan, Beulah dropped down on her knees next to Daisy. "What can I do?"

Needing no time for deliberation, Daisy gave instructions at rapid-fire speed. "Call Sue Lowell. Tell her my momma's hit her head, and she's unconscious. Or semiconscious. I don't know if it makes a difference, but she'll understand either way. Try her at the Glade Hill Fire & Rescue Squad first. She's usually there in the mornings."

Beulah jumped up and raced out of the room in the direction of the nearest phone. Her robe flapped behind her like a pair of angel wings. Daisy was too busy cradling her momma's bruised face in her lap to ask Ethan why he was examining the door frame.

"Daisy—"

"Huh?" She didn't raise her gaze.

"Does your mom have any other injuries?"

"No, I—" Daisy paused and did a quick survey of her momma's body. Her neck was straight, and her shoulders appeared even. Her arms and legs weren't twisted funny. Nothing seemed broken, at least not from the outside. Maybe there was a sprain somewhere, but hopefully that wouldn't be too serious. "I don't see anything."

"There's no blood?"

"There's no blood."

"You're sure? Because—"

Too agitated to listen, Daisy glanced over at the two drawers lying nearby. "Why are those on the floor? Do you think maybe she tried to grab the dresser as she was falling?"

"I think it's more likely that's where she kept her Colt," Ethan replied.

Daisy's head snapped up. "Her what!"

"Her Colt," he repeated placidly, gesturing toward the base of the nightstand.

Her eyes followed his finger. Less than a foot away at the crinkled edge of the throw rug, there was a pistol. A small bluish-gray Colt. Daisy recognized it immediately.

"The three-eighty," she whispered.

"You know it?" Ethan asked.

He sounded surprised, but not half as surprised as she was to see the gun in her momma's bedroom.

"My daddy gave it to her," Daisy answered, reminiscing

more to herself than to Ethan. "The Christmas before he passed. For years he told her she should have one, just in case. But she always laughed him off. Said that's what she kept him around for. My momma never really liked guns much. Her hands are so tiny she has trouble holding most of them. That's why my daddy got her the three-eighty. He said it was light and little and manageable."

"So manageable"—Ethan gave a grim smile—"she was able to get off two rounds even after she fell."

"Two rounds!"

"See that?" He pointed at a marred spot about waist-high on the door frame. "One's lodged there. And the other"—he waved a few inches lower—"based on that blood spatter across the wood, I'd bet is hurting somebody pretty bad right about now."

"You think she hit someone?"

"Absolutely. Best guess, in the thigh. Or his ass if he was already running."

Stunned, Daisy blinked at the Colt lying on the floor. "I didn't know she still had it. I assumed she sold it after—after we moved to the inn."

"Well, it's a good thing she didn't," Ethan replied, "because I doubt your mom would have pulled apart her dresser and started firing in here unless she seriously needed to."

Daisy's stunned blinking continued. The firecrackers. There had been two bangs. That must have been her momma with the .380. Then the clumsy footsteps thudding down the stairs and the door slamming. It was the person she had injured. Fleeing. And the other footsteps? The door slamming again?

As though he could read the progression of her thoughts, Ethan said, "That's the reason I didn't want you going after

Emily. I had a feeling it wasn't deer—or rabbits—she was shooting at."

"But why? Why would anyone—" Daisy cut herself off as a chilling possibility occurred to her. "Could it be them? Those big-city folks Zeke was talking about last night? He told me to watch out. He said they were going to come looking at us next. But I didn't really believe him. I never imagined they'd actually go after my momma!"

Before Ethan could respond, Aunt Emily appeared in the hall outside the room. Unlike the rest of them, she was fully dressed for the day. Her hair was smooth. Her jewelry was coordinated. Only her raspberry lipstick looked a tad smudged, most likely from all of her yelling earlier.

"That'll teach those lurkers!" she chortled with glee.

"Where is he?" Ethan asked hurriedly. "Is there any chance he'll come back into the house?"

"No chance. No chance in the world. Not when he knows what's waiting for him if he does." Aunt Emily patted the double-barreled 20-gauge she had perched on her shoulder.

"But is he still on the property? Does he need to be restrained?"

"Naw. He's gone. Went hobbling into the trees like a lame horse. If there'd been a smidge more light out, I could have put him down permanently. But as it was"—Aunt Emily clucked her tongue—"Lucy got him good. Hit 'em close to where it downright counts, if you catch my meaning. He'll be limping for a long time to come. Other things might not be working quite right neither." She chortled again, even more gleefully this time.

"How did you know he was here?" Ethan questioned her. "Was it the gunshots? Or did you actually see him?"

"I was about to go to the kitchen to ready the biscuits

for breakfast when I heard Lucy start talking. She was mad. I knew in a snap something was wrong, because Lucy's almost never mad. Usually she has more patience than a monk being stung by a thousand yellow jackets in the keester. Isn't that true, Ducky?"

She gave a slight nod. She was still wondering about the big-city folks.

"Just as I came out of my room to check on her," Aunt Emily went on, "Lucy let 'er rip. Twice, I think she fired. And he stumbled into the hallway with a sweet little bullet up in his right thigh. Fast as I could, I ran back to grab my Remington. He went down the stairs and out the back door. But it was easy enough for me to follow him. He left a nice trail of blood behind. I'm glad about it too."

"Glad?" Daisy raised an eyebrow.

"You bet your bippy I'm glad," Aunt Emily crowed. "Serves him right for skulking around the neighborhood. I told you somebody was out there spying, Ducky. Just waiting for an opportunity to prey on one of us. And to pick the sickest of the bunch! Like we're a herd of helpless antelopes in the middle of the Serengeti. The man ought to be ashamed!"

"So you saw him," Ethan said. "Can you describe him to me?"

"I didn't get much of a look at his face. Speaking of faces." She glanced over at Lucy. "Hers isn't looking the prettiest right now. But at least it's nothing a couple of aspirin and bag of frozen peas can't fix."

Daisy's mouth opened, ready to protest Aunt Emily's lack of concern over her momma's condition.

"Pish, pish. Don't gape at me, Ducky. You're not a sea bass. I love your momma dearly, as you well know. And she'll be just fine. It takes more than one bump on the noggin to bring down a lady like Lucy Hale. You know that too."

"It'd be very helpful if you could describe the man," Ethan pursued.

"All right. All right. Don't rush me." Aunt Emily stroked her beloved shotgun thoughtfully. "As I said before, I didn't get much of a look at his face. It was dark in the hall and dark outside. But I can tell you it was painted."

"Painted?"

"Camouflage-style. Green stripes across his nose and cheeks. Like he was heading for a tour in the jungle. His clothing also. Shirt, pants, boots, and hat. All green camouflage. The complete getup."

Full camouflage with his face painted. That puzzled Daisy. It didn't sound like big-city folks.

"Was he armed?" Ethan asked. "Did he fire back at you?"

"He didn't aim. He didn't even raise it," Aunt Emily said. "But if I'm not mistaken, he had a rifle with him. I only caught a glimpse as he was running. It was camouflage too."

Daisy's jaw stiffened and her eyes narrowed as an icy, bitter realization crept along her spine. Not many big-city folks used rifles with camouflage. Especially not out of season. But she knew someone who did. In fact, the last time she had seen him, he had been wearing camouflage and carrying camouflage.

"Bobby," she hissed.

Suddenly Lucy's shoulders twitched, and she gave a small cough. Daisy looked down at her.

"Momma, was it Bobby? Bobby Balsam. Rick's brother. Was he the one who was here?"

"Bo . . . Bobby," she mumbled.

It was enough of a confirmation for Daisy. The icy bitterness spread through every vein in her body, and she instantly made up her mind what to do next. But before she could act, Beulah and her flapping robe reappeared in the doorway next to Aunt Emily.

"I spoke to Sue," she reported breathlessly. "She's in the ambulance, and she's coming right away. But it'll take her awhile to get here. They had an early call over in Gretna. She says not to move your momma in case she's hurt her back."

"Thanks, Beulah." Daisy nodded gratefully. "Now if I could ask you for one more favor?"

"Of course. Anything."

"Will you stay with my momma until Sue gets here? I don't want her to be left alone."

"Of course," Beulah said again, entering the room and sitting down by her. "But what about you? Where are you going?"

"I"—she carefully transferred her momma's head from her lap to Beulah's—"have some business to take care of."

"Business?" Beulah frowned, not understanding.

Ethan frowned too, except he did understand. "Are you sure about this?"

Not responding to either one, Daisy grabbed the Colt from the edge of the throw rug, stood up, and marched into the hall. Ethan stepped in front of her to block her path.

"Get out of my way," she snapped.

"Daisy—"

"Get. Out. Of. My. Way."

"Just hold on a minute. Wouldn't it be wiser to call the sheriff? Let him handle it."

"*I'm* handling it." Her voice was steely. "You don't want to fight me on this, Ethan."

There was a fiery determination in Daisy's eyes, and he capitulated. "Then at least let me come with you. I'll drive.

You don't have a car anyway. We left it at the General last night, remember?"

She hesitated.

"You can use my car, Daisy," Beulah offered.

"You'll need yours if they take Lucy to the hospital," Aunt Emily countered. "She can have mine. Only I don't think she should take it. I think she should go with Ethan."

Daisy turned to her with pursed lips.

"Think smart, Ducky. If you're planning on confronting the Balsam boys, you're better off not doing it alone. Take someone who knows how to handle himself—and a weapon."

Although she wasn't keen to admit it, Daisy knew that Aunt Emily was right. She turned back to Ethan.

"Fine. You want to come, you can come. But *I'm* driving."

Aunt Emily let out a low, tittering whistle. "That means you, Mr. Kinney, need to put on a shirt *and* a safety belt."

CHAPTER
22

"If you had been born fifty years earlier, you would have made one hell of a bootlegger."

"If I'd been born fifty years earlier and become a bootlegger," Daisy retorted crisply, "you would have been chasing me instead of sitting next to me."

Ethan grinned. "I told you already. I'm not a revenuer."

"Then don't complain about my driving."

"I'm not complaining. But I do think you should seriously consider a career in NASCAR."

It was Daisy's turn to grin, just a little. She did it as she swerved fearlessly along a mountain ridge, not taking her foot off the gas in the slightest. She had no intention of slowing down. Not for tight curves. Not for obtuse possums. Not even for other vehicles. They could move. And they did move. It was as though they knew that she was focused on speed. Speed and Bobby Balsam.

The first peachy streaks of dawn were beginning to brighten the night sky, but they weren't yet strong enough to break through the thick pine stands that surrounded the Balsam homestead. Daisy barely noticed the darkness or the gradually increasing light. She was too enraged by what had happened to her momma, and she had driven that road so many times in years past that her memory simply took over. Handfuls of gravel spit out from beneath the car's tires as she accelerated deeper into the forest.

"You do know where you're going?" Ethan asked her, clutching the armrest with tense fingers.

"You'll see the signs soon," she said.

"The signs?"

"Then you'll hear the dogs. They've got lots of dogs. Rottweilers, blueticks, black-and-tan coonhounds. Normally I bring a bag of ham bones with me. That keeps them pretty well in check."

"And without the bones?"

"It'll be even noisier than usual."

The signs started. NO TRESPASSING. BEWARE OF DOG. PRIVATE PROPERTY. Ethan read them as they sped by. When they reached the more serious signs, he laughed aloud.

"Is there anyone they aren't threatening to shoot on sight?"

"There's a mighty good chance I'll be shooting Bobby on sight," Daisy replied, not laughing with him.

Ethan grew solemn. "How confident are you he's the person?"

"I don't have to be confident. All I've got to do is look at him. Either he has a bullet in his right thigh or he doesn't."

"I guess I can't really argue with that logic, but I can tell you I still think it'd be much wiser to call the sheriff and let him handle this."

Daisy slammed on the brakes. Lucky for Ethan, he had taken Aunt Emily's sage advice and put on his safety belt, so he snapped back against the seat instead of hurtling into the dash.

"Ow." He put his hand to his neck.

She turned to him without sympathy. "You're going to have to choose, Ethan. Get out now, wait here until I'm done, and I'll pick you up on my way back."

"Or?"

"Or quit talking about calling the sheriff and trust that I know how best to deal with a miserable little bastard like Bobby Balsam. This isn't any of your business."

"I'm a federal agent."

"This ain't federal."

Ethan met her gaze. The bitter, fiery determination from the inn was gone. Now Daisy's eyes were stony. So stony, they were almost to the point of colorlessness.

"I won't say another word," he promised.

She raised a dubious eyebrow.

"At least not about the sheriff," Ethan amended himself. "I can't swear I won't call the paramedics if it looks like somebody's about to bleed to death."

Daisy stepped on the gas. A few minutes later they pulled into the clearing. There was enough pale morning light to see Rick's and Bobby's ramshackle trailers at the far end. There was also enough light to see the dogs snoozing peaceably together in a large pen over by the fire pit. It was so early, no one had yet fed them and let them out. Their heads popped up as Daisy brought the car to a stop. She called out to them by name, and the pups greeted her with friendly yowls.

"So what's the plan?" Ethan said.

"The truck." She didn't elaborate.

Clasping her momma's Colt firmly in her hand, Daisy climbed out of the car and walked over to one of the two pickup trucks parked on the mixture of red clay and scruffy weeds in the center of the clearing. Ethan followed her.

"This is Bobby's," she told him, placing her empty palm on the hood. "The engine's still warm." Opening the door, she leaned over to examine the inside. "There's blood on the driver's seat. And the console. And the steering wheel. And yes, it's fresh."

"Okay." Ethan nodded. "I'll agree that's decent enough proof. But, Daisy, don't do anything rash."

"I should have left you back in the woods," she muttered.

"I'm serious, Daisy." He sounded serious too. "If you act on impulse now, you may do something you later regret."

"I regret giving him extra pecans on his waffles for all those breakfasts at the diner. And I regret bringing him a bunch of cookies and brownies the last time I came to this place. But I can guarantee you, Ethan, I won't be making those sorts of mistakes again."

Ethan didn't respond. He held back guardedly as she approached the trailer on the left. Daisy halted just short of the two steps that led up to the battered door with its peeling paint.

"Bobby!" she hollered.

Bobby Balsam didn't appear.

"Bobby, get out here!"

He still didn't appear, and Daisy's patience was thinner than a new blade of spring grass.

"Bobby, get your sorry ass out here right now!"

There was some noise from inside the trailer.

"Does it have a back exit?" Ethan asked. "He could be trying to escape that way."

"There's only one door. And one window big enough." She gestured toward a filthy pane of glass.

"You should pull back a little and move to a more covered spot," Ethan cautioned her. "Emily thought he had a rifle. He's probably got it with him."

Daisy didn't budge an inch. "I know you're in there, Bobby!"

This time the noise came from the other trailer. Several thumps and a small crash later, the shredded screen door flew open. Rick stumbled out in his athletic shorts.

"What the jiminy is going on! Who's doing all the shouting?"

"I am," Daisy calmly informed him. "And you can turn right around because it doesn't concern you."

Still half-asleep, Rick rubbed his face with his thumbs like a baby. "Daisy?"

"Yup."

He squinted in her direction. "What are you doing here?"

"I'll say it again. It doesn't concern you."

His squint switched toward Ethan, who had positioned himself strategically behind the bumper of Bobby's truck. "Is someone with you? I can't really see 'em. That's not Sue?"

"No," Daisy answered. "It's not Sue."

"So who is it?"

"Go back to bed, Rick. And whatever girl you've got in there waiting for you. Is it still the one with the pink tank top, or have you traded her in already for a new flavor of the month?"

"The one with the pink tank top? What pink tank—" Rick stopped as his drowsy vision cleared. "Wait a minute. I know that car. That's the car you were in at Fox Hollow."

"That's right," she confirmed tetchily.

"Why is it here? Why are you here? What's going on, Daisy?"

It was obvious from the escalating sharpness of his tone that Rick was quickly becoming tetchy too, but Daisy was in no mood to tread lightly.

"How many times do I have to tell you? Do you need me to spell it out? It. Doesn't. Concern. You."

"It sure as hell concerns me if you brought that goddam federal out here! Wasn't taking him to Fox Hollow enough for you?"

Her tiny remaining strand of patience snapped. Daisy wasn't there to deal with Rick. She was there to deal with his brother. Her arm raised the .380, and she leveled it at the elder Balsam.

Rick's stubbly jaw convulsed with surprise. "Jesus, Daisy."

He wasn't any more startled than she was. Daisy didn't ordinarily point guns at people. In fact, she never pointed them at anything at all. But she didn't lower her weapon.

"Daisy—" Ethan began, taking a step forward.

"Stay out of this," she growled at him.

"You did bring him here!" Rick exploded.

"He didn't come for you," Daisy retorted with equal vehemence. "And he didn't come because I asked him to. This isn't any more his concern than it is yours."

"Then exactly whose concern is it?"

"Bobby's."

That silenced Rick for a moment.

"Daisy," Ethan began a second time, "maybe you should put down the Colt."

She glared at him. "I'll put it down when I dang well feel like it, thank you very kindly."

"What makes it Bobby's concern?" Rick spoke slowly, his expression hovering somewhere between wariness and indignation.

Daisy turned her glare on him. "What makes it Bobby's concern? He did when he attacked my momma."

Rick's stubbly jaw convulsed once more. "What did you just say?"

"You heard me."

"But—"

"But nothing," Daisy cut him off brusquely. "Someone was in my momma's room at the inn this morning, and Aunt Emily saw him running out wearing full camouflage and carrying a matching rifle. Just like Bobby's got."

Rick frowned. "You can't really believe it was him. Bobby wouldn't—"

She cut him off again. "Before my momma was knocked unconscious, she managed to get off two rounds. One hit him in the leg. Bobby's truck has got blood on the seat, blood on the console, and blood on the steering wheel. And now I'm seeing there's blood on those steps leading up into his trailer and blood on the door frame. So yes, I can really believe it was Bobby."

His frown intensified. "How's your momma?"

"I don't know. She fell pretty hard, and she's got a bad bump on her head. When I left to come here, Beulah and Aunt Emily were both with her. They're waiting for Sue and the ambulance."

"Lordy, Daisy. I'm sorry."

"Don't feel sorry for me. Feel sorry for your brother." Her lips curved into a very slight, very grim smile. "Because if I find he's got a bullet in his right thigh like I think he does, he's going to learn what happens to people who mess with my family."

Not wasting any time, Rick jogged from his trailer to Bobby's. Daisy tracked him with her gun.

"You better not try to pull something tricky on me, Rick," she warned him. "Not today. Not when it involves my momma."

With his hand on Bobby's door, Rick paused and turned

toward her. His gaze was full of resentment, but Daisy could tell that it wasn't directed at her.

"If Bobby went into a woman's bedroom and threatened her with a firearm, he's gonna have to answer for it."

He disappeared inside the trailer. She expected a long wait while the two Balsams argued, or deliberated, or schemed. But to her surprise, Rick reemerged within seconds. He pushed Bobby out ahead of him. The first thing that Bobby saw was the .380 staring at him, and he immediately sunk to the ground.

"Don't shoot! Don't shoot me, Daisy!"

Shooting Bobby Balsam at that moment would have been like clubbing an orphaned, injured, baby otter. He was an utterly pathetic creature. The green paint on his cheeks was smudged and streaked as though he had been crying. The sleeves of his camouflage shirt were torn as though he had been scrambling through heavy brambles. And his right leg was a bloody mess.

"Please, Daisy. Please! Please don't shoot me." He clasped his red-stained hands together and shook them toward her in a wretched plea for absolution.

"Shut up, Bobby."

She said it with unconcealed disgust as she lowered the Colt. There was no question that he was the one who had been at the inn that morning. If his clothing and face weren't sufficient evidence, the condition of his thigh was incontrovertible.

"Your mom has nice aim," Ethan remarked, studying the wound.

"She does, doesn't she?" Daisy agreed. "Makes a daughter proud."

"Well, it doesn't make a brother proud." Rick gave his brother a hard shove in the shoulder with his knee.

Bobby whimpered.

"You better start explaining yourself," Rick snarled.

"I—" He whimpered some more.

"Now!"

Rick roared the command with such ferocity that Bobby's petrified eyes seemed to sink into his skull.

"I . . . I wasn't trying to hurt her."

At the mention of her momma, Daisy was tempted to raise her gun again.

"I don't care what you were trying to do," Rick spat back at him. "Did you or did you not have your rifle with you?"

"It wasn't loaded," Bobby whined.

Curling and uncurling his fists repeatedly, Rick closed his eyes and took a deep breath. He was clearly having a difficult time restraining himself from strangling his brother.

"Why, Bobby?" Rick said quietly, his eyes remaining closed. "Why were you at the Tosh Inn in Lucy Hale's bedroom?"

"If I tell you, they might hurt me."

"If you don't tell me, I *will* hurt you."

Bobby gulped. "They . . . they paid me to do it."

CHAPTER
23

Daisy stared at Bobby in astonishment. "Someone paid you to go after my momma? Who?"

"His . . . his name is Joe."

"Joe?" she echoed.

"Do you know him?" Ethan asked her.

"No." Daisy shook her head. "I don't think so."

Rick frowned at his brother. "Who the hell is Joe?"

"I don't know." Bobby shrugged. "He said that was his name."

The frown became a glower. "What was his other name, Bobby?"

He shrugged again. "I don't know. He didn't say."

"What the hell do you know then!" Rick exploded.

Bobby looked like he was about to burst into tears. There were deep wrinkles of pain mixed with fear etched into his forehead. "I . . . I know I met him at the General."

"The General?" Daisy responded sharply.

She looked at Ethan. He looked back at her and nodded. They were thinking the same thing.

"Bobby," Daisy said, "was this Joe you met at the General from around here?"

He sniffled. "I'm not sure."

"Well, I want you to think about it. I want you to think about it real hard." She tapped the Colt against her thigh. "Was Joe from Pittsylvania County, or was Joe from the big city?"

Clutching his injured leg protectively, Bobby answered, "He wasn't from these parts. He tried to act like he was, but he wasn't. I could tell. He didn't know things right. And he didn't talk right. I think he was big city."

Daisy drew a shaky breath. So Zeke had been correct. The big-city folks had come looking for her momma. Only they had gotten stupid Bobby Balsam to do the dirty work for them.

Ethan turned to Bobby. "What exactly did this Joe pay you to do?"

Bobby sniffled some more. "I was supposed to talk to her."

"To Daisy's mom?"

He nodded.

"About what?"

There was enough hesitation on Bobby's part that Rick was obligated to encourage him with another ungentle shove in the shoulder with his knee.

"Okay, okay!" Bobby wailed. "Joe wanted me to pressure her to sell the land."

"Sell the land?" Daisy squinted at him. "She doesn't own any land."

"That's what I thought. That's what I meant about him not knowing things right. But he said she did."

"Don't be an idiot, Bobby," Rick snapped. "You know I bought Fox Hollow at the beginning of the year."

"I told him that, and he told me I didn't understand."

Ethan frowned. "What's there to understand? If she

doesn't own any land, she can't sell any land. That's as simple as it gets."

Daisy's anger toward Bobby began to rise again. "So even though you knew Fox Hollow belonged to your brother, you decided to take your rifle and go threaten my momma?"

He responded with a sheepish shrug. "I already said it wasn't loaded."

"And that makes it all right!"

The shrug repeated itself. "I figured cuz she was sick, it'd be easy. She'd just agree. What does your momma want an ol' farm for anyway? She's better off at the inn with the other widows."

"Rick," Daisy seethed in warning, her finger twitching on the trigger of the Colt, "you better do something before I do."

Rick promptly reached down and grabbed the collar of his brother's shirt. "Look at me."

Bobby hung his head like a puppy that had just been caught piddling on the prized Persian carpet.

"Look at me!" Rick bellowed, yanking Bobby toward him without any consideration for the bullet in his thigh.

He lifted his wan, shuddering face and met Rick's livid gaze.

"If you go near Lucy Hale—or that inn—ever again, I swear to you, Bobby, I'll set the dogs on you and you'll be their next dinner. Kin o' mine or no kin o' mine. Do I make myself clear?"

The only reply was Bobby's teeth chattering.

"Do I make myself clear!" Rick thundered.

"Y . . . Yesh."

"Good. Now apologize to Daisy."

The wan, shuddering face turned toward her. She had never seen Bobby look so terrified.

"I . . . I'm sorry, Daisy," he stammered. "I'm very sorry."

With a grunt, she relaxed her finger.

Also grunting, Rick released his hold on Bobby's shirt. He slumped back to the ground.

"I have a question," Ethan said.

Both Daisy and Rick looked at him.

"It's for Bobby."

Bobby half-gurgled, half-moaned as he cradled his leg.

"What did Daisy's mom do when you told her she had to sell the land?" Ethan asked him.

"She shot me!" he sobbed.

"Obviously. But did she say anything before she shot you?"

"Naw. She just pulled her gun from the dresser without any warning and . . ." Bobby paused to rub his watery eyes. "Well, she did tell me she wouldn't ever sell it. Then she pulled her gun from the dresser and . . ."

Not waiting for the conclusion of the woeful tale, Ethan turned to Rick. "Is it possible you don't own all of Fox Hollow?"

Rick raised a surprised eyebrow. "I bought everything the bank had."

Ethan then turned to Daisy. "And did the bank have all of Fox Hollow?"

"Yes."

"Are you sure?"

"Of course I'm sure," she returned with irritation. "We covered this once before already, and I really don't know why we have to go over it again. The entire property was forfeit. The house, the crops, and the land. You took the whole thing. And the whole thing was mortgaged, so the bank had all of it."

"But there must be a reason why this Joe believes your mom still owns a piece of the property," Ethan mused.

"Now that you mention it," Rick said, "there were some folks up here acting like a piece might be missing."

Daisy snapped her head toward him. "A piece might be missing! What piece? And what folks?"

"They came a couple of weeks ago and—"

Thinking immediately of Zeke and what he had told her, she interrupted him. "Were they big-city folks? Did they ask you if you own Fox Hollow?"

Rick's eyebrow went up in surprise a second time. "Yes. How did you know? They did ask me if I now own it. I guess there was some confusion on the subject. Since old man Dickerson had been living there, they thought it belonged to him. Or maybe he even told them it was his. I'm not sure. But then they discovered it'd been sold to me."

"How did they find that out?"

"I think they looked at the property records. Same as Sheriff Lowell and everybody else who's interested in learning who owns what. The county must be slow in processing the paperwork, because nobody seemed to know I'd bought Fox Hollow until right around the time Fred died."

"That's not unusual," Ethan said. "Most places are at least six months behind when it comes to updating land records. But what I'm curious to know is whether—"

"Whether the timing with the records and Fred's death is just a coincidence," Rick finished for him, "or something else instead?"

Ethan nodded.

"I've been wondering that for a while too. I even looked at the records myself, but they didn't help any. Old man Dickerson wasn't listed at all. And there's no mention of the ATF either. Fox Hollow went from Paul and Lucy Hale"—Rick glanced at Daisy—"to the bank, then to me."

"That's not unusual," Ethan said again. "My office doesn't take possession the same way a normal purchaser

would. From a legal standpoint, governmental forfeiture—"
He also glanced at Daisy.

She gave him a sour look. "Is this really the best time
for a lesson on forfeiture?"

"Probably not. Sorry." Ethan cleared his throat gruffly,
then turned to Rick. "I do think the way you obtained the
property might be important. How did you learn it was
available?"

"From the bank." Rick leaned against the dented door
of Bobby's trailer and folded his arms across his chest.
"From the bank's president if we're being precise."

Daisy's sour look went to him. "Since when are you
and the bank's president pals?"

Rick smiled. "We've been doing business together for
many years."

"Doing business together?" She smiled back at him
wryly. "I don't believe that for an instant. What kind of
business?"

The smile grew. "Darlin', I sell more whiskey to him
than to any other man in the Commonwealth of Virginia."

Her mouth flopped open.

"We were drinking together one evening this past winter," Rick said, "and he told me he was on the verge of cel-
ebrating. You see, the bank had a property on its books that
had been giving him a whopper of a headache. For four
years they hadn't received a mortgage payment, interest
payment, property tax payment, or insurance payment. It
was just sitting there with the bills accumulating, and he
couldn't do anything about it. The feds had it all tied up
with their rules and regulations and endless red tape. But
at long last every necessary form had been signed and every teeny tiny technicality had been taken care of. The
bank could finally dispose of its albatross.

"It was a messy albatross too," he continued. "There was a tenant on the land who supposedly had a lease, but no one could find a copy of it. And without it, the bank didn't have a clue what to do about him. Their best option—their only option really—was to sell the property, wipe it from their list of defaults, and at least get a portion of their investment back. I was curious about it and asked where the property was. When I heard Fox Hollow, I almost fell off my chair."

"I bet," Daisy muttered.

Rick's voice deepened. "I immediately made an offer, he accepted it, and we shook hands on the deal over a jar. So now you know how it happened. How I became the new owner of Fox Hollow."

"Well," she said, sighing, "that explains why you were the only one who knew it was up for sale."

"Right time, right place."

"And the money?" It was a question that had been nagging her for weeks. "How could you afford it?"

"How do you know the Balsam family isn't worth millions?"

Daisy gestured toward the dilapidated trailers.

"Darlin'," Rick drawled, "you shouldn't be so quick to judge a book by its cover. For your information, I don't wet the whistle of just the lovely folks in Pittsylvania County or even good ol' Virginny. I supply half the eastern seaboard with my 'shine. And that keeps me flush enough to afford a lot more than your precious Fox Hollow."

"Damn." Ethan exhaled.

Rick looked at him. "Is that a problem for you, Mister Federal Agent?"

Ethan answered with a smirk. "Clearly I chose the wrong occupation."

"You and me both," Daisy agreed. "And to think how many stupid scones I've baked when I could have been brewing up brandies instead."

"I told you on the drive out here you should have become a bootlegger."

"Unfortunately that advice comes a little too late."

"Doesn't seem quite fair, does it?" Ethan remarked.

"Fair?" It was Daisy's turn to smirk. "Nothing in this world is ever fair."

As though to prove her point, Bobby mewed piteously.

"I think your brother is in need of some medical attention," she said to Rick. "And now I know you won't have any problem paying the bill."

Rick's gaze narrowed, and he was about to respond when Bobby interrupted him.

"Watch . . . watch out for Joe," he choked.

"There's another piece of advice coming too late." Daisy's sarcasm was mixed with frustration. "You saying that now doesn't do my momma and the humongous bump on her head a lick of good. Nor does it help me that everybody's constantly talking about who owns Fox Hollow and then telling my momma to sell it. She doesn't own it, so she can't sell it, and I really don't understand why that's such a difficult concept to grasp."

Ethan nodded. "That's why the first thing I'm going to do after we leave here is check with my office. I want to make absolutely certain nothing funny happened with the forfeiture. That something didn't get divided or split off along the way. So we know without any doubt what you think of as Fox Hollow and what the property records show as Fox Hollow are the exact same piece of land."

Daisy nodded back at him. "I appreciate it. Thank you, Ethan."

"Hopefully that'll clear everything up," he went on. "And if not, it should at least give us a better idea of how to protect you and your mom from any future problems." He frowned at Bobby.

"I won't. I won't." Bobby shook his head vigorously. "You won't have any problems from me."

"Even if your brother decides not to set the dogs on you"—Daisy restrained a grin—"should Aunt Emily catch a glimpse of you lurking anywhere in the neighborhood, she won't hesitate for a second to pop you full of holes. She's always itching for an excuse to blast something to kingdom come, and you'll make the easiest target she's ever had."

Bobby squirmed like an earthworm on a hot sidewalk.

"What about Sheriff Lowell?" Rick asked her pragmatically.

"Maybe you should try bribing him with a couple of jelly jars," she replied. "Have you been doing business with him too?"

Rick growled, and her nose twitched in amusement.

"We don't know what the others have told the sheriff by now," Ethan interjected.

Daisy's eyes went to Bobby, who was beginning to resemble a rather sickly and nearly desiccated earthworm. Albeit with some reluctance, she felt a smidge of sympathy for him. Punishing him further would be like scolding a recalcitrant hamster. There was simply no point to it.

"All right, Bobby," she said after a moment, "if the cat's not out of the bag already, I won't tattle on you to Sheriff Lowell. That's assuming, of course, my momma doesn't have any lasting injuries and you don't have any more dealings with Joe."

"I won't! I won't!" he cried again.

Bobby looked so grateful and relieved—and he sounded

so sincere in his promise—Daisy didn't regret her decision, not yet at least. She turned to Ethan.

"Could we go back to the inn now? I really want to check on my momma."

"Of course. But how about if I drive this time?"

They shared a laugh and started toward Ethan's car. Rick called to her.

"Daisy—"

She slowed but didn't stop.

"Daisy, will you let me know how your momma's doing?"

"I will." She continued walking toward the car.

"In the meantime," Rick said, "I'll track down a copy of the plat map. Maybe it'll show something about Fox Hollow that explains all the interest in it. And, Daisy—" He hesitated. "If you find out anything about the property or the forfeiture—"

Her back stiffened, and her feet stumbled on the gravel. Daisy didn't mean to sound so resentful and envious, but she couldn't help it.

"Don't worry, Rick," she hissed. "If we find there's a piece missing, you'll be the first one to know about it and the only one able to buy it."

CHAPTER
24

"I think it's about time for an explanation."

"What sort of an explanation, Ducky?"

They were sitting in her momma's hospital room, so Daisy kept her voice low. "Don't play dumb with me, Aunt Emily. We both know you've got a treasure trove of Pittsylvania County secrets stored in that brain of yours."

Her shrewd blue eyes were filled with laughter. "I'm not disputing that, Ducky. I'm just not sure which particular secret you're interested in at the moment."

"We can start with old man Dickerson and what you meant when you said he was responsible for the death of my daddy."

"I thought you didn't believe a word of that."

"I didn't, and I still don't. Fred didn't cause the accident. He wasn't at Fox Hollow when it happened. He wasn't anywhere near the place."

"Just because the man wasn't standing in the garden and didn't physically make that propane tank explode, doesn't mean he wasn't responsible."

Daisy tapped her heel on the floor with growing impatience. "So then how was he responsible?"

The shrewd blue eyes blinked at her. "Are you certain this is something you want to know?"

She stared straight back, resolved not to be sidetracked. "I think we're beyond that point, don't you? Considering Fred's dead—and Hank's dead—and my momma's lying unconscious in that bed over there."

"I suppose you're right, Ducky. I suppose there are times when what you don't know can hurt you. Although I doubt what I can tell you about Fred Dickerson is going to help you much."

Daisy leaned back on the seat of her folding chair expectantly.

"Fred had already been a recluse for a good long time when your daddy hired him," Aunt Emily began. "He didn't like talking to people or even being around them. That was obvious enough. But like all the rest of us, he still needed to eat and put a shirt on his back. Your daddy used to see him scrounging around for a decent meal and a dollar bill, and he felt sorry for him, so he started offering Fred odd jobs. Mowing in the cemetery, bushwhacking along the creek, digging out rocks from the fields."

"I remember that. I remember my daddy liked him and thought he was a hard worker."

"But Matt's daddy didn't like him," Aunt Emily said.

"He didn't?" Daisy frowned. "That I don't remember."

"There's no reason why you would, Ducky. You were married and living happily with your husband. Your pretty little head wasn't focused on an old wreck of a farmer like Fred Dickerson. Mine wouldn't have been neither, except your momma was worried enough to talk to me about it."

"She was? Did she tell you why Matt's daddy didn't like Fred?"

"She had a guess. A correct guess in my opinion. Your

momma thought Matt's daddy was using the cemetery as a giant pot field."

Daisy chuckled. "That doesn't surprise me. Clean living was never Mr. McGovern's strong suit. He must have tried his hand at a hundred different schemes over the years. Cooking up home brew. Organizing gambling operations. Peddling insurance pyramids. Everything illegal but with the potential to make him a quick buck."

Aunt Emily nodded. "And the cemetery was the perfect spot for it. Back then it was all overgrown, so he could have planted whatever he wanted in between the gravestones. Nobody would have noticed. Nobody except your family ever went there. Not until your daddy hired Fred to tidy it up."

"I can't imagine Mr. McGovern was too happy about that."

"He wasn't. According to your momma, Matt's daddy wanted your daddy to fire Fred, but he wouldn't do it. The two argued about it. Your momma told me they squabbled for days, just like a couple of obstinate roosters. They were still quarreling the morning of the accident. They were so busy fighting with each other, they weren't paying enough attention to fixing that dang tank and—" She paused awkwardly.

"I know what came next. There's no need to say it." Daisy sighed. "But you haven't answered my question. How was Fred responsible? It wasn't his fault something went wrong with the tank."

"It most certainly was his fault," Aunt Emily returned crisply. "Without Fred Dickerson, there wouldn't have been a fight. Without the fight, there wouldn't have been an explosion. And without the explosion, your daddy and Matt's daddy would still be with us today."

Daisy sighed again, more audibly this time. Aunt Emily clucked her tongue.

"Your momma agrees with me even if you don't. So did Hank. So did Fred himself. That's why he decided to live at Fox Hollow after the government took it from you. He felt a duty and obligation toward your family, so he wanted to watch out for the family home as best as he could."

She thought for a moment. "I wonder if that's why my momma asked Ethan whether Fred had been maintaining the place."

"Your momma always asks about the property whenever she hears somebody visited it."

"She's never asked me."

Aunt Emily reached over and patted Daisy's arm. "She doesn't want to cause you pain, Ducky, or burden you with more worries."

More worries? Daisy looked over at her momma sleeping soundlessly with the starched white sheet tucked snugly around her. There were so many worries already. Her health. The medical bills. The diner being closed. And now Joe and the other big-city folks and their unexplained interest in Fox Hollow. If her momma had been awake, Daisy could have asked her about a possible missing piece, some portion of the property that she might still own and could sell. But her momma wasn't awake, and the doctors didn't know when she would regain consciousness. They had done all the tests. Thankfully there was no sign of any permanent injury. She would be fine. They just had to wait for the healing process to move at its own speed.

"Aunt Emily?"

"Yes, Ducky?" She patted her arm a second time.

"Do you know anything about another piece of land? A part of Fox Hollow separate from the rest?"

The patting stopped. "Separate from the rest? I'm afraid I don't understand you."

"Bobby Balsam told me some big-city folks hired him to pressure my momma to sell the land, but that doesn't make a bit of sense to me."

"Big-city folks?" Aunt Emily raised a curious eyebrow. "Your momma wouldn't ever sell her land."

"Bobby said the same thing, and that's what puzzles me. Fox Hollow doesn't belong to her anymore. And I'm sure those big-city folks are aware of that. They might have been confused about it awhile ago, but they can't be now. Rick himself told them he's the new owner. So why are they still bothering my momma?"

Aunt Emily was puzzled too. "You're right, Ducky. That doesn't make a bit of sense."

"Ethan thinks maybe something funny happened with the forfeiture. A portion of the property got split off, and my momma went on owning it. But you've never heard about anything like that, have you?"

She shook her head regretfully. "I wish I could say I have, except I haven't. And that's not the sort of thing I'd forget."

"When Ethan first suggested it, I figured it was pretty improbable. If Fox Hollow had been divided into parts—inadvertently or not—I think somebody would have told us about it at some point, even if just by sending my momma a tax bill."

"Fox Hollow divided into parts?" Aunt Emily went on shaking her head. "Maybe there's been a mix-up with Chalk Level. Chalk Level has parts. It's got Fox Hollow and the cemetery and all those little parcels sprinkled around the edges."

"But everybody knows that. Those parts have been the

same for ages. The only thing that ever changes about them is how many people are living in which single-wide. And as far as I'm aware, the big-city folks never asked about Chalk Level. They asked about Fox Hollow. The only person to ask about Chalk Level recently is Ethan, and that's because of what happened to Fred. Chalk Level was listed as his residence."

"In a way you could say it still is his residence. Didn't your momma agree he could be buried there?"

"She did. They couldn't find any of Fred's relations to send his remains to after the autopsy, so my momma told them they should just put him in the cemetery. She didn't like the idea of a person never being laid to rest, even if he wasn't family. There's certainly plenty of room for him. The place is huge. And how often is there a new grave? Hank was the first one since my daddy passed."

"That was very generous of your momma, especially considering the circumstances." Aunt Emily fussed with a few errant strands of hair. "Although I'm not sure how happy Hank or your daddy would be if they knew Fred Dickerson was sleeping beside them for all of eternity."

"He's not beside them," Daisy corrected her. "Fred'll be in one corner, and they're in another. But does that really matter at this point?"

"It matters plenty if the curse has moved along with them—from Fox Hollow to the cemetery."

"What!"

"How many times have I told you not to gape, Ducky? You're not a baby seal waiting to be fed a mouthful of sardines."

"Aunt Em—"

"Nobody looks handsome when they're gawking. Not even you, Ducky. I'm sure Mr. Kinney would much rather have his romps with you when you know how to use your mouth properly."

"Aw jeez, Aunt Emily."

She smiled. It was that animated smile of hers that drove Daisy nuts. The one where it was nearly impossible to determine whether Aunt Emily was being terrifically canny or terrifically cuckoo. In this instance Daisy tended to think it was the latter.

"Cursed? The land is cursed and the curse could move? Be serious, Aunt Emily. You can't honestly believe that."

The smile remained.

"And there haven't been any romps between Ethan and me," Daisy added with some irritation.

"Not one?"

"Not one."

Aunt Emily wrinkled her brow. "Then I'm disappointed in you, Ducky. You haven't been using Mr. Kinney to your full advantage."

She rolled her eyes.

"Fiddle, fiddle. I'm only watching out for your best interests. The man is both attractive and convenient. I've said it before, but it bears repeating. He can help you get some of the answers you're looking for. And it's about time you tried bringing a new chap into your life, Ducky. Even if it's just for a couple of nice nights. You can't go on pining after Matt forever."

"I'm not pining," Daisy scoffed.

"Maybe. And maybe Fox Hollow isn't cursed. And maybe Fred Dickerson wasn't responsible for the death of your daddy. And maybe Hank's crash truly was an accident. But I doubt it. And when you think about it—honestly think about it—you'll understand what I'm saying. You'll agree with me too."

Daisy didn't bother arguing with her, knowing full well that arguing any further with Aunt Emily about sex and death and curses would be an utterly fruitless endeavor. And to be fair, not all of her words were kooky. She was most likely right about Hank. His crash most likely wasn't an accident. And Daisy was beginning to understand why. If Hank knew something about Fred and Fox Hollow—and he gave the big-city folks trouble about it—it could very easily have gotten him killed.

"Daisy? Oh good. There you are." Ethan stepped unexpectedly into the room.

Aunt Emily chortled. "My goodness. The timing couldn't get much better, now could it?"

Shooting her an admonishing glance, Daisy turned to Ethan. "Why are you here? I thought you were going to check with your office and we'd talk later at the inn."

"I did check with my office and it'd be better if we talked now. Assuming, of course, that's all right—" He looked over at her mom.

"It's all right." Daisy rose from her chair. "Outside?"

"Outside."

Not heeding the admonishment, Aunt Emily chortled again. "Full advantage, Ducky. Full advantage."

Daisy was not amused, but she didn't respond, figuring that it would only encourage her. She followed Ethan into the hall.

"Can you leave?" he asked as soon as they were out of range of Aunt Emily's sharp laugh and even sharper hearing.

The question surprised her a little. "Leave the hospital?"

Ethan nodded.

"I suppose so. If it's necessary. I'd like to be here when my momma wakes up, but that could be hours from now. Why? What's going on? What did you find out?"

He hesitated as a nurse hurried out of a nearby room, then he dropped his voice cautiously. "I know why they want the land."

Daisy put her hand on his arm. "You do?"

"And I know how Mr. Dickerson was involved. I know what he did, and I know why they poisoned him."

Her grip tightened.

"But I need some help from you, Daisy," Ethan said. "I need you to take me back to Chalk Level."

CHAPTER
25

"Watch my phone, will you? They'll send the plat map as soon as they get it."

Daisy cradled Ethan's phone in her lap with as much care as if she had been holding a rare egg from an endangered swallow.

"Left on Highway 40?" he asked her.

"Highway 40," she answered absently. "Left." She wasn't thinking about how to get to Chalk Level. She was thinking about why they were going there. "Are you sure? About the drilling?"

"I'm not sure if they've started or how far they've gotten. But I am sure they requested exploratory drilling permits for uranium. I found them when I was looking for information on the forfeiture."

"It must be a mistake." Daisy shook her head. "Doesn't it have to be a mistake? The wrong paper went into the wrong file?"

Ethan shook his head back at her. "It's not a mistake. I checked twice, and my office confirmed it. The permits are for Chalk Level. Or part of it at least. The Fox Hollow part from all indications. That's why we need the plat map. To see where exactly the property lines run."

"But how could it be the Fox Hollow part?"

"Is there really any other part?" he replied. "I thought Chalk Level and Fox Hollow were pretty much the same thing, aside from a few little lots along the edges. I seriously doubt anyone would go through all this trouble to dig under a trailer or two."

"I doubt it too. And I agree if it's Chalk Level, then it must be Fox Hollow. Except that's not what I meant. I don't understand how it could be either one. How could there be drilling permits, or even a request for drilling permits? Doesn't the owner of the land need to be involved in something like that?"

"The owner of the land was involved. He signed the request."

A surge of anger reddened Daisy's face. "Rick signed the request?"

"It wasn't—"

She didn't listen. "That rotten ass! The whole time he's been pretending not to have a clue why those big-city folks are interested in Fox Hollow when he's really known all along. They've probably been working together on this for months, maybe even before Rick bought the property."

"It wasn't—" Ethan began again.

"I should have seen it! I should have realized! I always thought Rick knew more than he was letting on."

"It wasn't Rick."

Daisy was so riled up, for a moment his words confused her. "Huh?"

"It wasn't Rick. Rick didn't ask for the permits."

They turned left on Highway 40 and were greeted by the blinding orange blaze of the sinking late-afternoon sun.

Ethan pulled down the visor on his side and squinted hard, but Daisy stared straight into it.

"Rick didn't ask for the permits?" she echoed. "But just a minute ago you said the owner of the land was involved. He signed the request."

"The supposed owner of the land was involved. Only he turned out to be the tenant instead. Fred Dickerson was the one who signed the request for the exploratory drilling permits."

Daisy's head snapped toward Ethan, except she couldn't see him. Her eyes were filled with a glowing tangerine blur.

"Fred Dickerson signed the request," he repeated. "He signed it about a month before his death."

Although her vision remained distorted, Daisy's mind wasn't muddled in the least. She immediately began putting together the dates. "According to Zeke, that's right around the time the big city folks first came to the roadhouse and asked about Fred."

"There's no chance that's a coincidence. Especially considering a couple of weeks later the sale of Fox Hollow to Rick became public knowledge and they started asking about him instead."

"And then"—she gave a little gulp—"Fred died."

Ethan nodded. "I'll tell you why that's not a coincidence either. Because just a few days before he died, Mr. Dickerson tried to rescind his request for the permits. It was too late by then. The permits had already been issued. But he tried nonetheless. Those big-city folks must have been real unhappy with him for doing that."

"So unhappy they poisoned Fred? He didn't want to be involved in the drilling anymore, and you think they killed him because of it?"

"I do. It takes a damn lot of time and money to get exploratory drilling permits approved. There's no way anyone serious enough to go through that process would let an old farmer's cold feet interfere with their plans once they'd managed to get the ball rolling in their favor. My guess," Ethan said, "is at the outset Mr. Dickerson didn't really understand the plan. They probably put the request for the permits next to a big stack of cash, and he signed it to get the money. Maybe he pretended to own the land, or they just assumed it belonged to him since he'd been living there for so long. That'd make sense considering how screwed up the property records were from the forfeiture, and it'd also explain why they were continually asking about the ownership of Fox Hollow. They could never get a clear answer who it actually belonged to until Rick finally confirmed he'd bought the place."

"They must have been real unhappy about that too."

"No doubt. I'd wager they've been interested in acquiring the land for quite a while now but couldn't because of the forfeiture. When the bank was finally able to dispose of the property—"

"Rick swooped in," Daisy finished for him. "Rick and his 'shine made a hush-hush agreement with the bank president."

"Exactly." Ethan gave a slight smile. "They've probably been spitting nails about that sale slipping beneath their radar from the minute they heard about it."

She frowned. "But now they'll just buy Fox Hollow from Rick. Or work out some sort of mineral deal with him. Uranium is just like coal and oil, isn't it? I assume you can buy and sell the mining rights the same way."

"In general, yes. Except when compared with uranium, coal and oil are barely more dangerous than a tub of lard and a box of Cubans. Uranium is open-pit mined. That means they dig up a huge area, both wide and deep. The radiation and toxic chemicals released from the site spread like dust blowing on the wind. It's seriously harmful stuff guaranteed to cause kidney damage, birth defects, and a dozen different cancers. But on the upside, uranium is extremely valuable to the people who own the land with the deposits and the executives of the company that extract them."

"Lovely," Daisy muttered grimly. "They'll all become filthy rich before going safely back to whatever big city they came from, while the rest of us are left behind in Pittsylvania Count to wither and die."

"They've got to go awfully far away to be safe," Ethan said. "From what I understand about the degree of impact, the ground and surface water contamination from uranium mining and milling is so bad, the vast majority of Virginia would be affected, along with at least half of North Carolina. And that's assuming it's successfully contained. If at some point a remnant of a hurricane passes over the region—or any heavy flooding occurs—or a severe storm with a tornado—"

"All of which we get around here pretty regularly," she interjected.

"Then the affected area could be massive and potentially catastrophic for the southeast. The contamination would last for decades and generations. That's millions of sick people to dig up something there's not even any shortage of. Not here or in the rest of the world. Apparently we've got well over a hundred-year supply of uranium stockpiled already."

Daisy raised a suspicious eyebrow. "You seem to know an awful lot about all of this."

Ethan shrugged. "I did a little research on the subject

after finding those drilling permits. Trust me, I've learned my lesson about not doing enough research in advance."

The eyebrow remained lifted. "Thinking about trying to get in on the action? See if Rick'll cut you a piece of the uranium pie?"

"Hell, no. I don't want that much blood and suffering on my hands. Money or no money. From what I read this afternoon, uranium mining makes a smidge of explosives and a few questionable firearms look downright harmless. And I'm ATF."

She responded with a sigh.

"But even ignoring all of that," Ethan continued, "I don't think Rick wants to sell the property."

"What makes you say that?"

"He seems to me to be fairly content as its new owner. Maybe because it's a good place for his whiskey business. Maybe because he likes having Fox Hollow when you can't."

Daisy sighed again. Ethan was probably right on both counts.

"I think if Rick was interested in getting rid of the property, he would have done so already. But the last time we saw him, he didn't give any sign he was even contemplating it. When his brother said he'd been paid to talk to your mom, Rick appeared just as surprised as you. His reaction would have been different if he were in the middle of negotiating the transfer of two hundred prime acres to the same people."

"There are still the mineral rights."

"True." Ethan nodded. "But if Rick sold or leased those, the land itself would be worthless to him. No more corn. No more stills in the old tobacco barn. No more Fox Hollow as it looks today. The place would become one giant poisonous pit."

She shuddered.

"And Rick didn't understand their interest in the property any more than we did. He was the one who first suggested taking a look at the plat map to see if it could give us any answers. So he's not even aware of the uranium deposits."

Daisy shook her head. "Even after everything you've told me, I still can't figure out why those big-city folks are pestering my momma to sell the land. They're not trying to convince Rick to sell the land, and he's the only one who can sell it."

"I can't explain that," Ethan said. "I looked pretty hard at all the documents relating to the forfeiture, and there's no indication whatsoever anything funny happened with it. Nothing got divided or split off along the way. At least not that I could find. Fox Hollow appears to be fully intact and the same as it's always been. For better or worse, there's no missing piece that still belongs to your mom."

"So if there's definitely no missing piece, then my momma's definitely got nothing left to sell. Which means those big city folks are not only evil and greedy, they've also got a screw loose. Bothering a sick woman when she doesn't have anything they could possibly want? That's cruel and just plain stupid." Daisy scowled with contempt. "It makes me wonder if maybe that's the reason Fred came into the diner the morning he died. He wasn't trying to warn Rick about the bad 'shine. He was trying to warn me about the stupid big-city folks."

"Maybe he was trying to warn both of you. Rick because of the arsenic. You because of your mom." The car abruptly slowed, as though its driver had a sudden revelation. "And maybe Hank too."

"Hank?"

"It's possible. He was always at H & P's, right? Mr.

Dickerson might very well have gone there to talk to him about the uranium and the drilling permits. Tell him all his secrets before he died. Maybe Hank was privy to some of them already. Maybe he even played a part in persuading Mr. Dickerson to rescind his request for the drilling permits. It's hard to say for certain, but I think it's clear Hank knew something."

"He must have," Daisy agreed. "Otherwise he never would have been at Fox Hollow. And before the crash, Hank hadn't been in a single accident with his bike. He was probably one of the safest motorcyclists in the history of motorcycling."

"You can lock your doors, bolt your windows, and slap on a suit of armor," Ethan replied gravely, "but none of that's going to help you if somebody with a lot of money at stake is afraid you're going to start talking and lose them that money."

She winced. "And now they're focused on my momma."

Reaching over, he put his hand on her thigh. "Don't worry, Daisy. I won't let anyone hurt your mom. Or you."

It was a sweet promise. Protective and reassuring. Daisy found herself smiling. Not from Ethan's kind words, but from her own ludicrousness. Her momma was lying unconscious in the hospital thanks to some big-city folks who intended on making a fortune by turning her childhood home into a toxic pit while poisoning a good portion of Virginia and North Carolina in the process. Except instead of thinking about what she could do to stop them, she was fixated on the fingers caressing her leg. And she liked them. She liked them so much and she was in such desperate need of comfort and escape, Daisy was seriously tempted to tell Ethan to make a U-turn on Highway 40, head to her room at the Tosh Inn, and spend the rest of the night with him forgetting everything else.

The only problem with that idea was everything else wouldn't allow itself to be forgotten. The moment she put her hand on his, Ethan's phone buzzed.

"Damn," he muttered. "Lousy timing."

Daisy started to withdraw her hand, but his fingers grabbed hers.

"Daisy—"

She checked the screen. "It's your office."

"Really lousy timing." With a sigh, Ethan released his hold on her. "Did they send the plat map?"

"I think so, but we just lost the signal."

"What do you suggest?"

"Keep driving. Eventually we'll hit a good spot." Daisy could see the bridge over the creek not too far away. "We're almost at Fox Hollow. We can pull in there. It usually gets a pretty strong signal."

She unsnapped her seat belt in preparation for getting out and opening the big red metal gate, but when they swung into the driveway, she discovered that the gate was already open. Ethan stopped the car anyway.

"Shouldn't it be closed?" he asked her.

"I was wondering that myself."

He took the phone from her. After a few seconds of fiddling, Ethan tossed it on the seat. "The signal's still too weak."

"Let's try closer to the house," she said. "It's higher."

They traveled down the long broad drive in silence. Daisy kept thinking about the gate. Why was it open? With some anxiety, she waited for the car to reach the top of the ridge. She wasn't quite sure what to expect on the other side. Would someone be there digging up Fox Hollow? Ethan had explained to her that exploratory drilling permits were just what they sounded like. The holder of the permits could drill in various locations and test the deposits for their precise uranium content.

Her breath caught in her throat as the house appeared. It stood alone and untouched on its kingly rise. No drilling equipment sat nearby. No humongous holes marred the garden. Nor was there any sign of any big-city folks. There was a truck sitting in the pebbly circle at the front of the house, however. It was Rick's pickup. The driver's side door was wide open. Rick wasn't in sight.

Ethan frowned at the vehicle.

Daisy was too happy to worry about the truck. "At least they haven't started drilling yet."

"Maybe they have and maybe they haven't. We won't know until we take a look at that plat map."

He pulled behind Rick's pickup. Daisy immediately climbed out of the car, but Ethan hesitated. She turned to him questioningly.

"That truck." He shook his head. "I don't like it."

"It's Rick's."

"I know. Only the last time we were here he had it parked behind the barn."

Daisy called Rick's name and waited for an answer. There was none. She tried again, louder. Still no response.

Ethan went on shaking his head. "I really don't like that truck there."

"Rick's probably in the house or barn and can't hear me."

With a dubious expression, Ethan picked up his phone. He grumbled a curse. "Stupid technology. Never available when you actually need it."

"The porch is the best spot for a signal. The left side porch," Daisy corrected herself hastily. The right side porch presumably still had the pair of canning jars filled with arsenic-laden moonshine sitting on it.

Ethan shut off the car and followed her toward the left side porch. As she headed up the stairs, Daisy made a cursory inspection of the back garden and the path leading to the tobacco barn, but she didn't see Rick anywhere.

"Finally!" Ethan exclaimed, grinning at the phone. "Success!"

With a weary smile, Daisy sank down on the aged porch swing. Waiting for him to examine the plat map, she watched the sun slip beneath the horizon in a deep red ball of flame. The mountains in the distance reflected its light like a row of fiery volcanos, and the ponds scattered throughout the meadows glowed like pools of molten lava. In contrast, the land closer to her was already growing dark. The trees lining the creek and the cemetery on the opposite bank were gray and hazy.

Ethan grunted.

"Any luck?" she asked him. "Does it show the permits?"

"It does. My office highlighted the area in yellow. Except the whole thing is tiny." He squinted at the screen. "I've managed to find Highway 40, but I can't line up the road with the property. And there's an FPC on here. What's an FPC?"

"FPC?" Daisy's brow furrowed.

"Here. You take a look." Ethan handed her the phone. "Maybe you can decipher it. You know Chalk Level better than I do."

She studied the plat map. It was small and hard to read, especially with the gradually diminishing daylight. Like Ethan, she found Highway 40 without much difficulty. Then came the tricky part—finding Fox Hollow. Daisy turned the screen several times until she finally got her directions straight. North. South. East. West. There was the mobile home park and the Round Pond Baptist Church. Head west.

The pastor's house and the playing field. Head farther west. The next big piece of land should be Fox Hollow. And there it was. The plat map was so detailed, even the driveway was shown. At its far end lay the farmhouse, followed by the old tobacco barn that Rick was now using for his whiskey business.

"And?" Ethan glanced at her from the porch railing, where he was admiring the view.

"I've got Fox Hollow," she said.

"You do? Good! Now do you see the area highlighted in yellow? That's where the permits are for."

The area highlighted in yellow. Daisy looked at it. It was west of the driveway and west of the house and west of the tobacco barn. It was also west of something labeled FPC. What was FPC?

Ethan stifled a yawn. "It's been a long day."

Daisy blinked at the map, then she figured it out. FPC was Frying Pan Creek.

"All this fresh air is making me tired." He yawned again. "And hungry."

She went on blinking at the map. The highlighted area was west of Frying Pan Creek. That meant it was across the creek. The exploratory drilling permits were for the other side of the creek.

"You know what I've got a taste for—"

The phone fell from her fingers and clattered to the porch floor. Daisy stared at it in stunned disbelief, as though it had suddenly come to life in her palm and whispered the answer to a very perplexing riddle.

"Burger," she whispered back.

CHAPTER
26

"A burger? No," Ethan said, "I've got the taste for—"

"Not burger," Daisy cut him off. "Berger."

"Huh?"

She dropped her head into her hands and groaned. "Oh, it makes so much sense now. How could I not have realized it before?"

He took a step toward her. "What makes sense now? What did you realize?"

"He wasn't saying burger. He was saying Berger."

"What?"

"Not a burger, like a hamburger you eat. But Berger as a name. A surname. A proper noun."

Daisy looked up and found Ethan frowning at her.

"Do you remember how I told you when old man Dickerson came into the diner on the morning he died he ordered a burger?"

"Yes."

"Well, I was wrong. He wasn't asking for a burger. He wasn't *asking* me for anything. He was *telling* me something. Fred didn't want breakfast. He wanted to tell me why he'd been poisoned."

Ethan stared at her just as she had stared at the phone a minute earlier.

"At first"—Daisy drew a shaky breath—"I thought it was just bad luck and poor timing that Fred happened to stumble into H & P's and collapse there. After we learned how he died, we were all thinking he was trying to warn Rick about the bad 'shine. But now I see it had nothing to do with Rick. Or Hank neither. It was me. Fred came to the diner because of me."

"Because you know somebody named Berger?"

"I'm a Berger. Or partially so at least. But my momma's a true Berger. Berger is her maiden name. Lucy Berger Hale."

"And that's something Mr. Dickerson would have known?"

"Without a doubt. Until the forfeiture and Rick Balsam came along, Fox Hollow was in the Berger family for generations. Everybody in Pittsylvania County knows that."

Ethan's frown returned.

Daisy responded with a mournful smile. "Fred thought I'd be the one who'd understand, and I should have. I should have understood right away. I should have put it together in a snap. But I didn't. It all happened so fast. And I got distracted when I found out Rick had bought the property. I didn't really think about what Fred had said—or why he said it—or that he said it to me."

"It was one word." Ethan shrugged.

"But it was an important word. A word that should have had special significance to me." She sighed. "Maybe Hank figured it out. He didn't need the plat map like I did. Maybe he realized what those big-city folks wanted, and they killed him because of it."

"Do you think that's why he came here? To tell Rick about the uranium, so he wouldn't sell Fox Hollow to them?"

"Hank may have come here to tell Rick about the uranium, but not to stop him from selling Fox Hollow."

"How do you know that?"

Daisy glanced at the phone still lying on the porch floor. "Because those big-city folks don't want to buy Fox Hollow."

Ethan squinted at her. "But the uranium is under Fox Hollow. And we know they want the uranium. They've been killing people to get it. You do remember the exploratory drilling permits?"

"Of course I remember them. Except the permits aren't for Fox Hollow."

"They're most definitely for Fox Hollow. It says Chalk Level right on them. I saw it with my own eyes."

"Chalk Level, yes. Fox Hollow, no."

"I'm confused." Ethan shook his head.

"I was confused too," Daisy said. "Until I saw that plat map. Then it all became clear. And I'm pretty sure for a long time those big-city folks were even more confused than us. That's why they were asking so many questions about Fred and Rick and Fox Hollow. They weren't trying to figure out who owned this land." She pointed at the ground below them. "They were trying to figure out who owned that land." She raised her arm straight ahead.

Ethan followed her outstretched finger. "The creek?"

"The other side of the creek."

"Isn't that the cemetery over there?"

"It is. The old Berger family cemetery."

His mouth opened, but no words came out.

Daisy lowered her hand. "It was the forfeiture. That was the problem. Before it, everybody knew my family owned Fox Hollow and the cemetery next door, which was logical considering the names carved into the tombstones.

But afterward, nobody knew anything. The property records didn't say what had happened, so it was just a big guess. And the natural assumption was if Fox Hollow was forfeit, the cemetery was forfeit right along with it. Only it wasn't. The cemetery was never in my daddy's name. He wasn't a Berger. The cemetery was always only in my momma's name. Fox Hollow was different. After they married, it became my daddy's too."

"Son of a bitch," Ethan muttered.

"You were right," she went on. "Nothing funny did happen with the forfeiture. There was no missing piece. The land was there the whole time. And my momma owned it the whole time. We were all just thinking about the wrong piece of land. All of us except for those big-city folks. They knew it was the cemetery they wanted. It had the uranium, and it needed the permits. The only issue was finding out who it belonged to after the forfeiture dust settled. They did a good job of narrowing it down. When it wasn't Fred—and it wasn't Rick—only my momma was left. And they sent Bobby after her."

"So that's what your mom was talking about when she told Bobby she wouldn't sell her land."

Daisy nodded. "My momma wouldn't ever sell the cemetery. Uranium or no uranium. The world could be coming to an end. The stars could be raining down from the heavens. She'd never let it leave the family. It's her heritage—and my heritage too. Our kin have been laid to rest there for hundreds of years. We had a great uncle, Jacob Berger, who was chief wagoner in the American Revolutionary War. Born December 21, 1745. Died January 25, 1837. I can show you his grave and dozens more like it. All with the name Berger. That's why I can assure you without the slightest reservation there is no way in this lifetime those big-city folks will lay one dirty, money-grubbing finger on that property. My momma wouldn't allow anyone to desecrate the family name by poisoning babies and their parents in this county—or the state—or any other state. Not with the good lord as her witness."

A lengthy silence followed. Ethan sat down next to her on the porch swing. It creaked gently beneath them. Daisy watched the shadows crawl from the cemetery to the creek to the farmhouse as the last remnant of rosy glow from the sun faded away.

"Do you think they're over there?" she asked Ethan after a while.

"I don't know. I was wondering that myself. I don't see any lights or hear any machinery. But they do have the permits. They could be doing something. And your friend Zeke at the roadhouse told us they were going for burgers. I have to assume that meant they were planning on heading to the Berger cemetery at some point."

"I'd forgotten all about that."

"Tomorrow I'll look into what we can do about those permits. Without the real landowner's permission, I don't think they're still valid. But I'm not sure how that works exactly. And considering what they did to Hank and Mr. Dickerson, I doubt those big-city folks are going to just walk away and give up without a fight."

Daisy shivered. Ethan wrapped his arm around her shoulders.

"You don't have to worry about them," he said. "Not anymore. I'll call my boss and your sheriff. Together we'll take care of them."

She leaned against his chest. The swing moved with the rising night breeze. It was a clear evening. The moon was a bright crescent shimmering high above the creek. Frying

Pan Creek. Such a silly name. She had no clue where it came from. A century or two ago somebody had probably used the creek for washing the grease from their skillet and it just stuck. But as silly as the name seemed, the creek was now of great importance. It divided Chalk Level. Fox Hollow from the Berger family cemetery. Rick's land from her momma's land. Corn whiskey from uranium deposits.

Ethan's arm tightened against her body as the darkness spread over them like a soft mist. It was quiet on the porch. And so very peaceful. Daisy remembered how as a little girl she used to sit on the swing with her daddy counting fireflies before bed. She had planned on sitting there with her own children one day. But that dream was gone. The house was lost. She would never sit on the porch again. This was the last time. At least she wasn't alone. It was nice being close to someone. She hadn't realized before quite how much she missed it. She could feel Ethan's heart beating into her back. She hoped that Rick wouldn't suddenly appear. Then she'd have to explain. The plat map. The exploratory drilling permits. And Ethan. She would have to explain sitting with Ethan on Rick's swing—on Rick's porch—at Rick's house.

Frogs burped. Whip-poor-wills called. Cicadas buzzed. It was such a hypnotic refrain that Daisy barely noticed the shout off in the distance. It sounded like Rick. Was Rick shouting? Then came the explosion.

CHAPTER
27

She ran. As the scarlet plume of fire hurtled into the sky, Daisy forgot the cicadas and the porch swing. The only thing that she could think about was the blazing cloud ahead of her. And Rick. She had heard his voice just before the explosion. He was somewhere in the middle of it. She had already lost her daddy and Matt's daddy. She couldn't lose another person to the flames.

"Daisy!"

It was Ethan. He was calling after her. Maybe he was running after her too. She didn't know, and she didn't really care. She couldn't worry about Ethan. Not at that moment. Not when he was perfectly fine and Rick very possibly wasn't.

"Daisy, stop!"

Her feet went faster. She was already down the porch stairs and across the gravel driveway. She had reached the side garden and was heading toward the creek.

"You don't know what's out there, Daisy! You don't know *who's* out there!"

Ethan must not have heard the shout. Or if he had, he

didn't connect it with Rick. But she did. She knew that it was Rick out there. And Daisy knew Rick. He didn't shout without a reason. Especially not right before an explosion.

"Damn it, Daisy! Stop! It could be—"

The words became garbled in her ears, like static filtering through a radio. Daisy didn't listen anymore. She couldn't. She was too busy watching the red-hot sparks rocket into the air. They were coming from the cemetery. But what could burn like that in the cemetery? Nothing. At least nothing natural. There was only grass and gravestones. A brush fire expanded gradually. It didn't detonate with the force of a missile.

The night was warm and humid. Whether it was made any warmer by the sudden inferno Daisy couldn't tell. The land in the distance glowed crimson, but there was little light directly in front of her. She moved into the dark shrubs with only a general sense of direction. The hollies scratched her arms and legs. The forsythias slapped her face. But she pushed determinedly through the brambles and branches, knowing that they wouldn't last long. The thicket wasn't wide. On the other side lay the creek.

Daisy stumbled down into the muddy water. There wasn't much of it. A trickle no more than a generous inch at its deepest. Not the swift knee-high current from a week or two earlier. The mud was sticky, and within half a dozen steps, she lost a sandal to the gummy mire. She stopped and tried to search for it, but it was no use. She couldn't see well enough, and the sandal had been sucked beneath the glop.

Slipping over the damp rocks, she crossed the creek. Daisy almost smiled as she reached the opposite bank. It was her momma's land that she stood on now. It would always be Berger land. The soil firmed beneath her, and she tried to run again, except she found that she couldn't. Not with only one shoe on. She pulled off the remaining sandal, tossed it over her shoulder, and started up the embankment.

The dirt slid out from under her as she climbed. It was powdery dry from too much sun and not enough rain. Daisy scrambled higher. Only a few more feet. Then she would be at the top. She could take a good look at the situation and have a better idea of what to do about it. The smell of scorched earth struck her like a violent squall as she crested the hill. It was acrid and stung her nostrils. Her foot struck a stump, and she tumbled to the ground. When she lifted her head from the clover, Daisy saw them. And she froze.

There were men. At least ten, maybe more. Inky figures racing toward the fiery ball, trying to douse it. They weren't firefighters. She knew that instantly. They weren't dressed like firefighters. They didn't move like firefighters. And they didn't have the equipment of firefighters. They had other equipment though. Bulldozers and massive shovels and towering rigs. They were drilling. Or preparing to drill. To test the uranium no doubt, as the exploratory permits allowed. But something had exploded, without any warning from all indications. It was most likely a storage tank. Gasoline or propane. Whatever powered all that machinery.

For a long minute Daisy gaped at the scene before her. She hadn't expected it. Not anything like this. And then she thought of Rick. Rick shouting. She looked more closely at the men. Was Rick among them? Daisy didn't recognize him. But she couldn't really recognize anyone. They were no more than bulky shapes moving hurriedly around the blaze. Could she have confused Rick's voice with someone else's? It was possible, of course. Except she had been so certain that it was him. She hadn't hesitated for even a second jumping off the porch swing and racing away from Ethan into the darkness.

Ethan. She had forgotten all about him while struggling through the brush and muck to reach the cemetery. He had come after her, and Daisy saw him now standing not far from where she lay. His gun was in his hands in front of him. His body was turned toward the flames. She whispered his name. He didn't respond. She tried again, a little louder. Still no success.

Daisy wavered, debating how loud to get. She was afraid of attracting the attention of anyone other than Ethan. There was plenty of noise around her. Snapping and crackling from the burning vegetation. Men hollering back and forth. Surely they wouldn't notice one extra yell. One name called out. Her mouth opened. She promptly snapped it back shut. There were more men. A small group that she hadn't spotted before. These men weren't darting around. Nor were they dealing with the fire. Instead they were talking together intently. She couldn't hear their words, but she could guess who they were. Big-city folks.

She had to get away. Daisy understood that immediately. She was too close to them. Dangerously close. They had murdered Hank and Fred. And several of them were carrying what appeared to be AR-15s. That was a serious rifle with a clip holding something in the neighborhood of thirty rounds. At least Ethan had his Glock. If only she had her momma's .380. It might have been a small pistol, but when push came to shove, it fired bullets just like the big boys. Bobby and his bloody thigh could attest to that fact. But the Colt wasn't there. She had left it at the inn before going to see her momma in the hospital.

Her eyes went to Ethan. Did he see the group? He did. His head was turned straight toward them. And he must have seen the AR-15s too, because he was walking slowly backward, trying to slink silently to the creek. Daisy held her breath as she watched him. Step by stealthy step. Only another couple of yards. Then he could disappear down the hill. Meanwhile the men continued talking. They didn't seem to notice Ethan or his retreat. Now was the perfect time for her to follow suit. She wouldn't stand up. She would just crawl away. And they wouldn't know that either of them had ever been there.

Daisy rose to her knees. She crouched as low as she could, like a panther trying to pass undetected through the pampas. First one knee back, then the other. One palm, then the second. Inch by precarious inch. No noise and no rapid movements. The ground was so rough in spots, it tore open her hands, but she ignored the pain. A few cuts and bruises were nothing in comparison to the barrel of an AR-15 pointed in her face. And if their past acts were any guide, she had little doubt that the men would be more than willing to pull the trigger. She glanced over at Ethan. He was closer to the embankment than she was. He was almost out of sight now.

A soundless sigh of relief passed through Daisy's lips. At least one of them would make it. Then Ethan could get help. He would know who to call and what to do. If he was fine, she would be fine. But in an instant everything changed. Without warning, a man suddenly appeared behind him. Ethan began to turn, but it was already too late. The AR-15 in the man's hands went up, the butt of the rifle came down with a startling crack against Ethan's temple, and he slammed to the ground.

"Hey!" the man with the rifle hollered to his comrades. "Look what I caught!"

The group went over to examine Ethan. A flashlight clicked on. They were studying his face.

"You messed him up good, Joe."

Daisy bit her tongue. She knew that name. Joe was the one who had paid Bobby to go after her momma.

Joe shrugged. "I couldn't let him leave."

One of the other men kicked Ethan hard in the gut. When Ethan didn't respond, he said with a laugh, "Doesn't look like he's leaving now."

The rest of the group laughed with him, and Ethan received several more hard kicks.

As hot as it was outside, Daisy's bones felt numbly cold. Ethan was in trouble. Serious trouble. He lay stiff and motionless on the grass, like a sack of feed somebody had pushed from the back of a pickup. There was no moan. No twitch. Nothing at all. She had to help him. Again she wished that she had her momma's .380. She couldn't have shot all the men by herself. The Colt had only seven rounds at most, and her aim was far from perfect. But any shots—even just one—would have scattered them. Then she could have run. Run back to Fox Hollow. Called Sheriff Lowell. Found Rick and his ever-present arsenal. And helped Ethan.

Even without the gun, she still had to run. It was her only option. Daisy understood that. She couldn't stay crouched in the clover forever. They would see her at dawn. And there was a darn good chance that they would discover her before then. She was awfully close to them. All they had to do was shine their flashlights a bit to the right, and there she was. A field mouse just waiting to be pounced on.

Ethan provided a distraction. As long as they were focused on him, they wouldn't be looking around for her. Speed had suddenly become far more important than silence. Daisy had to get to the creek. Even if the men noticed her before she made it down the hill, she could lose them when she hit the thicket on the other side. No one knew Fox Hollow as well as she did. She could have hidden on the property for days. Not even her momma would have been able to find her. Except Ethan didn't have days. He needed her help now.

Daisy fixed the plan in her mind. Jump up, whirl around, race toward the embankment. Don't look at anything. Don't listen to anything. Don't stop for anything. Just go. Go fast. Worry about everything else—her soon-to-be-raw feet, the proximity of the AR-15s, her strategy when she reached Fox Hollow—later.

Taking a deep breath to steel her nerves, she counted to three. Then Daisy went. She stood up. She turned around. She took four or five flying steps. There was a yell. It was rapidly succeeded by more yelling. The men were yelling in her direction. They had spotted her. She pumped her legs furiously. She could see the shadowy drop-off leading to the creek up ahead, waiting for her like a shimmering, beckoning oasis. Just a dozen more steps. Then the odds of her getting away shifted significantly in her favor. They couldn't shoot after her into the thicket, not with any real accuracy. Six or seven feet farther and then—

And then the ground vanished. It dropped away beneath her without the slightest warning. One moment there was steady, solid dirt under her toes, and the next moment it was gone, replaced by open air. She began to fall. Instinctively Daisy kicked and flailed about, but she touched nothing. There was nothing to hold her or for her to grab onto. She simply continued to fall, until she landed with a jarring thud on a rough surface that was as dense and unyielding as concrete.

Black, pulsating waves of confusion followed. Daisy lay sprawled on her side with one arm twisted painfully under her. Her brain was jumbled, and her spine sent searing lightning bolts up into her neck and along the length of her back. There were voices. Men's voices. They were loud and sounded agitated. Who were they? She shook her head, trying to clear it. What had happened?

She remembered running—and falling—and crashing down hard. Why had she been running? Daisy shook her head again. It made her neck throb violently, but the waves pounding through her brain subsided somewhat. Slowly she sat up. Her shoulders hurt. Her hips and ankles hurt. One of her arms really hurt. Her whole body felt weak and clumsy, so much that she didn't try to rise any further.

Where was she? She was surrounded by darkness. Daisy blinked. Still darkness. She put out a tentative hand. Clay. There was clay in front of her. She knew it even though she couldn't see it. Nearly every inch of Pittsylvania County soil consisted of heavy, compact red clay. Daisy reached behind her. More clay. Shifting on shaky muscles, she felt around gingerly. Clay beneath her. Clay on all sides. She was in a clay pit. She was sitting at the bottom of a clay pit.

A pale light fell on her face. Daisy looked up and blinked some more. She could make out the top of the pit. It was eight feet high, give or take a few inches. The edge was too dim for her to judge exactly. A row of eyes stared back at her. She could see their reflection like a group of raccoons clustered around a Dumpster in the middle of the night. One pair of eyes was more distinct than the rest. The flashlight shining down on her was closest to this pair and to the thick shock of curly silver hair above them. It wasn't a raccoon. It was a poodle. A wet poodle. It was Carlton Waters.

CHAPTER
28

In an instant Daisy's mind cleared and she remembered everything. The explosion. The big-city folks and their drilling equipment in the cemetery. The butt of Joe's AR-15 cracking against Ethan's temple. She didn't know how, but she had found help. She didn't know why he was there, but Carlton would help her and Ethan.

Daisy looked up at him eagerly, waiting for an explanation—and reassurance—and instructions on how to get out of the strange pit that she was sitting in. Carlton looked back at her for several long seconds, then he laughed.

"How convenient," he said.

"Isn't she that waitress?" Joe asked, squinting down at her.

"She is." Carlton went on laughing. "And she's saved me a hell of a lot of bother. I've been trying to find a way to trap that little bird for some time now. But I don't need to no more."

All the men laughed. It was a harsh, contemptuous laugh that seemed to increase with wicked glee as it echoed down the clay walls toward Daisy.

"Oh, my dear," Carlton drawled in his raspy Appalachian accent. "You look so surprised."

Surprised wasn't a sufficient description. The shock paralyzed her. Daisy's mouth didn't move. Her eyes didn't blink. Even her brain was partially frozen. She couldn't understand. Why was Carlton laughing? Why was he talking to Joe and the other men? Why wasn't he helping her out of the pit?

"Well, I suppose we should get down to business." Carlton shrugged. "Since you're here you must know what I want."

Daisy didn't respond. She couldn't.

He clucked his tongue at her. "Don't play dumb with me."

She struggled to breathe. To think. *Think smart, Ducky.* That was what Aunt Emily always said. She had to think smart.

"So I'll ask you again. Do you know what I want?"

What did Carlton want? He was with Joe. That had to mean he wanted the same thing Joe wanted. Her momma's land.

Carlton's voice rose. "Do you know what I want?"

This time Daisy answered with a small nod.

"Good. And are you gonna give it to me?"

"I—" Her lips were stiff. "I can't give it to you. It's not mine."

"I'm aware of that, but you can tell your momma what she ought to do with it."

"My . . . my momma feels very strongly about family. And it's her family cemetery."

"Hank told me the same damn thing. I told him family's only as good as what they can do for you today."

At the mention of Hank, Daisy's stomach churned and a thick lump swelled in her throat.

"He was loyal to you," Carlton said. "Like you and your momma were his real family, even though you weren't. I'll give Hank that. Stupid loyal he was. I offered him a deal. Told him I'd give him a cut of what I got out of this place if he'd take care of you like I took care of old man Dickerson when he started getting in my way. I figured it'd be easy for Hank. You ate his food every day. What's a little rat poison mixed in the chicken stew? Nobody would find out. Nobody would even care after a week or two. That's how it is when you die. Here yesterday, forgotten tomorrow."

Her stomach churned harder. It wasn't the big-city folks. It was Carlton. Carlton had poisoned Fred.

"But he wouldn't do it. Not stupid loyal Hank. Said he wouldn't betray your daddy by hurting his baby girl. Of course I couldn't have him go squealing to you afterward. Or to the sheriff neither. Something had to be done with him. So Hank ended up taking a long drink from a short creek."

Daisy felt all the oxygen go out of her lungs. It wasn't just Fred. It was Hank too. Carlton had killed Hank. Hank had been his friend, and he had murdered him. He had even gone to Hank's funeral!

Carlton chortled. "Will you listen to me? Crowin' like a fool cock. Telling you all my dirty secrets. I guess now I'll have to do something with you too."

A wave of panic rose in her chest. It seemed impossible to get any air. The stench of charred earth was so strong, and the pit was so deep and dark. It felt as though the clay walls were closing in on every side.

"The funny thing is"—Carlton chortled even harder—"you're already in a grave. It's not one of our holes you fell into. We haven't started drilling yet. So it's an honest-to-goodness gravesite. I don't know who it was dug for, but it looks like it belongs to you now!"

Daisy cringed in horror. Aside from Hank's final resting place near her daddy, there had been only one new grave dug at the cemetery recently. Fred Dickerson's. And as far as she was aware, it remained empty. They were still waiting for his remains to be sent back from the autopsy. That meant she wasn't sitting in the bottom of some pit. She was sitting in Fred's grave.

It was a gruesome realization. And in that moment Daisy knew she had to make a decision. She could either cry and beg and curl up in a ball like a petrified possum, or she could fight. It was an easy choice. She was a Berger. The Bergers were a family of fighters. Just ask Great-Uncle Jacob. Did he lie down and wait for the redcoats to roll over him and his wagon? Of course not, as proven by the fact that Virginia was no longer a British colony. And she wasn't going to be rolled over either, not if she had anything to say about it.

"One Berger almost dead," Carlton continued cheerfully. "That leaves just one to go. It shouldn't be too hard to get rid of your momma. She's a sickly croaker as it is."

Daisy forced herself not to get mad. Fear and rage were futile. She had to think smart. That was the only way to get out of the damn grave.

"So we're dead," she replied with a coolness that surprised even her. "You kill us. There are no more Bergers in Pittsylvania County. What good is that going to do you? You're still not going to own the land."

For the first time since he and his silver shock of hair had gazed down on her with his flashlight, Carlton Waters grew solemn. Daisy hoped that was a good sign.

"Not right away," he admitted. "But eventually the property will belong to me. After you and your momma are gone, who's going to stop me from getting it? Nobody knows how long I've wanted it. Nobody knows why I want it. And nobody is going to pay a lick of attention when I become the new owner. It's a useless old cemetery. Worthless—on the outside and above ground—to everyone but a Berger. And there won't be any Bergers around to interfere with my plans."

"Okay, you buy the land. What then? You still need approval to mine the uranium. All you've got now are some exploratory drilling permits, which might not even be valid. And even if they are, they're not the same as being allowed to actually dig up the stuff and sell it to the highest bidder."

Daisy was making it up as she went along, but she figured the longer she talked, the longer she survived. Carlton frowned at her.

"I can get anything approved. That's not a problem. They trust me. The whole county does. I've been auctioning off their meemaws' and pawpaws' bedroom sets and wedding china for more years than some of them have been alive. I've gotten them a lousy buck for their mismatched salt and pepper shakers and another for their chipped cow creamers. I know better than anyone how to convince people to buy crap. Mining and milling equals employment. All I've got to say is that pulling out the uranium will bring a whole lot of jobs to this area, and everybody'll applaud me for it. Hell, they might even raise a statue in my honor."

"But we're all gonna get cancer!"

Carlton snorted. "I won't. And no one cares about that. Not at the outset. As soon as they hear the word *job,* they aren't capable of thinking about anything else. So they'll gladly give me all the approvals I need, I'll get rich beyond your wildest imagination, and when people eventually do become sick, they'll blame someone other than me for it, because I'll be enjoying the good life far away from here."

His callousness was stunning. Daisy knew what Aunt Emily would have said to him. *It's easier for a camel to go through the eye of a needle than for a rich man to enter the kingdom of heaven.* It was one of Aunt Emily's favorite sayings, but Daisy doubted it would have the slightest impact on Carlton. He had probably hawked a few lame camels in his day.

Suddenly the ground trembled beneath her and large hunks of clay crumbled down from the walls around her. There was a tremendous boom, and the sky flashed crimson. It was another explosion.

"Goddammit!" Carlton jumped in surprise.

He and all the other men in the group spun away from Daisy and the grave. They turned to look at what she could only assume was the ensuing fire. The surrounding noise level quickly doubled, then tripled. There was frenzied shouting, loud intermittent crackling and popping, and grinding machinery. It was the din of chaos.

"Goddammit," Carlton said again, only this time it was accompanied by a growl.

A new man sprinted up next to him. "Mr. Waters—" Halting to catch his breath, he glanced over at the grave and saw Daisy. "What the hell—"

"Don't worry about her," Carlton cut him off. "What is it, Sam? Have you figured out what's causing these damn explosions?"

"No. But Larry sent me. There's too much burning now. We can't get it all. He thinks we better leave. Somebody's going to see it."

Carlton ran his fingers through his silver shock of hair. "He's got a point. I don't want that much attention. Not like this. The sheriff will come. And the fire and rescue squad. They're going to have questions. I'm not ready for them yet. I've got to get the story right. I need a couple of hours to pull it all together. And then . . ." He let the sentence trail away.

"And then?" Sam prodded him.

Carlton turned back to the grave and looked down at Daisy. Although he no longer shone the flashlight on her, she could see his face illuminated by the red glow behind him. He was smiling at her. It was a small impish grin from one side of his mouth, but it wasn't jolly. It was cold. So cold and utterly emotionless that Daisy found herself crawling instinctively backward, trying to get as far away from it as possible. It was going to kill her.

"What about him?" Joe asked Carlton.

"Who?"

He pointed the barrel of his rifle toward the ground in the opposite direction. "The guy I caught earlier?"

"Right." Carlton ran his fingers through his hair once more, then he shrugged. "Throw him in with her. Two birds, one stone."

Joe frowned. "But you just said the sheriff was going to come. He'll find them, and they'll start talking."

"Right," Carlton said again. "Except we can't shoot them."

Daisy exhaled a shaky sigh of relief. They weren't going to shoot her and Ethan. Sheriff Lowell would come. He would find them. Everything would be okay.

"But she knows what you've done," Joe argued. "They've seen what we're doing here."

"Right," Carlton agreed a third time, calmly. "That's why we can't just shoot 'em and leave 'em. We've got to get rid of 'em completely."

Her heart froze. Everything would not be okay. On the contrary, it was going to be the exact opposite of okay. They were going to get rid of her and Ethan. Completely.

She huddled into the back corner of the grave. What could she do? Daisy's eyes flew around frantically. Was there any way out? The walls were high, and the clay was flat and solid. There weren't many holes or ledges to hold onto, at least not that she could see. The light was poor at best, just what was cast off from the fire and a flickering flashlight or two. She thought she might be able to climb up if she had enough time, but she certainly couldn't do it with all the men standing around the edge. They would never let her make it to the top. Maybe when they were gone. Carlton had seemed to want to leave.

There were some scuffling and dragging sounds, then a black shadow blocked the scarlet sky. Daisy looked up at it, and as she did, the shadow rushed down toward her. She scrambled to get out of the way. It landed close to her with a heavy thud. Her first reaction was that Carlton and Joe had dropped something into the grave that would hurt her. It was how they were going to get rid of her. But an instant later the shadow shuddered and groaned, and she realized it was Ethan.

Daisy hurried over to his side. When she saw his face, she gasped. The man hadn't exaggerated. Joe had messed Ethan up good with the butt of his rifle. There was a welt the size of a potato on his forehead. His left eye was swollen shut. And a long gash ran from his temple over his cheek down to his jaw. It was bleeding heavily. For once she was glad she couldn't see well. She was pretty sure the injuries were far more severe than they appeared in the darkness. And she didn't know how else he was hurt. They had kicked him so hard, and there was the fall.

At least he was breathing. Daisy could feel his pulse, and Ethan moaned slightly. She wished she had a piece of cloth to put on his face to slow the bleeding, but she had nothing other than her hands. She lifted his head into her lap, hoping the elevation would help a little. His blood felt warm and sticky as it coated her palms. She tried to wipe it away, but it just kept coming.

A flashlight clicked on. Daisy looked up hurriedly. There seemed to be fewer men at the top of the grave than before. The flashlight clicked off again.

"Now that we've got that taken care of," Carlton drawled, "let's go talk to Larry. I'm afraid we don't have much time. We have to decide what equipment we need to take and what can stay behind."

"He's over by the . . ." Sam began.

She didn't hear the conclusion of the sentence, but Daisy could tell from the way the voices dropped that Carlton and Sam had turned around and were walking away from her. A tiny wellspring of hope bubbled in her veins. They were leaving. They were leaving while she and Ethan were still alive.

Joe called after Carlton. "So what do you want me to do with them?"

Daisy pressed her lips together so fiercely waiting for the answer, she tasted blood.

Carlton didn't stop. He kept on walking. And in a casual, inconsequential tone—as though he was telling Joe to throw a couple of extra steaks on the grill—he responded over his shoulder, "Bury 'em."

CHAPTER
29

Deafness, blindness, and muteness followed. Daisy lost every sense all at once. She was going to die. Not in fifty years. Not with a chubby grandchild perched on her knee. Not with a bouquet of stargazer lilies pressed to her nose and an extra-large piece of peach pie in her hand. She was going to die here and now, in a lonely corner of the Berger cemetery, at the bottom of a dark hole that had been dug for somebody else. At least she wasn't alone. At least she had Ethan with her. But she found no comfort in the fact that he was going to die too. He didn't deserve such a miserable fate any more than she did. It shouldn't be his time either.

Then she screamed.

"CARLTON!"

Daisy had never screamed so loudly or fervently in all of her life. But it was in a desperate attempt to save that life. And Ethan's.

"CARLTON!"

Carlton didn't reply. Nor did anybody else. Daisy stared at the top of the grave. There was no one there. All the men had disappeared. There was still noise. There was still fiery reflection. And there was still a lot of yelling. But it was all off in the distance. At the edge of the grave, there was no movement and no sound.

Daisy cleaned the blood from Ethan's jaw and temple as well as she could with the hem of her shirt, then carefully set his head down on a little incline of clay. She stood up. Carlton was gone and wouldn't return. She was convinced of that. But what about Joe? Where was he? She had to talk to him. She had to persuade him not to do what Carlton had said. There had to be a way to stop him from burying them.

"JOE!"

Was he getting a shovel?

"JOE! JOE!"

Was he getting other men with lots of shovels? Once more Daisy's eyes flew frantically around the walls that trapped her. There was only one possible route for escape. Up. She had to try it. She had to try it now. No one seemed to be watching. It was a tiny open window that might slam shut at any moment.

Her fingers were wet with Ethan's blood. As Daisy wiped them dry on her already stained shirt, she searched through the darkness for a place to start. There were some small cavities in the clay as a result of the explosions. She found a spot for one hand, then the other. And she began to climb.

It was tough going. One of her arms worked much better than the other. Her weaker arm smarted terribly, and the muscles strained to the point where they felt like they could snap in half. Daisy guessed it was because of how her arm had been twisted under her when she fell, but she forced herself to ignore the throbbing. She understood what would happen if her arm suddenly gave out or she lost her grip. There would be another fall. Another hard landing.

And she would have to start the climb all over again. Precious seconds would be irretrievably lost. Precious seconds that could very possibly mean the difference between survival and entombment.

Daisy glanced down at Ethan. He lay in the same position as when she left him. There was no more moaning. She wondered how much blood he had lost. But a part of her was glad that he wasn't awake. He couldn't feel the pain or know that he might never feel anything again.

With each inch that she progressed, the sky became brighter. The air seemed somehow fresher. Daisy had a bit more hope for success. The edge of the grave was now clearly in sight. Like the glittering summit of a mountain, the peak was almost within her reach. Just another couple of minutes, another foot or two, and she would be at the top. She could get out, and she could get help. Then it wouldn't matter if Joe brought a shovel. It wouldn't matter if he and the other men brought a dozen shovels. She would be gone. They wouldn't be able to bury her or Ethan.

There was the hum of an engine. Daisy didn't pay any attention to it. She knew they were moving equipment and machinery. Carlton was trying to hide what he could, as quickly as he could. But he wouldn't be able to hide it for long. Sheriff Lowell and the Glade Hill Fire & Rescue Squad would be there soon. The hum was getting louder. It was accompanied by the grinding of metal and the dry crunch of earth. It was a strange noise, but she didn't think about it. She was too close to freedom to focus on anything else.

Her weak arm felt like it was going to shatter into a hundred pieces. She had smacked her knees against the clay wall so many times, they had become swollen and ached. But it wasn't important. Nothing was important except escaping from the grave. The engine sounded awfully close to her now. Daisy wondered if they were driving the machinery next to the grave, or maybe even right over it. Would they see her climbing? Should she wait to go further until they had passed? She decided that she had better peep out before jumping out. Better to be safe than very sorry. Joe and the other men still had their AR-15s.

Stretching her hand up, she touched grass. It was warm, soft, wonderful grass simply because it wasn't clay. Like a prairie dog slowly poking its head out of its burrow, wary of lurking predators, Daisy raised her eyes cautiously over the edge of the grave. She expected to find fire, hustling men, and lots of commotion. They were all there, but she didn't see any of them. The only thing that she saw was the bulldozer. And the dirt. The towering mound of dirt that the bulldozer was pushing straight toward her.

She tried to leap out of the way. Daisy made one feverish attempt to get her body up onto the grass and roll to safety. But there wasn't enough time. The bulldozer was already too near, and the dirt started pouring into the grave with the force and speed of a torrential waterfall. She lost her hold on the clay and tumbled downward. Like a battered tennis ball, she bounced from one wall to another. There was dirt in her eyes, dirt in her nose, and dirt streaming into her clothes.

With all her might, Daisy struggled against the flow. She fought to keep her head up and breathe. She seemed to be swimming in it, paddling furiously against the tide. Except it was a rip current, sucking her inexorably away from shore. The pounding dirt was pulling her to the bottom. To the bottom of her grave. And there was absolutely nothing that she could do to stop it.

They were burying her, and they were burying Ethan somewhere below her. They were burying them alive.

Daisy's mouth filled with dirt, and she began to choke. Within seconds she was gasping so violently, it felt as though every cell in her body was on the verge of bursting. She was suffocating under a mound of Pittsylvania County clay. She clawed wildly at the walls, searching for a pocket of air. When she found one, she gulped what she could. Instinct told her it wouldn't last long. The dirt was crushingly heavy. She couldn't see, and she could only partially move. But she could still dig, and that was what she did, thrusting her arms forward and kicking her legs together below her like a flipper.

It was impossible for Daisy to tell if she was making any progress. She knew she was going up, but she had no way of knowing how far she needed to go. The dirt had to end somewhere of course. The question was whether she could get there before her air and muscles gave out. Her strength was already beginning to fail her. She felt her legs sag uselessly beneath her as though they were no longer attached to her body. She forced her arms to keep working, using every bit of energy she had left. Except the gasping had started again—and her head was pounding in agony—and instead of pushing dirt away from her face, now something was pushing it at her.

All of a sudden, there was a light. It was a dim red glow, followed by a hand. She reached for it. As her fingers grazed the palm, it grabbed her. It pulled, and she crawled, until she could crawl no more. That was when it lifted her. The dirt fell away like a coat of chain mail, and she was free. Rick's arms were wrapped around her. Daisy coughed, and her body shuddered with such exhaustion it seemed as though her spine might crumble. But Rick held her tight and upright. Then came his drawling voice.

"Looks like you owe me one, darlin'."

CHAPTER
30

"Have you decided on a name for the bakery yet?"

Daisy raised her head from the stack of paperwork in her lap. She was sitting in one of the white pine rocking chairs on the back porch of the Tosh Inn. Aunt Emily stood in front of her with a sweating glass of lemonade in each hand.

"No. Brenda wants to keep it H & P's, in memory of Hank and my daddy and to thank Hank for leaving the diner to us in his will, but—" She hesitated. "I think maybe it's time for a change. A new business should have a new name. A fresh start all around."

Aunt Emily nodded approvingly. She set one glass on the little table next to Daisy, then settled down with her own glass in the neighboring rocker. Daisy shifted in her seat to pick up the lemonade with her left hand. Her right arm was in a sling. It still hurt on occasion, but the pain was now just an annoying twinge compared to what it had been a week earlier.

"How are you coming with those?" Aunt Emily gestured toward the papers as half of them tumbled to the porch floor.

"I'm seriously beginning to hate forms." Daisy pushed the rest of the stack out of her lap. "Forms from the hospital for my momma. Forms from the government for closing the diner and opening the bakery. Forms from the sheriff and a bunch of mining bureaucrats for the mess in the cemetery. Forms, forms, forms. I'm supposed to go back to the doctor for one last look at my arm, and I really don't want to because it'll mean more forms."

"Wait until you get older." Aunt Emily chuckled. "It only gets worse. Forms and bills. That's what our existence on this earth boils down to at the end."

"Don't even get me started on the bills. How Brenda and I are going to buy the supplies we need to bake anything and sell it is a mystery to me." Daisy lifted the lemonade to her lips. She was expecting a pleasant mix of sweet and tangy but got a mouthful of lighter fluid instead. "Lord almighty, Aunt Emily! What did you put in here?"

"Just a dash of something to take the edge off, Ducky. You can't tell me you don't need it after what you've been through."

She had no argument there. Being very nearly buried alive did make a person think much more fondly of both life and liquor. Daisy took another drink, only this time she was careful to make it a sip.

"And somebody's got to give that Rick Balsam a shot of friendly competition," Aunt Emily continued with a sly gaze. "If he's doing as well as you say with his 'shine, then there's no harm in me expanding my repertoire. Branch out a bit from my usual brandies. It is medicine, after all. I'd be doing the fine folks of southwestern Virginia a service, medically speaking."

Daisy laughed.

"Unless you've caught wind of an impending crackdown

by our favorite ATF agent. In that case I'll stick with the gooseberries."

"Oh, I think you'll be safe. Ethan's on sick leave right now. And after he goes back to work, he'll be staying firmly attached to the desk in his office for the foreseeable future. He's got a broken leg and about a dozen facial fractures. He'll be okay, but he needs to take it easy for a while until everything heals."

"So he hasn't made any plans for a return trip? Even unofficially?"

"Not anytime soon. At least not that he's told me about. I believe Special Agent Kinney's had his fill of Pittsylvania County. And you can't really blame him. He saw a lot more than he bargained for."

"But surely he wants to see you again, Ducky."

She could only shrug. Daisy didn't know quite where she stood with Ethan. She had spoken to him twice since his release from the hospital. Both conversations had been brief and slightly muddled, because Ethan was on a slew of painkillers.

"He'll come back 'round when he's feeling better," Aunt Emily said with confidence. "You just wait. He'll find another assignment out here."

"Maybe." Daisy shrugged again. Then she smiled, remembering what Ethan had said about not being a revenuer. "Maybe he'll discover a sudden need to smash a still or dump some pints of whiskey into the creek."

"Are we talking about Rick's still and Rick's pints of whiskey?"

"Not unless Rick causes a mighty stink somewhere. If there's any really big trouble, Ethan won't protect him. But at this point—considering he saved our lives—Ethan's willing to turn a blind eye to Rick and his 'shine."

"I guess that's only fair. You were lucky Rick showed up when he did."

"I was lucky I could scream so loud," Daisy replied. "That's how Rick found us. He was already trying to stop Carlton and the others. He figured out what they were up to from the plat map—just like I did—and he thought the best way to shine a little light on their activities was to blow them up. So Rick was setting off the explosions when he heard me hollering my head off."

Aunt Emily sighed. "I still can't believe it was Carlton behind it all. He always seemed like such a harmless chap to me."

"He was dreaming of money, more than he could ever make selling everybody's old junk. And he can keep right on dreaming—in prison for the rest of his life."

"I suppose I should invite Rick over for dinner this weekend," Aunt Emily said after a slight pause. "Show my gratitude properly."

"I don't know if that's such a good idea."

"Oh?" She raised a curious eyebrow.

"I'm grateful to him, of course. Very grateful. I just—" It was Daisy's turn to sigh. "Well, I've learned over the years it's unwise to act too grateful to Rick for anything. He has a tendency to remind you of it. A lot."

"And he's always looking for reimbursement?"

"Especially a certain type of reimbursement, if you catch my meaning."

Aunt Emily frowned. "It seems to me you two should be nearly even. You didn't hurt his brother a stitch after what he tried to pull with your momma. You let Bobby walk away scot-free."

"Bobby's actually walking with a bit of a limp these days. Although I've been told it'll go away over time as the muscles in his thigh mend. He's paying another price too. Bobby's volunteered to clean up the cemetery for me. Collect the burnt brush. Plant some new azaleas. Even scrub and polish all the scorched gravestones."

The curious eyebrow went back up. "Volunteered?"

"Let me put it this way—" Daisy couldn't restrain a grin. "My momma's three-eighty is now my three-eighty. And it appears I can be rather convincing when I'm holding it, even with one arm in a sling."

Aunt Emily hooted so hard, she almost dropped her drink. "Now that's thinking smart!"

For several minutes she went on tittering to herself in amusement. Daisy watched the condensation trickle down the side of her glass.

"You were just kidding, weren't you, Aunt Emily?" she said at last. "You don't really believe Fox Hollow—or the Berger cemetery—is cursed, do you?"

At first she didn't answer, then Aunt Emily smiled. There was an unmistakable glint of excitement in her shrewd blue eyes.

"Don't you worry about that, Ducky. You just think about what you and Brenda are going to call the new bakery." She leaned over the arm of her rocker and pecked Daisy on the forehead. "Take it from an old biddy like me, some secrets are better off left buried."